WIRED JUSTICE

PARADISE CRIME THRILLERS BOOK 6

TOBY NEAL

"I am no bird; and no net ensnares me: I am a free human being with an independent will."
Charlotte Brontë

CHAPTER ONE

THE BEST PLACE TO *think about life was on a volcano.*

Sophie Ang tried to hold that thought as she held a hand up to shade her eyes, watching Alika Wolcott, ex-MMA coach, friend, and possible lover, pilot the chopper that had dropped her off up and away from the desolate lava field.

She couldn't suppress a pang of anxiety as she turned to view the plain. *What had she gotten herself into now?*

Kalapana on the Big Island was a landscape of stark contrasts. The deep blue sky arched overhead, depthless and unbroken. Desolate as a moonscape, acres of black lava stretched away in every direction to the ocean, where a restless sea beat against the fresh stone. The only sign of human presence was the remains of what had once been a two-lane highway, engulfed periodically by shiny black rock that gleamed iridescent in the sun of high noon.

"Come, Ginger." Sophie's yellow Lab had been nosing for smells around a rock, and came to Sophie's side at her call. Sophie attached the Lab's leash to her belt with a clip and tightened the straps of her backpack once more, settling the weight so that it rested evenly on her hips. She set off toward the area of active lava flow that she had been able to see from the helicopter as they flew over the plain.

All the tourists visiting the lava flow site had made a road of sorts across the expanse. It was easy to follow their tracks. As the morning wore on, Sophie encountered people riding rented bikes, other hikers, and tourists of every stripe, age, and build. Even a quad rumbled past her, towing a flat trailer loaded with tourists.

Sophie reached a crude viewing area taped off with yellow caution tape and found a good vantage point, slightly out of the gusty wind that whipped over the wide flank of the volcano, hitting the ocean like a cat batting the surface with its paw.

The lava ran in a sinuous, slow-moving, hypnotic glowing river to the edge of the cliff of new stone. Molten red chunks of liquid rock dropped into the sea in a relentless stream, causing explosions of steam and a crackling sound like breaking glass as extreme heat met its match in the water.

Sophie watched the majestic sight from beside her stone bulwark, one hand on Ginger's ruff. The dog whined, but calmed under her hand as hours passed with no sense of time. They watched the blood of the earth ooze forth inexorably, hit the ocean in sizzling bursts, and slowly build the island.

Sunset bloomed spectacularly to the west over the sea in reds and yellows that echoed the colors of the lava. The light faded into purple and indigo. Stars appeared, the moon rose, and the tourists mounted their bikes, shouldered their toddlers, and headed back toward the parking area some miles away.

Sophie ate a couple of energy bars, drank some water, and fed Ginger some kibble, still watching the lava trickle into the sea. The gleaming surface brightened even more as darkness fell.

She felt no urgency to leave. *This was all, and it was enough.*

Eventually, she undid her bedroll and sleeping bag. She lay down with the dog close against her, still enthralled by the lava's pageantry.

The soft breath of next morning's breeze caressed Sophie's face, waking her. She had come to no conclusions nor had any deep insights about her bizarre and fragmented life, lying there on the cliff and watching the lava drip into the ocean—but she reveled in that elusive sense of freedom she'd been seeking.

Still meditative, Sophie eventually rolled up her sleeping bag and headed out. She didn't feel ready to deal with people right now, and was glad of the early morning emptiness on the lava plain. She glimpsed a whale spout in the nearby ocean as she and Ginger, unleashed, walked over the raw lava back toward civilization.

The dog gave a sudden bark, signaling her interest in something, and lunged off of the rough path worn by hundreds of feet. Sophie grabbed for her collar, but the Lab galloped away across the razor-sharp rock.

"Ginger, no!" Sophie cried. Ginger's feet could be cut on the keen-edged lava! "Ginger, come!" She scrambled after the dog, continuing to call as she ran as fast as her forty-pound pack would allow.

Ginger could be impulsive, but this level of disobedience was rare. Sophie dropped the backpack to the ground to gain speed. "Ginger! Come!"

The lava rose in frozen, broken waves around her like a sea captured in black stone. Coruscations of lightweight *a'a* lava created banks and waterfalls, mounds and shelves. Sophie labored over the rugged surface, gleaming with iridescence and sharp as glass.

Ginger seemed to be heading for a stand of burned trees on a mound of a hill, emerging like an island in the ocean of the rugged black plain. Sophie had heard that these protrusions of unburned land were called *kipukas.* She scowled with fear and concern, noticing steam wafting up from cracks nearby. They were running around on an active hot zone! "Ginger! *Daughter of a diseased warthog!*"

Ginger wasn't even listening to Sophie's Thai cursing this time. The Lab disappeared into a stand of hardy *ohia* trees marking the edge of the *kipuka.* Sophie, a few seconds behind, entered the sheltering forest, her heart pounding with anxiety and frustration. "Ginger! Bad dog! You are not getting off the leash anymore!"

The dog's answer was a sharp yap, followed by a frantic whine.

Something was wrong.

Sophie crashed through a screen of dense, brittle underbrush made up of ferns and bushes, swatting aside branches. Another time she would have enjoyed exploring the old-growth *koa* and *ohia* trees towering around her, the air filled with the melody of native birdsong.

The sweetish rotting smell of decomposition hit Sophie's nose: *Of course!* Ginger was so excited about some awful dead animal. Nothing made the dog happier than rolling in a nicely aged piece of roadkill. Sophie had to catch the damn dog before she rolled in whatever had drawn her all this way.

Sophie parted the branches of a hardy guava tree, and stopped short, covering her mouth and nose with a hand.

Ginger stood, tail waving, amid a pile of dead bodies.

CHAPTER TWO

Security Specialist Jake Dunn prided himself on his focus. Yeah, people said he was impulsive, but they just didn't understand how he worked. When Jake was interested in something, he zeroed in on it like a heat-seeking missile and followed his instincts, which could look like a series of tangents to others—but he always ended up in the right place at the right time, nailing his objective. He'd seldom been wrong following his gut, and now it was telling him that something was wrong on the Big Island.

Security Solutions' newest clients, a couple in their late fifties wearing the golf shirts and chinos of the well-to-do, sat in chairs across from Jake and his boss, President of Operations Kendall Bix.

Bix was doing the interviewing. "So how long has your daughter been missing?"

"A week." Kent Weathersby spoke, petting his wife's hand over and over. Jake wasn't much of a toucher and the tenderness in the gesture looked strange to him—but Betty Weathersby seemed to find it comforting. She snuggled into her husband, her immaculately coiffed head nestled on his shoulder.

"We reported Julie missing after she didn't check in with us for our scheduled weekly talk. She had been on a backpacking trip through the islands, and we'd agreed she would check in with us every week. She'd been on the Big Island for a week, then we stopped hearing from her, so we contacted the authorities. The Hilo Police Department closest to the area where she was last seen has not been able to find her." Weathersby spoke mechanically, as if he had rehearsed the speech so it would flow smoothly, even as his wife winced visibly with each mention of their daughter's disappearance.

Jake cleared his throat. "I hope we can be of help, but you understand we will need to work closely with local law enforcement, and not step on anyone's toes or duplicate efforts on the investigation."

"Julie usually found a group of other campers to hang out with both for safety and fun. We'd only had two short check-in talks since she arrived on the Big Island. She was camping outside Volcanoes National Park. She hadn't found anyone to hang out with yet that we knew of." Betty's wet blue gaze brought on a twinge of guilt. She reminded Jake of his mom.

His mom had flown all the way from the mainland to be at his bedside when he had been recovering from a recent gunshot wound. His sisters had come over too. Totally unnecessary, but at least they'd all been able to get a Hawaii vacation out of it.

Jake looked out the windows of Security Solutions' conference room to where he could see a sliver of ocean in the distance between the buildings. The ocean was his favorite thing about living in Honolulu; just looking at it soothed his restless soul.

"I think we should be able to get some more answers for you," Bix said. "A week isn't long to be missing for a young woman of your daughter's age. She probably met a guy and...you know." Bix smiled. The expression perched uncertainly on the man's stern mouth.

"We've been getting that same feeling from the police department that you're giving us now: they don't take us seriously. They think our daughter is shacked up with some man. That's the message we've been getting over and over. But our Julie is not like that,"

Weathersby said starkly. "Something's happened. Something's wrong."

Jake slapped his thighs and stood up. "I believe you. I'll go to the Big Island and find her." He turned to look at Bix. "And I know just the woman to help. Our field agent, Sophie Ang."

CHAPTER THREE

S<small>OPHIE</small> <small>BREATHED</small> <small>THROUGH</small> <small>HER</small> <small>MOUTH</small>, overwhelmed by the stench and the sight before her. "Ginger! Come!"

The dog finally obeyed, whining anxiously over the discovery. Sophie clicked the leash onto Ginger's collar, her eyes scanning the scene. She dragged the dog back behind an *ohia* tree for cover, assessing the area and its horror.

The bodies were distorted with bloating, still dressed in their clothing. Gender and age were difficult to determine except by size, clothing, and length of hair. Five people, probably a family, had been piled into a shallow depression, but the killer hadn't bothered to cover them.

Sophie identified a Caucasian male and female adult along with two boys and a girl. Their clothing was better quality; the kids wore name brand shoes, and the parents' outfits were classic middle-class garb for Hawaii: aloha shirt and jeans on the man, capri pants and a tank top on the woman. Cause of death appeared to be gunshot; one of the bodies, the little girl dumped on top, faced Sophie. A bullet hole in what had been her forehead crawled with flies. Her eyes were missing, probably pecked out by mynah birds.

Sophie backed away, scanning the area. Most likely she wasn't in danger; this site appeared to be a straightforward body dump. Still, she needed to get back to her pack where her gun and phone awaited, and call it in.

Jogging back through the lush foliage of the *kipuka,* alive with birdsong and the green of mature trees, Sophie shook her head to clear it of a sense of unreality. *She hadn't come to the Big Island to investigate yet another crime in a remote place!* She was supposed to be having a vacation!

Who would shoot an entire family and just dump them out here?

Sophie'd been avoiding the news lately, but something like the disappearance of five well-off white people tended to get into the news. *Why hadn't she heard about this?*

"Not my circus. Not my monkeys," Sophie murmured one of Marcella's sayings. But the little girl's empty eye sockets had stared at her, making this her problem in a horrifying way.

Sophie reached her pack, secured Ginger to a clip, and dug out her phone. She had one bar of reception and her battery was low from her overnight on the lava without charging it. She called 911. "Hi. This is Sophie Ang. I'm a hiker in Kalapana, and my dog led me to a *kipuka* off the trail where we discovered the bodies of a Caucasian family." It felt good to identify herself by her legal name, now that the events of her past had been resolved. Law enforcement would run her name, and discover her background as a former FBI Agent. "I will wait for your team to arrive."

The sun was high overhead by then. Sophie took out her solar battery cell phone charger and hooked it up to the phone. She hiked back across the hot lava to the edge of the *kipuka,* where she and Ginger could wait in the shade under one of the towering *ohia* trees. She had given the team the best instructions she could, and it wasn't long before she spotted a couple of ATVs roaring toward her.

The responding detectives, accompanied by a couple of uniformed officers, introduced themselves. "Detective Kamani Freitan and Detective Fred Wong. Point us to the area of the discovery," the female detective said.

"Decomp has set in," Sophie said. "You're going to want proper crime scene wear."

Freitan, a statuesque woman with thick, black hair in a braid and tilted brown eyes, looked at her quizzically. Sophie met the woman's gaze squarely. "I'm former FBI. I'd say the victims were killed five or six days ago. Family of five. Execution style body dump."

The detectives looked at each other. "Wait here while we check it out. Where is the location?" Wong said.

Sophie pointed. "Through the trees there. Follow your noses—the smell will be your guide."

One of the uniformed officers stayed back with a clipboard. "I'd like to get your statement, Ms. Ang."

All of this was standard operating procedure, but Sophie still felt the usual suspicion coming from the investigators elicited by anyone discovering a body. She breathed through her frustration and gave her statement of events leading to the discovery to the officer as the detectives left.

Detective Freitan reappeared, visibly pale under her tan. "I need to find a cell signal out from under these trees." She walked a distance away and Sophie could hear her, working both the radio and her cell phone, calling for her commanding officer, the medical examiner, and crime scene investigators. Presumably her partner was still with the bodies.

Sophie's phone buzzed, and she jumped. *Only a few people had this number.* She glanced at the little window, and answered. "Hello, Jake."

"Hey, gorgeous. How's the hiking?" Jake sounded upbeat and energetic.

"Not so terrific. Ginger's nose led me to a body dump in the lava field. A whole Caucasian family, executed."

"Do not discuss an active investigation!" Freitan snapped, walking toward Sophie. "Who are you talking to?"

"My partner at a private security firm," Sophie said, as Jake fired questions in the background. "I will not discuss it with him further."

11

Freitan folded her arms. "I'm going to want to speak to him. And your boss."

"I'm on leave from Security Solutions," Sophie said. "Personal leave. I won't discuss what I found. Can I continue my conversation, as long as it stays away from that subject?"

"Give me the phone." Sophie handed it over. "This is Detective Freitan with the Hilo Police Department. You are not to say anything to anyone about this discovery, do you hear?"

Sophie overheard squawks from the phone, presumably Jake agreeing.

"Good. If we have a leak, I will have your head. Here's your partner." Freitan handed Sophie the phone and turned her back, still fully listening in.

Sophie tightened her lips in annoyance, returning her attention to Jake. "I have happened upon a situation."

"When do you not? Jeez, woman, you're a magnet for trouble in paradise! But as it happens, I called to get your help on a case over there."

"A case?" Sophie walked a little further from Freitan. "What kind of case?"

"Missing person. Julie Weathersby, age twenty-four, tourist-hiker, has vanished from her camping trip around the island."

Sophie glanced back toward the gruesome body dump. She couldn't be totally sure, but none of the bodies seemed like a single young female. "Want me to come back on the payroll to help you here on the Big Island? My vacation trip isn't exactly going as planned."

"Just what I was hoping you'd say. I'm coming over. Can you meet me at the airport?"

Freitan turned to Sophie with a look in her eye.

"Not sure, Jake. I don't have a car. Call you back later." She pushed the END button on Jake's loud protest, and slid the phone into the pocket of her pants.

"I ran a background check on you. Your story checks out," Freitan said.

"It would be incongruous to lie about being an FBI agent. Very easy to verify the truth."

"I've heard crazier things." Freitan smiled. "Know anyone in the department over here?"

"In fact, I do. Dr. Wilson, your psychologist, is an acquaintance. I am close with Sergeant Leilani Texeira. She is stationed on Maui but started her career here, I understand, under Captain Ohale."

"Yep, Ohale's my commanding officer and I remember Lei. We graduated from the academy around the same time. She was a good cop." Freitan's attitude visibly thawed. "Weird that you found this body dump while just out hiking."

"Indeed it is. But not when you consider Ginger." The dog, seated beside Sophie, pricked her floppy triangle ears at the sound of her name. "Ginger's got quite a nose for dead things. So, was this family reported missing?"

"That's what's interesting. Empty wallet with ID was on the adult male body, and we called it in. Not reported missing, but the family does have an address in Ocean View." Freitan gestured inland. "Big area of unregulated development and small landowners. Lot of weird shit goes down there. But I shouldn't be talking with you about it, really."

"I understand." Sophie looked away across the lava. Hot air shimmered over the black stone. Hiking across it in the afternoon did not appeal, and the heat would likely blister Ginger's paws. "Will you want to interview me at your station or anything?"

Freitan's lips tightened. "Not sure yet. Got to check in with Captain Ohale."

Sophie nodded and sat back down under the now-familiar *ohia* tree as Freitan left. She took out her canteen and poured some liquid into a collapsible pet bowl for Ginger, then drank the rest. She peeled an energy bar and gave Ginger some kibble, then rested her back against the tree's rugged bole. The area was like an island in the sea

13

of the lava; that was the gist of what *kipuka* meant, and it was aptly named.

Sweet-singing native birds flitted among the red blossoms above her, and Sophie reached out to touch one of the scarlet, tufted flowers.

"The legend of why the *lehua* blossom lives on the *ohia* tree is a sad one." Her friend Lei's voice filled her mind, telling her the story as they sat by a fire in Lei's backyard on Maui. "The legend says that one day the fire goddess Pele, fiercely jealous, met a handsome warrior named Ohia, and asked him to marry her. Ohia, however, had already pledged his love to Lehua. Pele was furious when Ohia turned down her marriage proposal, so she turned him into a twisted tree. Lehua was heartbroken, and the other gods took pity on her. They decided it was an injustice to have Ohia and Lehua separated, and they turned Lehua into a flower on the *ohia* tree, so that the two lovers would be forever joined together. That's why, if you pluck a *lehua* flower, you are separating the lovers, and that day it will rain."

A little rain might not be a bad thing—the lava was too hot to walk on. Sophie plucked the *lehua* blossom and tucked it behind her ear.

"That's bad luck, you know." Detective Wong came out of the forest. The mixed Hawaiian-Chinese man was pale and sweating under his sterile gear. He tore off his mask. "You never pick the *lehua*."

Sophie removed the blossom from behind her ear. "I heard a legend that picking one meant rain. That didn't seem so bad."

Wong fisted his hands on his hips and tipped his head back, sucking in deep breaths of fresh air. "Rain would wreck our crime scene. I thought I'd seen some things, but that was bad back there. Those kids. What the hell motive could there be for that kind of slaughter in a place like this?"

"I know." Sophie stroked Ginger's head, gazing into the dog's soulful eyes, wishing she could erase the memory of the little girl's bloated, mutilated face. "Looked like a mob execution to me. I've heard there are a lot of witness protection folks hiding on the Big Island. Have you checked in with the U.S. Marshals?"

Wong's eyes narrowed. "Who did you say you were?"

"Witness protection leak—not a bad theory. Fred, this is Sophie Ang. She's ex-FBI." Freitan addressed Sophie as she stripped off her gloves and joined them. "I called some friends and they gave the thumbs-up about you. Said you're a whiz with tech."

"I am a whiz with tech." False modesty wasn't useful. "I am happy to help in any way I can." Sophie didn't want to compound her bad luck by throwing away the *lehua* flower, so she slid it out of sight into her pocket, regretting crushing the delicate blossom.

"It's weird that the victims aren't reported missing anywhere— but they wouldn't be if no one knew who they were, and some federal agent thought they were safely stashed." Freitan gestured to Wong. "Let's run this by the chief and then reach out to Witness Security."

"Can I get a ride to town? My partner is flying into Hilo for a missing persons job we're going to work together." Sophie needed to detach from the case. They weren't going to let her be a part of it— but having found the bodies, seen that little girl . . . *she always would be.*

"Sure, we can give you a lift. We were about to head back to the office anyway, now that the techs and the ME are processing. It's going to be awhile before we have any more information than we gleaned on our pass through the crime scene."

CHAPTER FOUR

JAKE PICKED up his duffel from the checked bags section at the Hilo airport. He hated checking a bag, but carrying his weapons demanded it.

Flying commercial was such a buzzkill.

Security Solutions was expanding its transportation fleet, but it looked like it would be a while before the company jet was whisking anyone but their CEO, Sheldon Hamilton, around the world.

As soon as he picked up his rented Jeep, Jake phoned Sophie.

To his surprise she answered. "Jake. I'm on my way into Hilo with some detectives. Where can we meet?"

His heart didn't just give a great big thunderous squeeze at the sound of Sophie's sexy accented voice. No, his hands weren't sweaty, gripping the steering wheel at the mere thought of being alone with her. He hadn't just jumped on this job so he'd have a reason to track her down. Nope. Not at all.

Jake cleared his throat. "Let's meet wherever they're taking you. We need to start working with the local PD on this missing persons case, anyway. What station are you headed for?"

He listened to a muffled conversation, then Sophie said, "I will meet you at South Hilo Station in an hour." She hung up.

Sophie often hung up on him.

What did it say about their relationship that she was usually either hanging up on him, leaving him, or getting a new burner phone with a number he didn't have?

But he had *this* phone number. Her latest number. He'd memorized it immediately.

Jake glanced down at the inside of his forearm where she had written a series of digits in ink. She crossed her sevens and drew a line through her zeros. Only a faint tinge of blue still showed. Not that he had been consciously trying to keep the number from disappearing or anything—that area up there by his elbow was just out of handwashing range.

Jake remembered that moment in the restaurant vividly. She'd written the number on his arm with a ballpoint pen from the hostess stand; he'd said something funny and as she finished writing she froze suddenly, holding his wrist. He heard the deep inhale of her breathing. Electricity surged between them. She held his arm for a long moment, the pen pressed against his skin, not moving.

The atoms in him streamed toward the atoms in her—it felt weirdly metaphysical.

"Sophie," he whispered.

This wasn't the only time attraction had zapped them out of nowhere. They'd almost crossed that invisible line several times.

They'd saved each other's lives more than once. Saving someone's life tattooed the person on your heart a little bit—*especially when that someone was so utterly awesome.*

Sophie had flung his arm down and practically ran out of the restaurant. Jake was so repulsive to her that she'd jogged away to join that bastard Alika with his helicopter and smooth moves.

He was fooling himself, imagining that he could be the one to get past the ways Sophie's sick, abusive ex had messed her up.

He'd tried to get over Sophie on their last job together by having a thing with Antigua, the estate manager at their client Shank Miller's.

Antigua was great: gorgeous, a wonderful cook, hot in the sack, a really quality person. She'd given him the heave-ho after a month. "Make a move on Sophie, Jake. I won't be anyone's second choice." *Ouch.* The lady was right.

He had to make a move on this trip. Sophie was still on the rebound from her boyfriend Todd Remarkian's death. She was going to get scooped up by that rich player Alika if he didn't do something.

Jake's belly knotted. He'd already been stung by the nettle of rejection more than once when Sophie shut down his flirting. He'd never had trouble getting a woman he wanted before; but Sophie had ignored or refused his various tried-and-true gambits, shit that always worked with chicks in the past.

Jake was stuck in the friend zone, trapped between the pillars of work partnership and the way he annoyed her.

Yeah, he was too restless. Too loud. Too impatient. Had too much energy. Always wanted to take the lead. None of that was going to change.

Tough. They'd find a way somehow to rub along and give each other space—they already had, as partners. And he'd make up for how irritating he was by being so fucking good to her in bed she wouldn't be able to walk or do anything but sigh and say, *"Oh, yes, Jake. Yes."*

Jake missed the turn onto the highway because he was so caught up in his thoughts. He shifted in his seat, hot and uncomfortable, and pulled the Jeep over onto the side of the road to put down the soft top and get some more air, since the AC didn't seem to be working.

"Dream on, Jake. She's not into you. Why are you torturing yourself?" *She was making him crazy.* He was talking to himself like an idiot. He never got this twisted up about women!

Jake looked around at the urban sprawl outside of Hilo's old town area. All vegetation was bright green, saturated by the Big Island's frequent east side rains. Traffic was heavy on the busy freeway going into town. Hilo had the look of a place that had once been sleepy and small, but had sprawled into utilitarian growth.

Jake programmed the South Hilo PD location into his phone's GPS, and fifteen minutes later was pulling up to a small, older building wedged between a Vietnamese nail salon and a laundromat. After parking, he pulled open a bulletproof glass door covered in peeling reflective coating, entering a tiny lobby guarded by a duty officer.

The individual was the size of a mountain and held a Sudoku tablet in front of him. He looked up at Jake and narrowed his eyes. "Help you?"

Jake showed his Security Solutions ID, introduced himself and his errand. "Our firm has been hired to find a missing person. I'm looking for Julie Weathersby. Anyone assigned to the case that I can interview?"

The behemoth typed in the name on his computer as Jake surveyed a row of hard wooden chairs, scuffed linoleum, and a crowded bulletin board. He recognized his client's face on a missing persons printout thumbtacked to the board, issued by a company called FindUsNow.com. Her sweet-looking smile stood out among the most-wanted posters and a homemade ad for pet sitting. *"Social Media can Find Us Now! Forward to a friend on Snapchat, Twitter or Facebook!"*

The Weathersbys had probably employed that company, too. Jake took one of the several flyers and tucked it into his pocket.

"Detectives Wong and Freitan have that case. They are on their way back from the field." The giant pointed to a hard wooden chair. "Sit and wait."

Jake sat and waited.

Sitting and waiting was not something he enjoyed.

He worked his phone first, checking in with the office on Oahu to report that he had arrived and was meeting Sophie; then he logged into his case file. He already had one started for the Weathersby girl; he added a quick phone photo of her missing persons poster. He ran a search for FindUsNow.com and checked out the write-up they'd done on Julie. Apparently, she wasn't big on any social media but

Instagram; her last photo was of the big lava tube in Volcanoes National Park.

Bored, he stepped outside and got into the Jeep. He extracted a hand exerciser and a couple of heavy duty rubber bands from his bag, and using those, with his seat tipped back, he was able to run through a fairly complete upper-body workout. He was just getting ready to do another set of curl reps when an extra-duty truck towing an ATV on a trailer pulled up.

A male and female detective exited the truck along with Sophie and her dog.

Everyone looked overheated from being on the lava; their shirts were sweaty and their skin was gleaming. Sophie, dressed in a black tank and ripstop hiking pants, still managed to look stunning even with dark circles under her big brown eyes. He hated how she didn't take care of herself.

Jake opened the Jeep's door and stepped out. "Sophie!"

Ginger yanked loose from her owner to run over to him, thrusting her nose into his crotch and then lashing him with her sturdy tail.

Sophie grinned at the sight. "Someone is happy to see you."

"At least Ginger knows a good thing when she sees it." Jake joked. He wanted to grab Sophie and kiss her; he made do with a casual half wave, catching Ginger's collar to drag the Lab, now investigating a trash can, back over to her mistress.

Sophie took the leash and introduced him to the cops. "Detective Freitan and Detective Wong, this is my partner Jake Dunn. The detectives responded to the crime scene I found, and were kind enough to bring me here."

Jake sized up the two. Freitan looked like a multi-ethnic Wonder Woman; tall with a curvy build and a shiny thick braid, her hand-shake wrung his hand like a truck driver's as she ran an eyeball over him in a frank, full body check-out. Wong was wiry and short and disliked Jake on sight, judging by the squint of his eyes and his refusal to shake.

Jake forged ahead, adopting a confident manner. "Just the people

I came to see. My agency, Security Solutions, has been retained to investigate the disappearance of Julie Weathersby. I hear you're the detectives on the case."

"Yeah. We are looking into that one. It's early days yet. Her parents seem a little overprotective. She's probably holed up with a dude, which can be fun." The detective licked her lips and showed her teeth like she wanted to take a bite of him. "Can't blame a girl for getting swept away by the right man."

Jake ignored the byplay and grinned his most charming. "Well, since my friend Sophie here just found you a big case with that body dump, maybe you wouldn't mind letting us run with the ball on the missing persons a bit."

"Sure thing." Freitan narrowed her eyes at Wong, who had opened his mouth to object. "Fred, the Weathersby case is back burner right now with this other discovery. Why not let the private dicks run with it?" She emphasized *"dicks"* in a way that made Jake squirm internally, though with an effort, he kept his expression neutral and his stance relaxed.

Wong gave an almost imperceptible head jerk towards the bull pen area through a closed gate. "We can give them what we have, at least."

CHAPTER FIVE

"LET me just tie Ginger up and get her out of the way," Sophie told Jake and the detectives.

The three of them waited while Sophie secured Ginger's leash to a handy little railing and provided her with a dish of water. They filed inside, weaving through a work area of tight cubicles to a section in the back. There was barely room for the four of them to wedge into Wong and Freitan's office area.

Sophie's arm brushed Jake's and she felt a surprising *zing!* of sensation as her partner leaned forward, his elbows on his knees in the cramped cubicle. He was trying to peer at Detective Freitan's computer to see the case file she had pulled up on Julie.

"Never underestimate the power of the rich parents of a white girl," Freitan drawled, glancing back at them. "Wonder what would have happened if this *haole* girl had been local and poor. We'd still be trying to fit her in with all our other cases. It's actually a good thing you showed up when you did."

Sophie pulled her arm away from Jake's. "Is there a problem with missing people on the Big Island?"

"Yes," Wong printed the meager Weathersby file, and caught the pages spitting out of the printer, slipping them into a blank folder. "A lot of people go missing here. For a lot of reasons. This island is a big area to cover and being understaffed is one reason we have trouble closing cases."

"But we seldom have anything like that body dump you found," Freitan said. "Let me put it differently: never have we had something like that. A whole new level. I've got a call into WITSEC and it's looking like there might be something to your mob hit idea, because a couple of Marshals are coming to meet with us in an hour. They wouldn't discuss it further, but that they're making the trip says a whole lot."

"I'm sorry to hear that I might have been right," Sophie said. "Doesn't make sense for anyone to kill the whole family."

"Maybe they all saw something. Who knows?" Freitan shrugged. "We'll do the best we can, as usual. Now as to this missing Weathersby girl . . . we went to her last known camping spot the day we got the report. She was staying at Volcanoes Park. When we showed her picture around, no one had seen her. Her equipment was gone. She had a permit for two nights; she had arrived by unknown means. That's as far as we got."

"Any leads from different campsites? Her parents said she often found other travelers to group together with," Jake said.

"We only had the case a few days. That's as far as we got with it."

Jake's arm brushed Sophie's again as he reached for the folder from Wong. She shoved her chair back and away to get space. Freitan turned a level stare on her. "You guys a thing?"

"A thing?" Sophie frowned. *Some sort of vernacular.* The woman's pursed lips and raised brows implied it was sexual.

"Yeah, we are." Jake put a big hand on Sophie's knee and squeezed.

Sophie froze. Was he saying . . . they were a couple?

"Too bad," Freitan smiled, a long slow smile. "I like a little white meat now and again."

"By the sweat of Ramses!" Sophie swore, all of the innuendoes coming together in an excruciating moment of mortification that heated her face and chest. "There is no sexual relationship between me and my partner!" She took hold of Jake's wrist, but it took both hands to pry his grip off her leg. "You may indulge your sexual interest in Jake if he is agreeable. He has frequent liaisons."

"I don't think he's agreeable," Freitan said regretfully. "But he might be if you joined us."

"Hey. I'm right here, Freitan, and we're on the clock," Wong said. "Keep your pants zipped in our cubicle, please."

Jake stood up. His face was expressionless. A muscle ticked in his jaw. "I do believe I've just been sexually harassed, and I can't say I like it overmuch, Detective Freitan. Is this all the information you've got?"

Sophie stood as well, her eyes down, fighting the urge to bolt. *Why had Jake said that about them being a couple?* Was he claiming a faux relationship with her to fend off Freitan's advances? And why did it bother her that he did?

"That's all. Hope you get somewhere with it, big boy." Freitan was unfazed by Jake's rebuke to judge by her insouciant tone. There might even have been another innuendo hidden in her parting words, but Sophie didn't want to figure it out. She squeezed past Jake and did a very rapid walk, not technically a run, through the bull pen and out the front door of the station.

Outside, Sophie rushed over to Ginger and untied her. She tossed away the remaining water and stowed the foldable dish in her backpack. She felt more than heard Jake come up behind her.

"That was embarrassing."

Sophie didn't look up from fiddling with the dog's leash. Her skin still felt hot and prickly.

"I think we should go look at Weathersby's earlier camp sites." Jake's tone was nonchalant, as if being propositioned for a threesome was a normal event. *Maybe, for him, it was.* The thought made her stomach hurt. "It seems like these guys barely got started and didn't

25

really take the case seriously. I think there's a lot of room to develop some leads."

"Yes. The campsites seem like a good place to begin." Sophie straightened and tugged the dog's leash. "Perhaps I can camp tonight in whatever park we end up in."

"I have no intention of anything but a hot shower and a soft bed tonight," Jake said. "And you look like you could use one or both, too."

"I'm sure Detective Freitan would be happy to share hers with you." Sophie wished she could take the words back the second they were out of her mouth. She tweaked Ginger's leash and headed for the Jeep.

"Jealous?" Jake sounded almost cheerful. "Because I think I made it clear I wasn't interested in her."

If only she were quicker at repartee! Sophie's tongue felt thick and her throat choked with inarticulate exclamations that didn't clarify her confusion about Jake and his behavior one bit. *"Son of a yak!"* she muttered. She loaded her backpack into the rear area, secured Ginger on the back seat, and took her place in front beside her partner. He started the rental, and they roared out of the South Hilo Police Department parking lot with more throttle than necessary.

The open road leading out of Hilo led toward a campground in the Waimea area, where Julie Weathersby had stayed before Volcanoes National Park, where she'd disappeared. The wind blowing through the open vehicle gradually swept the awkwardness away. Sophie enjoyed the plethora of bright flowers, tall grasses, and overarching tropical trees as they drove.

"I wish I didn't get drawn into these situations," she said, and the wind whipped her words away.

"What?" Jake shouted.

Sophie glanced into the back seat of the Jeep. Ginger's eyes were slitted shut as the breeze ruffled her fur. The dog looked totally content. *If only life were even an eighth as simple for her as it was for her dog.*

"I wish I didn't keep getting into these things. Body dumps. Missing people. So much violence."

"That's the nature of the job. You could always go back to working behind a computer." Jake's gaze was compassionate. He felt sorry for her. It was not acceptable.

"I'm well aware of that, Jake Dunn. I have chosen this path, and for some reason I am here to help find answers, help people who cannot help themselves. I thought I was going to be a tourist for once, that's all. I feel like my walkabout has been hijacked. First by the body dump, then by you and this case."

"I'm sorry." His hand landed on her leg for the second time. She removed it with both of hers and set it back on the steering wheel.

"That's quite enough of that. We are not a 'thing,' Jake. And I don't know why you said we were."

Jake was silent. Sophie sneaked a glance at him, and his profile was stony. She couldn't leave it alone. "I don't understand why you said that we were a couple."

"I was just trying to get Freitan off my back."

"But it did not slow her down a bit."

"No, it did not." Jake's knuckles gleamed white on the wheel. "That was awkward. I apologize if I made you uncomfortable."

"Yes, you made me uncomfortable. I accept your apology. Freitan was inappropriate." Sophie hated how stiff and wooden she sounded.

"Would it be so bad?"

"What?"

"If we were a couple. A thing."

Sophie glanced at him. That muscle in his jaw looked like a cable. His gunmetal eyes were glued to the road. His arms were so tight she wondered that he didn't break the steering wheel. She glimpsed a smear of blue ink on the inside of his arm near the elbow. *Was that where she'd written her number?*

"It would not work. We . . . irritate each other." Sophie's heart was pounding so hard she felt it in her temples.

"And yet . . ."

"And yet, what?" She turned to face him.

"And yet. That's all I'm saying." He refused to look at her.

She flounced around in the seat, fiddled with her seatbelt. "I would never be one of your . . .bed buddies, Jake."

"Nor would I be one of yours. I told you that when you propositioned me. Remember?" His eyes seared her. Gray was just the wrong word for them. They were definitely silver. Silver with blue.

"Oh. That. I was drunk." That awful prickling on her chest and neck had returned. "Drinking lowers inhibitions. Everyone knows that. That's why I don't drink."

"And sometimes they call booze a truth serum. Dutch courage. Drinking gets you to tell what's really going on. Were you telling the truth that day on Maui, Sophie, when you asked me to have sex with you?"

Sophie couldn't breathe. All this air whipping around, and she couldn't breathe. "I can't be in a relationship right now. I told Alika the same thing."

"That slick asshole. I knew he was making a move."

"Alika's not an asshole. He is a good person. Really good."

"And I'm not?"

"You know you're not, Jake." Sophie didn't flinch when she met his eyes. "You're selfish. Sometimes you cheat. You're a dirty fighter. You like this line of work for the thrills and danger, not because you enjoy helping people."

"I like helping just fine. Helping people is fun, and I like having fun. And as far as good—I could be *good* to you, Sophie. *So* good."

The Jeep wandered across the center line as their eyes locked.

Jake overcorrected. They wove a bit, and Ginger yelped from the back seat.

"I think that's the turnoff to the park." Sophie pointed. Jake turned the vehicle down the side road, and made no further comment.

Sophie exhaled a long slow breath.

"*So* good," he said again, and Sophie shut her eyes because she could feel the shape of the words on her skin.

CHAPTER SIX

JAKE TURNED THE WHEEL, heading down into the park. The narrow, two-lane road wove along the side of a canyon draped in varying shades of vegetation. He unclenched his hands on the wheel—they'd begun to cramp.

That was his big move? Grabbing her leg and pretending they were "a thing" in front of those detectives?

Smooth one, Jake. Nice. She was really impressed by your promise to "make it good."

Jake sneaked a look at Sophie. Her face was turned away as she looked out the window and her eyes were shut, but blotchy color showed on the golden skin of her neck.

She was blushing.

He'd gotten to her.

Yeah! His opening move had sucked, but she was thinking about what he'd said.

It was a start. He could work with it. The key to success was exploiting every angle toward an objective. And his objective had just shown a chink in her defenses.

They reached the bottom of the canyon and a small parking lot beneath the high, graceful arch of a freeway overpass. That bridge spanned both the canyon and a small river that tumbled over rocks and between banks of tall native grass.

Jake pulled the Jeep into a parking spot and they sat for a moment, surveying the park.

A camping area toward where the riverbank met the ocean was clearly marked. Off to the right, tucked up against the steep wall of the canyon, hunkered a cement block bathroom. A brisk wind blew in from the sea, smelling of the ocean. Jake's nostrils flared instinctively, taking in the salty goodness.

Sophie gestured toward a small group of tents clustered in the designated camping zone. "We should begin by canvassing there. You have a photo of our client?"

"Sure do." Jake took out his phone and texted a photo of their client to Sophie.

Julie Weathersby was five foot six, one hundred and thirty pounds, with light brown hair and blue eyes. She had freckles on her nose and a hopeful smile with the perfect teeth of good orthodontia. In the photo, she wore hiking clothes and carried the backpack she'd disappeared with.

"She looks so young." Sophie said.

"She's twenty-four."

"That's how old I was when I escaped from Assan." Sophie's lips folded tight. "I didn't feel young."

She so seldom said anything about her fucked-up marriage. "That bastard stole your . . . your youth and innocence." Jake growled. "May he rot in hell."

"It's some comfort that I sent him there." Sophie opened the door of the Jeep and got out. *Yeah, she'd sent him there, all right—Sophie had slit the man's throat.* Not that he didn't deserve that, and more. Jake would've liked a little time to work on Assan Ang with a knife, himself.

They left Ginger secured in the vehicle with some water and a dog biscuit.

The two approached the first tent. A young mother sat on a beach

32

towel near its entrance, playing with a baby wearing a *puka* shell necklace and a diaper. Sophie squatted to smile at the child, who reached out a hand, grasping her finger. "She's darling."

"Thank you. We think so," the mom said.

Sophie was such a softie when it came to kids. Every case they'd worked so far, she seemed to get attached to any children involved. He'd never forget climbing over that fence at a cult's headquarters in Waipio, carrying a couple of terrified children, with dogs and armed men on their trail.

Sophie chatted up the mother as Jake surveilled the camp. A young man strolled towards them, wearing a pair of board shorts and a battered tee. He carried a fishing pole and a stringer.

"Good fishing?" Jake loved fishing on any days he had off. Spin casting, stream fishing, reef walking, deep-sea—it didn't matter, as long as he was near the water.

"Got a few *papio* for dinner." Jake recognized the Hawaiian word for a small jack as the young man held up his catch. "What can we do for you, Detective?"

Jake laughed. "I'm not a cop. But Ms. Ang and I are private investigators." He held up his Security Solutions ID, and Sophie showed hers as well. "We're looking for a young woman who camped here around a week ago." He held up his phone so they could see the photo of Julie Weathersby.

The young woman shook her head. "We've only been here a week. But I think the couple down by the creek has been here long enough to have seen her."

Taking their leave, Jake and Sophie walked toward a battered tent set close to the water, away from the rest. Disorderly bins of personal clothing and objects were piled nearby. The door was zippered shut.

Jake flicked a finger at Sophie, cueing her to speak first. Women elicited less caution in an initial encounter. Sophie approached the tent. "Hello? Anyone inside? We need to speak with you."

Rustling. Muttering. These people did not appear to be as friendly as the small family they'd first spoken to. Jake stepped aside out of view, his hand falling to the holstered weapon at his hip. Finally, the zipper moved upward slowly. A young woman poked her head out. Her blonde hair was snarled, falling over sunken eyes. He spotted a scabby sore on the back of her hand. "What do you want?"

Dark shadows moved behind her.

Sophie held up her phone for the young woman to see. "We're looking for our friend Julie. She seems to have gone missing. Have you seen her?" The woman reached for the phone, but Sophie moved it up and away so that the photo was more visible. "Julie Weathersby. She would have been here a little more than a week ago. Traveling on her own. We were supposed to meet her at Volcanoes Park, but she never showed up."

A flicker of something showed on the woman's face, but she shook her head. "No. Haven't seen her."

"I'm Sophie. What's your name?" Sophie was still trying to get a connection that Jake had already decided wasn't going to happen. The woman didn't answer. Sophie showed the phone again. "Maybe your friend has seen her?"

A rough masculine voice rumbled from behind the woman. "She told you we haven't seen her. Buzz off."

Sophie glanced at Jake. He gave a quick negative shake of the head. Maybe they could find out something more about these campers from the other park dwellers, or from sending a ranger to check the couple's permits. He glanced at the tent pole. *No permit.*

Jake took his phone out, stepping away to call the park service.

They worked their way through the rest of the campsites, letting Sophie be the face of the operation while Jake kept an eye out and provided backup.

Sophie was letting Ginger stretch her legs by the river when a Hawaii State Park truck rumbled down the road to pull in beside the Jeep. Jake intercepted the green and white vehicle with its distinct logo.

"Hey there. I'm Jake Dunn, a private investigator with Security Solutions." He held up his ID. "We're looking for a missing person, and in the course of interviewing these campers, came across what might be some permit violations."

The ranger slammed the door of his truck with a thump. "Oh yeah?" A mixed-race male of five-ten, approximately a hundred and seventy pounds, his ID badge read Hernandez. "Getting me out here to do your investigation for you, eh?"

Jake raised his brows innocently. "Just thought you'd want to know. There's a couple over there that looks like they're making this park their permanent home." He gestured toward the riverside camp-site with its assorted piles and bins. "Would you mind taking a look at a photo of our missing person? Maybe you've seen her."

"Sure." Hernandez squinted at the picture of the smiling young woman as Sophie put Ginger back in the Jeep and approached. She introduced herself, and Jake narrowed his eyes as Hernandez checked her out and clearly liked what he saw.

Jake glanced at Sophie, remembering meeting her for the first time.

Yeah, Sophie was hot—five-nine and one thirty-five, all muscle, bone and tender curves. That caramel skin, those gorgeous arms and legs with their secret tattoos . . . Her eyes. That sexy scar. The weird way she seemed both badass and vulnerable. And her voice! *That accent.* It slayed him.

Even in a pair of hiking pants and a tank top that had seen better days, she was unusual and stunning.

Would this be his life with her if they ever got together? Every man they met checking her out, wishing for the impossible?

If so, *worth it.* He could deal.

Jake reached for the phone and took it back from the ranger. "So, you haven't seen Julie Weathersby? Not just here, but at any park? We heard from her parents that she was camping on the Big Island for a week or two before she disappeared."

Hernandez shook his head. "Nope. We've had a lot of missing persons on the Big Island this year. Doesn't surprise me some folks are hiring private eyes to supplement the police. Police department is pretty overwhelmed. Park Service is stretched thin." The man folded his lips together suddenly, as if regretting saying so much. He brandished a metal clipboard holding citations. "Could you stay back here and let me do my job?"

"Of course." Jake nodded respectfully. He needed this guy on his side. Hernandez headed for the hostile couple's campsite, and Jake's hand fell to his weapon, just resting there. Waiting.

CHAPTER SEVEN

SOPHIE WATCHED Ranger Hernandez approach the tent containing the illegal campers. The two reluctantly emerged at his direction, but they were too far away for Sophie to hear.

The couple were poorly groomed. They held themselves in defensive postures with folded arms and sulky stares as the Ranger lectured them, obviously directing that they break down their camp and move along. Sophie wondered if he were allowed to conduct a search, and surmised not, as Hernandez pointed at the tent, and they shook their heads. Finally, Hernandez returned in their direction as the couple began packing their belongings.

"Where will they go?" Sophie asked the ranger. "Is there a shelter that will take them in?"

"There are a couple of places in Hilo, but I suspect they will just go somewhere else and squat. There are a lot of encampments on private land here on the island where the homeless congregate."

"Kinda seems like a problem." Jake had his arms folded in an unconscious imitation of the campers. "Is there another park toward Waimea? Our client's parents said Julie camped somewhere on the Kona side, but she never told them the name of it."

"There are a number of places. East Point is one of the most popular." Hernandez described a park near a lighthouse on a bay that faced Maui. "It's got a good beach, snorkeling. Tourists on foot seem to like it."

Sophie felt compelled to defend the choice to camp. "I am enjoying my own backpacking and camping trip. It's a great way to really see and experience the island."

Hernandez nodded, his eyes softening. "I can recommend the top five places on this island to hike," he said. "Some of them you won't find in any guidebook. Let me write down the details for you."

Sophie followed him over to the hood of his truck. The ranger removed a blank piece of paper and made a list of destinations for her to explore, including whether or not they had facilities.

Jake paced up and down behind her. She could feel his restlessness, and the way he kept an eye on the campers as they continued to break down their area.

Eventually Hernandez continued around the park checking everyone's permits, and Sophie and Jake got back into the Jeep. Jake looked up at the overcast sky, already beginning to darken to the west. "I don't know about you, but I'm ready for some food, a shower, and that aforementioned soft bed."

Sophie's belly gave a grumble of agreement. "I guess we could head in that direction, and see what we find."

They drove into the town of Waimea and had an early dinner at a burger joint featuring a specialty of the ranching area, local grass-fed beef. Jake was a rapid and efficient eater, consuming his burger in about four bites. Sophie ate hers much more deliberately.

Jake gestured to her with a fry. "You need more meat on your bones. You're getting skinny, Sophie."

"I know." Stress over recent events, combined with haphazard packing and nutrition on the camping trip she'd finished in Kalalau, had not helped. "Marcella said the same thing. Some people eat when they are stressed. I work out."

Jake's blue-and-silver gaze pierced her. "You're not in danger any longer. Assan Ang is in the ground." He pushed the big basket of fries toward her. "Eat all of the rest of these."

She did, and enjoyed his story of a river raft trip on the Congo to deliver needed supplies to an outpost there. She tipped her head back, laughing at the details of his encounter with a hippo.

"Don't laugh," Jake admonished. "Hippos are bigger killers than crocodiles, even. They top the charts ahead of wildcats and piranhas."

Sophie shook her head. "I did not know that. I would like to see a hippo someday."

"No, you wouldn't. They have awful breath."

Soon they were checked in to the hotel with a pineapple theme on the edge of the quaint town of Waimea. Jake got them two rooms and put the accommodations on his Security Solutions credit card. Lathering up in the shower, and later, washing Ginger's muddy coat in the same space, Sophie had to admit that Jake had been right. There was nothing quite like a hot shower—*and now she had a soft bed to look forward to.*

A knock came at the door when she was on that bed, dressed in her favorite lightweight, yet warm, leggings and vest-style top that doubled as a cold weather outfit. Ginger, on the bed beside her, lunged off and gave a happy greeting bark as she ran to the door.

"Hello? Sophie?" Jake's voice.

Her heart hammered. *What was he doing here?* She and Jake alone in a hotel room after dark seemed like a profoundly bad idea. She undid the bolt and chain and peered around the jamb. "What is it, Jake?"

"I come bearing an opportunity to log business hours and a nightcap." Jake held up a laptop and a bottle of some sort of alcohol. "May I come in?"

"For the business hours. Not for the nightcap." Sophie held the door open and he stepped inside.

Lemony aftershave and the smell of clean skin hit her nostrils as he passed. The hairs on her arms stood up and her nipples tightened.

The room suddenly seemed too small because, *son of a cockroach!* Jake took up a lot of space leaving nowhere to sit but on the queen-sized bed with its exuberant display of pineapples in a repeating pattern.

Sophie drew pineapple-patterned drapes closed as Jake sat on the bed and booted up the laptop. She spotted a single side chair resting against the wall and perched on it. Jake held up the bottle and waggled it. "Best I could do at the corner store. How do you feel about amaretto?"

"I love amaretto." Sophie's mouth watered thinking of the taste of the almond flavored, sweet liqueur. "I guess I will have some, after all."

"I've been stealthily studying Sophie Ang's favorite things." Jake winked and pointed to the pair of sterilized water glasses wearing little ruffled tops that rested on the sideboard next to the coffee maker. "Nothing beats a good drink at the end of a productive day."

Sophie fetched the glasses and he splashed a couple fingers' worth of dark amber liquid into each. *"Cheers."* They clinked glasses. Sophie swirled the alcohol and closed her eyes, inhaling the almond scent, before she sipped. She so seldom drank. *She would have to be careful.* This situation was a set up.

"So. I am writing up notes from today and thought we could check the details." Jake's big fingers typed rapidly on the slim silver laptop. "I'll begin with our meeting at the station, leaving Detective Freitan's harassment out of it."

Sophie's skin prickled, remembering the uncomfortable scene at the station. She sipped her drink, savoring the delicious taste and the ball of heat it ignited in her belly.

"I'm more interested in finding out what happened with the Marshals and the body dump I discovered. I wonder if Freitan and Wong would give me any information if I called them." She tightened her lips. *She didn't need to call them.* She could use DAVID to hack the case file and see for herself.

DAVID, her rogue data mining program, was designed to penetrate law enforcement databases and collect and search data based on keywords, then use a comparison algorithm to test hypotheses. She could ask DAVID if there was a pattern connecting the family's shooting with any other killings . . .

"Let's not get into that kettle of fish—Hilo PD working with WITSEC on a quintuple homicide has no room for private agencies getting nosy. Instead, why don't you use that laptop of yours to look for our girl online?"

"DAVID needs secure bandwidth to be used safely. What I mean is, the wide open Wi-Fi signal at this motel is not a place I'd like to use it. The program has firewalls, of course, but anyone in range of this signal could pick up some of the highly confidential data DAVID might access. I only like to use it when I have a cable uplink in a secure location." But still, her fingers itched to input all the information about their missing girl. She went to her backpack and dug out her waterproof, satellite-capable laptop. "Even if I set up a secure hotspot with my sat phone, the data is vulnerable."

"Look around you, Soph." Jake gestured to the hideous décor. "We're in Hawaii cattle country in a small town in the middle of the Pacific. What high tech cyber thief is going to be driving around Waimea with an antenna out, trying to steal data?"

"You never know," Sophie said darkly. *Because you never did know.* People wanted DAVID and might be tracking it, and there was one particular Ghost that was . . . not an enemy, but no doubt watching her every move.

CHAPTER EIGHT

"Come on, Sophie, take a chance."

Don't just take a chance by using the DAVID program—take a chance *on him.* Jake willed Sophie to understand his double meaning. She glanced up, her golden-brown eyes a little surprised. It almost seemed as if she understood him; but he'd been wrong before.

"All right." She opened the laptop. "Where is the client information?"

Jake passed her the file containing all of the relevant data on their client submitted by the parents. Sophie had her program open, and began inputting. Her long tan fingers flew, her eyes flicking rapidly back and forth between the files' contents and the screen of the computer that she was logging data into. Her ability to submerge into the cyber world was amazing. While he appreciated the function of that world, he'd never found it absorbing. He was a man of the outdoors, most at home doing something physical, and he made no apologies.

Jake sipped his amaretto. God, he hated the syrupy stuff, but he'd taken notice of what she liked; a good operative always knew everything about his objective. She liked Blue Hawaiians, too, and those frothy tourist concoctions made amaretto seem like hard alcohol.

Sophie drank a certain kind of tea, smoky and dark, from Thailand. She suffered from depression that could drag her down for days. She loved her dog. She slept in the buff.

Jake's mind stuttered on that one. He'd overheard Marcella teasing Sophie about her private nudity habits, and had never been able to forget it. His gaze flicked over Sophie's form, hidden in a body-concealing loose top and leggings. *Ugh.* He hated those clothes, too.

Whiskey, neat. And Sophie naked in bed. Now that would be a better evening.

"If you aren't careful, we'll devolve into actual working." Jake handed Sophie her glass of amaretto after he topped it up a bit. "Medicinal purposes. We've had a long day."

Sophie took it without looking at him and sipped. "That is certainly true." She was barely paying any attention. *Good.* If he could just maneuver her into position . . .

Jake leaned against the headboard and patted the comforter beside him. "Come over here. You need back support."

Sophie moved onto the bed next to him, leaning against the headboard, her eyes never leaving the screen of the laptop on her knees. She trusted him, and that gave him such a good feeling. She saw him clearly, knew he would cheat, lie, steal, and fight dirty to get what he wanted, and she still trusted him. Kinda made him wish he was a better man. Maybe he could be a better man, for her. Anything was possible—*but tonight he was bent on seduction.*

Sophie eventually finished her drink and he observed her for any signs of effect, taking her glass and filling it again. She slipped up, made a typo. Giggled as she corrected it. *The booze was working.*

"What's so funny?" He drew a line down her bare arm with a fingertip, gratified to see her shiver.

"Just feeling good. Kind of floaty. I am a lightweight, as they say." Sophie gazed up and to the left, considering. "What keywords, besides our client's name, should we have DAVID search for?"

"I don't know. Camping? Female hiker? Come to think of it, I don't know how much about Julie Weathersby's current travel is going to be online in any form. She didn't do much social media, according to her parents and that commercial location media group that's posting about her."

"I know not what is available about Weathersby on the Facebook. But we must try all of the avenues." Sophie's voice had become pedantic and measured as she attempted to hide her amaretto buzz. She closed the laptop and set it on the nightstand. "And now we conclude our evening's plan of collegial investigation work and alcoholic beverages." She gave a little burp and hid it behind her fist.

God, she was adorable.

Time to make that move.

Jake slid an arm around behind Sophie's back and drew her close against him. He loved how she felt against him; warm, strong, and soft in all the right places. He lifted her chin with his other hand. Sophie's eyes fluttered shut as her face tilted toward him. Her lips parted. He waited to see if she would pull away, but she didn't.

So, he kissed her.

Softly, at first. Like a gentleman. But she made a tiny sound, and that was the end of that.

He hauled Sophie over into his lap, and the kiss was bold and graphic. She gave as good as she got, pulling his hair, tugging at his shirt, nipping his lip with her teeth. Their hands were everywhere they'd wanted to be on each other. Thought disappeared in a red buzz of hungry sensation.

They eventually came up for air.

Sophie blinked, her gaze foggy. "I thought it might be that good," she said. "But now you have to go." She pushed at his chest.

Jake's arms tightened around Sophie, but he made them let go. He was playing a long game. It would never be a good idea to rush a goal this worthy.

"No means no." He gently disentangled himself and kissed her one last time, a touch on the nose, a brush of his lips behind her ear.

"You're the boss." *Leave her wanting more. Leave her believing she was in control. Leave her knowing she could trust him.*

But that didn't mean walking away was easy.

THEY MET at the Jeep the next morning. After they'd settled their belongings in the vehicle and secured Ginger, Jake handed Sophie a bamboo stick with three sugar-dusted malasadas speared on it. "Eat these. And drink this." He handed her a large cup of the strongest tea he had been able to find.

"Thank you. I slept very well." She wouldn't look at him. That wasn't a good sign.

"Me too. Let's drive over to that park Hernandez suggested and continue canvassing. Did your computer program turn up anything?"

"Not yet."

Ginger thrust her head between the seats, and Jake caressed the dog. The Lab shut her eyes and rubbed against his hand wantonly as Sophie watched. Blotchy red appeared on her neck and she turned away, taking a bite of the local Portuguese pastry. *She was thinking about him touching her.* Wishing he'd touch her like he was stroking her pet.

Good.

Jake brushed her arm as he put the Jeep in gear, and once they were on the road, he took her hand.

It was a bold move, and he knew it was the wrong one when Sophie pulled her hand away and tucked it into her lap. "Jake, we have to talk. Last night . . ."

"Last night happened, and I'm not sorry." *Talking was a mistake. Talking would make her withdraw back into her shell.* "There's nothing to talk about."

"I won't be one of your . . ."

"I know. You told me. And I told you . . . what I told you." He cleared his throat. He didn't want to have to try to define what they were to each other at this stage. "Can we just move on? Do we have to analyze this?"

"Do we?" She eyed him. "I think you were a little generous with the amaretto last night."

He cracked a grin. "Was I? Didn't notice."

She rolled her eyes and groaned. "You're what they call a bad boy, Jake."

"You have no idea." He winked.

She punched him in the arm, hard, and this time he was the one who groaned.

East Point Park was on the dry side of the island's volcanoes. Golden brown hills covered in dried grasses swept down to a horseshoe bay of gleaming turquoise water, black sand, and stunted *kiawe* trees. The area was sheltered from the prevailing wind by a rocky promontory. Tents were clustered under the overhanging trees.

Jake and Sophie began their questioning at the edge of the campground.

They had no luck with the campers, nor the beachgoers enjoying the sun and sand. Finally, the pimply young man occupying the ticket booth on the way into the park nodded at the sight of Julie's picture. "Yeah. I saw her. She was here for two days. Let me see where." He typed into a laptop and looked up. "She stayed in campsite 19A."

"Was she with anyone? Did she share the campsite?" Sophie's voice was low and urgent, and the young man looked up, really taking her in for the first time. His eyes widened as he tracked her face, her scar, both of their utilitarian black clothing.

"Who did you say you were?" They showed their Security Solutions IDs.

"This young woman is missing. We are trying to find anyone who might have seen her."

"Well, people are not supposed to share campsites, and it didn't seem like she did. But she was sharing a fire with a couple."

Jake took out his phone and showed the couple from the park outside of Hilo. "Any chance it was these two?"

"Yeah, as a matter of fact. The three of them were barbequing. I leave the ticket booth when it closes at six, but they already seemed to be having a good time before I left." The tops of his ears turned red. "We're not supposed to allow alcohol in the campground, but it's hard to call people on it."

"Did they camp that night?" Sophie asked.

"Yes. The couple only stayed the last night that your missing woman did." He tapped some buttons, and nodded. "Yep. Spot 19B right next to her."

"What were their names?"

"Jim Webb and Holly Rayme."

Jake and Sophie thanked him and walked through the campground to the site in question. Jake surveyed the level, sandy sites with their tidy enclosed metal fire ring. "So she met them here. Probably went to the next park with them. They know something, I'm sure of it."

"I agree. Is it time to contact Freitan and see if we can get that couple picked up?"

"Time to update Freitan, at least. We've got a lead. We need to share it." Jake made prayer hands. "Please, Sophie. You call her."

Sophie laughed. "Big bad Jake is scared of the detective! All right, I will call her." She dialed the detective directly, and he listened to Sophie updating Freitan on speakerphone.

"All right. I'll put out a Be On Look Out for this couple. Can't do anything more at the moment." The woman's voice came through a bit fuzzy.

"What about the dead family? What's happening there?" Sophie asked.

"Can't discuss it, unfortunately. But I will say—that idea you had? Spot on." Freitan clicked off.

Sophie looked at Jake. "So, I was right. That family who was murdered was in Witness Protection. There must be some kind of leak."

A WITSEC leak was serious. "I don't see what we can do about that," Jake said. "The Marshal Service doesn't like working with local law enforcement, let alone private investigators."

"I do not know what we can do either," Sophie said, but she was frowning thoughtfully as she walked toward the ticket booth, away from Jake. *What was she thinking?* Jake wished he knew.

CHAPTER NINE

Maybe she should call the Ghost about the WITSEC leak and the body dump. Connor would be able to investigate that in a way no one else could.

But no. Sophie couldn't reach out to him—her ex-lover would misconstrue it, and the last thing she needed was more confusion with the men in her life.

Sophie checked back in with the park attendant. She met the young man's eyes. "Is there anything else you can tell us about this couple? Did you hear anything about where they might be going, and where people like them—homeless transients—might have gone?"

"Yeah. I think they were all talking about heading for Volcanoes National Park, and that Oceanview area outside the park. A lot of homeless end up camping around Oceanview. It's pretty unregulated out there, kind of a new Wild West. My cousin lives there and says the parties are off the hook." The young man had a gap-toothed grin.

"Thanks a lot, man." Jake came up from behind her and handed the kid a twenty-dollar bill. "We really appreciate it."

Sophie took him to task back at the Jeep. "Wasn't that kind of like a bribe? Isn't it part of his job to help us and protect the people who come through the park?"

Jake scoffed. "C'mon, Sophie, don't be naïve. Money makes the world go 'round."

Sophie puzzled over that saying as they drove. *Money go round?* English had so many colloquialisms that didn't make sense. The earth was a sphere! Oh, but perhaps Jake meant, "go around." In which case, he was justifying paying off that park employee, who should be cooperative and helpful because it was part of his job. But the young man probably didn't make much, in which case Jake's gesture was more altruistic?

People were so hard to understand . . .

Maybe she spent too much time wondering about turns of phrase and their hidden meanings.

But there had been no hidden meaning in that kiss with Jake last night. She definitely needed to avoid alcohol, Jake, and anything to do with a bed.

The mere thought made her chest tingle.

Sophie sneaked a glance at her partner. His eyes were on the road, those big hands loosely gripping the wheel. She liked looking at him more than she wanted to.

She had woken up determined nothing further would happen between them, but faced with malasadas and Jake's upbeat mood this morning, she found herself just as conflicted as before.

He intended to wear down her resistance.

Knowing that was his strategy didn't make it less effective. She'd always found his determination and single-mindedness sexy. That Jake's focus was trained on her made her kind of hot. There was no doubt they were attracted to each other physically.

But on the other hand, she was attracted to Alika as well. She didn't know her own heart, or body! Her bad choices with Assan and then Connor had wounded and confused her. No, she shouldn't be having a relationship until she could clearly pick someone she wanted to be with.

But maybe her problem was that she was too old-fashioned. "Conservative as my grandmother's chastity belt," Marcella had teased her a few years ago. *Did sex have to mean something?* Just because she was inexperienced and recovering from domestic violence didn't mean she had to be celibate in this day and age. Now that she was getting over the scars left by having a sexual sadist be her first lover, could she indulge in an "adult relationship" with a man and have it be just physical?

Jake irritated her, challenged and annoyed her, but she also liked him. She trusted him. And if that kiss had been any indication, he would be very good in bed.

A memory of the creative and healing lovemaking she'd shared with Connor made her curl up tight against the window, withdrawing further from Jake.

She'd thought Connor was *the one*. She'd found her soul mate, if such a thing existed. He'd been so perfect for her in so many ways.

Except for that one, glaring, impossible problem: *Connor's heart was already given to something she would never agree with.*

After her mistake with Connor, she didn't trust her own judgment. Which is why she was trying to be done with men, and that wasn't going well at all.

"I'm considering whether or not we could be bed buddies after all." Sophie hadn't meant to say the words out loud, but now that she had, she pressed on. "Though I prefer the phrase, "partners with benefits.""

Jake's gaze shot to meet hers. The Jeep swerved, hitting the center line, and Jake over-corrected in a replay of another conversation. The juxtaposition made Sophie laugh.

"But I thought you just said . . ."

"I know I did. But I kind of want to have sex with you. No, I really want to have sex with you. And I don't want to be . . . a 'thing' with you. If we agree on that, I think we can proceed."

"Proceed. Huh." Jake sped up. It was a long drive of an hour or so to Oceanview, along a scenic highway that passed above Kona. Vista views of the ocean and the great sweep of the side of the volcano they were circumnavigating tumbled into a horizon line blurred by voggy mist, reminding Sophie of a glimpse of infinity.

Jake finally spoke. "My whole body wants to say yes, I'll take you however I can get you. In fact, the thought is making me rather uncomfortable right now. But to be honest, I don't think I want just a casual lay. Because when I think of you with someone else . . ." Jake's hands tightened on the wheel. The bone of his knuckles shone through the flesh. "I want to rip him apart. With my bare hands. So I guess that's a no for me, unless we're going to be exclusive."

"Oh." Sophie rubbed sweaty hands on her hiking pants. "That's too bad, but good to know because the last thing I need is another homicidally jealous man in my life. It's a big turnoff to me, Jake, as you can imagine. So I regret to say that, until something about the scenario changes, we won't be having sex."

"I guess not. But what do you say to a little friendly making out?" Jake bounced his brows at her.

This was her chance to cut off further contact with him, but Sophie found herself unwilling to do so. *Maybe a little friendly making out might still happen.* The thought gave her tummy a warm glow. "Perhaps."

They drove the rest of the way in silence until they stopped for lunch at a café in a tiny hamlet called Captain Cook outside of Kona. A gauzy haze softened their view of the long stretch of land below them, ending in black rocks and the sea.

Sophie pointed out to the horizon with a carrot stick. "The vog must make some pretty sunsets with all the particulate matter in the air."

"Yeah, I'm sure we can see one firsthand now that we're on the south side of the island. The east side is much clearer, in general."

They discussed the ongoing volcanic emissions from the active site of Kilauea volcano that had been going on for more than ten years. "I think I like a lot about the Big Island. So much variety in the microclimates, and it's so big that you forget it's an island. But the vog seems like a health hazard," Sophie said. Conversing about something other than their case and their relationship was easy. She was relieved. Whatever happened, she didn't want to lose her friendly partnership with Jake. *They were good together.*

On the way back to the Jeep, Jake took her hand again. This time, she didn't remove it. It did no harm to allow the connection—it felt nice to have him hold her hand.

THE FIRST PLACE they stopped when they arrived at the sprawling area of Oceanview was a small general store. Sophie perused a bulletin board thick with notices. "Let's look for anything that seems like a clue." She frowned at several missing persons posters. "There are many of these." She pointed to one of their client. "There's Julie Weathersby."

"Yeah, I'm beginning to see a trend."

"I think DAVID would find this many missing persons in one area statistically unlikely," Sophie said. "I'll have to set up a hypothesis and test it, but I predict the confidence interval to be low that this is a normal phenomenon occurring within the population."

"Speak English, woman." Jake put his hands on his hips.

"DAVID works on keyword searches for input data, developing correlations between possibly related pieces of information accrued under search parameters. This many missing persons, in the relatively small area of this island, being the result of random occurrence or statistically normal disappearance patterns—well, I think it has to be at least partly the effect of some other factor."

Jake towed her around the building into shadow, where they would not be overheard by the comings and goings through the store's battered doorway. "What are you saying? That there is a serial killer at work?"

"Perhaps more than one." Sophie rubbed her arms briskly at the chill that had passed over her. "I want to input all of these people, try to get a number of how many are missing on the Big Island, and work up a larger picture of what might be going on. This data could be the beginning of a case for the FBI's Behavioral Analysis Unit."

Jake scowled. "That investigation is not going to pay the rent, my friend. You are not an FBI agent any longer. We need to stay focused on the case we have, and if it turns up something more, great. Why go looking for trouble?"

"It's what I do." The truth of that insight burst across her brain. Sophie turned to Jake. "It's what I do, Jake. I find things. I fix things."

Jake's silver-and-blue eyes were intent as they locked gazes. He was the first to look away, thrusting a hand through his short, dark hair. "I don't like it."

Sophie shrugged. "I don't answer to you. Or Security Solutions, for that matter."

Jake snorted through his nostrils in obvious frustration and stalked to the front of the store. He opened the door and went inside.

Sophie followed. She paused to photograph each of the posters on the bulletin board with her phone, and the bulletin board as a whole. One small notice in the corner caught her eye.

LOOKING FOR SOMEONE? Call me! I might know what happened to them.

A Hawaii cell phone number was listed in tear-off tags at the bottom. Three of the tags were missing. She tore one off, and made it a fourth.

Jake was likely canvassing the store owner with Julie's photo as they'd discussed doing. She had time for a quick call to investigate this lead. Sophie walked around the back of the store and took out her cell phone, and called the number.

CHAPTER TEN

JAKE RECONNED up and down the aisles of the store, discharging the spike of anxiety and frustration that Sophie's words had ignited in him. The shop was a typical rural mom-and-pop place. The shelves were stocked with everything from kerosene to flashlights, with a limited food aisle.

Why did he care if Sophie uncovered a serial killer?

Honest answer? Because she might put herself at risk by doing so, and he might not be able to help if she did. If she got into some big solo investigation without him, God knows what danger she might be in. She certainly wouldn't pause to count the cost to herself.

Jake was still shaking inside from their talk in the car and confronting his feelings about her. He couldn't believe she'd brought up sex and propositioned him so matter-of-factly, but it had clarified things for him.

He was in it for the long haul; he wanted Sophie not just to sleep with, but to be with always. *The whole white picket fence enchilada.* Being at the party where mutual friends Marcus and Marcella had become engaged a few weeks ago had done something to him, tipped him into thinking of that kind of life, love, and stability.

"Son of a bitch. How did that happen?" Jake had spoken aloud.

His gaze focused. He'd stopped somewhere midway through the store, and he was staring at a rack of fishing gear. The bell over the store's door dinged; he smelled mildew and the dusty scent of bags of beans on the shelves behind him. *What a place to be standing when he realized he was in love.*

He would just have to stay with Sophie until this rabbit hole was thoroughly explored, and he was going to continue his current strategy of slow encroachment and seduction. Yep, he was going to wear her down, and hopefully, he'd win her over to care about him like he cared about her. If not, at least he'd given it a hundred percent effort. No one ever accused Jake Dunn of giving up easily.

A profound sense of relief loosened the knots in Jake's gut. He wasn't fighting his feelings for Sophie any more. He'd just stepped up his game to the next level.

Jake walked back to the checkout counter. A slender Filipino man wearing trifocals and a tonsure of gray hair around a shiny brown pate stacked boxes of Marlboros on the cigarette shelf behind the cash register.

"Excuse me." Jake held up his phone, showing the picture of Julie Weathersby. "Have you seen this young woman?"

"Let me get a closer look." The man took the phone, blew up the image by expanding it with his fingertips. He gave a regretful shake of the head. "No, I have not." He looked up at Jake. "Don't tell me. She's missing."

Jake frowned "That's right. How about these two?"

He handed the phone back, showing an image of the two campers they were pursuing.

"Yah. Those two tweakers came in just this morning. All flush, for once."

"For once? What do you mean?" Jake tried not to leap on the man with too much intensity.

"Those two, they lowlifes. They come and go. I keep a good eye on them when they in the store." The man's voice had drifted into pidgin English. He turned away and continued his stacking, as if regretting saying so much. Sophie entered, and came to stand beside Jake.

"You know where they stay when they're in this area? We think they might have something to do with this girl's disappearance," Jake persisted.

"For shame. I sorry to hear that." The man continued his stacking.

Sophie stepped up to the counter and laid a couple of twenties down. "I'm sure these people have stolen from your store. Here's a little cash to make up for that. We just want to make sure this couple doesn't hurt anyone else."

The man turned to look at Sophie, and his eyes warmed. He got off his stepstool and pushed the money back to Sophie. "I never like to get involved in anything that could come back on me and my family. We gotta live heah too. But those two, they're bad news. Maybe you can help get them busted."

The storekeeper reached under the counter and drew out a detailed map of the area. "This is Oceanview. If you take this road off to the left . . ." he traced the branching veins of a small artery of road. "There's a big camp back here, squatters and da kine folks li'dat. Lotta these roads not marked. You take a picture of my map, you be okay finding it."

Jake stood back while Sophie photographed the map. She gave the older man a brilliant smile. "Mahalo. And please, keep the money. You have to deal with so much out here, and your store is important to everyone in this area."

The man folded the map and tucked the cash into his pocket. "Mahalo to you, miss. I hope you get'um."

Jake followed Sophie out of the store. He touched her elbow at the Jeep. "You get to do all the talking from here on out. And nice touch with the money. You're a fast learner."

Sophie blinked. "I really meant it. Rayme and Webb probably stole a lot more than forty dollars' worth of merchandise from that man. He works so hard, and he's just trying to make a living."

This woman. Jake's chest was tight as he got into the Jeep.

CHAPTER ELEVEN

SOPHIE FIDDLED with Ginger's collar as they drove down the bumpy road into the heart of Oceanview. The potholed road was lined with christmasberry bushes, an invasive species from Brazil that had been aggressively taking over many areas on the Big Island. Most of the ground was rough lava, still being tamed by lichen and small, hardy ferns. Small native *ohia* tree saplings raised silver-green branches, part of the new landscape.

"I am not certain why they call this Oceanview. I cannot see much ocean from this area," Sophie said.

Jake nodded. He had been uncharacteristically reserved since they left the store.

Sophie's phone buzzed, and she saw a text from the number she had found on the bulletin board. *"Come meet me at Aweo Park, and we can discuss your concerns. Let me know a time that works for you."*

Sophie held her phone up. "I have an interesting lead here. There was a number on the bulletin board advertising information about the missing people, and the subject just sent me a text message with a place to meet."

"That could be something." Jake shot her a glance. "What do you think is going on?"

"I do not know, but anyone who claims to know something about the missing people probably has a motive or information worth investigating."

"Agreed. Now where are we going? We need that map. This road is getting sketchy."

The road had split, but no road marker delineated the fork. Sophie opened her phone photo of the storekeeper's map and traced their route with a finger. "Take a left here."

The need to navigate forestalled any further discussion. In half an hour, they arrived at a crude archway over a dirt parking area. *"Travelers' Rest"* was spelled out at the top, hand painted on a section of wood.

Sophie pointed. "Looks like we've arrived. The name over the camping area is a good portent."

They drove beneath the archway into a crude parking area marked by painted boulders and filled with ramshackle parked vehicles. Jake jerked his head toward the back seat. "Kevlar back there."

"I don't think that's necessary."

"You're speculating that we might be venturing into the hunting grounds of a serial, and you're arguing about wearing Kevlar?"

Jake was right. Who knew what their questions would unleash? Sophie reached in the back for the gear bag. "I don't want to advertise wearing this."

"Then put your shirt on over it."

Sophie bit her lip. "I will. Look the other way and give me some privacy."

Jake gave a brusque nod and got out of the Jeep, reaching into the back to grab his vest. Sophie stripped her shirt off over her head, feeling self-conscious in her plain black bra. The area was deserted as she slipped the vest on, tightened the Velcro, and then wriggled her tee shirt back down over it.

Jake's naked upper torso caught her gaze through the window as he similarly changed.

No, she wasn't looking. It would be wrong to look when she had instructed him not to. But . . . *damn*. His back was a wall of rippling muscle stippled with scars. Every one of those scars probably told a story of the adventures he'd been through. She loved his stories, and she'd loved touching that warm, solid body the night before . . .

Sophie tore her gaze away.

They checked weapons, got their IDs ready, and Sophie let Ginger out of the back, clipping on her leash. "She can't hurt anything."

"Agreed." Jake shoved his pistol into a hip holster and ran his hands through short dark hair, rearranging its messy spikes. He tugged his shirttail out to cover the gun. "People talk to us more easily with Ginger there. She looks friendly."

"And we do not?"

"No. We look like cops. Let's stay focused on asking about Webb and Rayme. Work this like a normal canvass."

"Do you still think I should take the lead?" The dynamic of Sophie initiating contact and Jake backing her up seemed to work.

"Yeah. Our line is the truth: we're wanting to talk to these two campers because we think they might have seen our missing girl. And then we can show Julie's photo, too."

They found a trail leading between rough boulders toward the camp area. They paused to evaluate at the edge of the settlement.

A central pathway fanned out into rows of crude dwellings made of pallets, plywood, roofing tin, tarps, and transparent plastic. Small, hand-painted signs identified people's dwellings: *Jones. Mikelson. Imua. Rashan.*

"Looks like a real little town," Sophie said. "I wonder who owns this land."

Jake shrugged. "Someone who doesn't care what's going on with it."

They worked their way through the village of motley homemade dwellings. Most of the residents eyed them with suspicion and denied knowing anything, but halfway through the encampment they encountered a family with several young children. The father scowled. "Yeah, I know where those two are holed up." He pointed. "Last shack on the left. Watch out, they have a mean-ass dog and a terrible attitude."

Sophie and Jake approached the shack with caution.

A dark, cramped-looking dwelling made of roofing tin and tarps, there was nothing inviting about it. Sophie wondered how well the crude shelter would even keep out the frequent rain.

The dog they'd been warned about started a barking that unnerved Sophie and made Ginger whine anxiously. Sophie secured the Lab to a nearby *ohia* tree, straightened her shoulders, and boldly walked forward toward a doorway framed in rough logs. A tarp hung over the crude opening.

There was nowhere to knock, so Sophie called out instead. "Hello! Anyone home?"

The dog barked louder. It sounded as big as a tank and just as deadly. A rustling noise inside the dwelling confirmed that it was occupied. Jake took up a position beside her, and she knew that he had drawn his weapon; they'd worked together long enough that she could predict his behaviors.

Sophie called again: "Hello in there! We need to speak with you!"

The tarp moved back. The woman Sophie remembered from the campground stuck her head out, scowling. Holly Rayme's snarled blonde hair didn't look like it had been touched since the last time they saw each other. "You again. What do you want?"

"We need to speak to you. Where is your companion?"

"I got nothing to say." The woman dropped the tarp and it fell back into place.

Anger swelled in Sophie. She swept the tarp aside and barged through the doorway, reaching for the woman.

Her eyes didn't have time to adjust to the dim interior as she was slammed from the side and knocked sprawling.

CHAPTER TWELVE

HEARING A SCUFFLE, Jake thrust an arm through the flimsy tarp doorway to follow Sophie. He swept the covering back to throw light on the scene.

Sophie was down.

The dog was tied just out of range, but its snapping, snarling jaws were way too close to her face. The male tweaker, Jim Webb, loomed over his partner, holding a wooden club.

Sophie lashed out suddenly with a foot, and caught Webb in the knee. The man's leg buckled and he went down with a cry, landing on the dog. The big pit bull yelped pitifully.

Sophie rolled out of the way and sprang to her feet, ready for action. Webb lumbered up and rushed her, but Jake saw his chance to help. He stepped in and backhanded the guy with his weapon, dropping him like a bag of rocks. Jake hauled the tweaker up by his armpits and leaned him against the doorway. Webb's nose dribbled blood, but he was already coming around as a shrieking, demon-possessed banshee rushed Jake from the back.

Sophie very efficiently stopped the woman with an elbow to the midsection and an uppercut to the jaw. Rayme crumpled, and Sophie hauled the woman by the armpits over to the wall and propped her beside her partner.

Jake held his weapon on the two. "This didn't have to be so unpleasant. We just want to know where Julie Weathersby is. Don't bother telling us you don't know her. We have an eyewitness who puts the three of you together, partying around a campfire at East Point."

Webb shushed the barking dog with a curse. The black-and-white pit bull, scrawny under its swagger, sank to its belly, backing away and whining in distress.

They couldn't leave that poor animal here. Hopefully, Sophie would agree. They could at least take it to an animal shelter . . .

The couple glanced at each other and Rayme twisted her hands together. A gold chain winked on one of her wrists. "We don't know anything, I swear," she whined.

Sophie pointed to the chain. "That bracelet looks new. And I think I see a charm on it. Hand it over."

"No. It's my private property," the woman said. "And I'm gonna report you for assault."

Sophie took out her phone. She held the picture of Julie Weathersby out toward Rayme. "Examine what is on this woman's wrist. Look familiar?"

Rayme squinted at the phone, and then covered the chain on her wrist protectively with a hand. "That girl gave this to me. Screw you."

"And show us some ID if you're cops," growled Webb.

"We're not cops." Jake growled. He was downright eager to inflict some pain on these two. He dropped the tarp, and the room went dim. "It's your word against ours what went on here, and we can do this easy, or we can do this hard."

The couple picked easy.

WALKING BACK TO THE JEEP, leading the scrawny black-and-white dog on a rope and carrying the gold chain in his pocket, Jake glanced at Sophie walking ahead. She had just hung up from calling Freitan again to let the detective know the tweaker couple had admitted to robbing Julie Weathersby and dropping her off alone in a wilderness area, which was where he and Sophie were headed next.

"I hope you're okay with taking the dog. Tank deserves a better life," Jake said.

Sophie laughed. "Of course. You must have read my mind, because Ginger likes him too."

Jake kept a wary eye on their six o'clock, glancing back toward the camp as Ginger, tugging at her leash to get close to her new friend, licked the pit bull's face. "Tank complicates things a bit. We need to take him to the shelter in Hilo."

"The area where Rayme and Webb dropped Julie is on the way to Hilo. Not that I think she'll still be there." Sophie frowned. "But hopefully someone will have seen her around there, and we can pick up her trail, at least. I'm beginning to be very worried for Julie Weathersby."

CHAPTER THIRTEEN

SETTLING the dogs in the back of the Jeep was a bit of a struggle for Sophie. Tank was confused, trying to jump out of the open area, and Ginger, taking this as a sign to play, tangled their leashes on the back seat. Finally Sophie got the dogs situated, Jake pulled the vehicle out of the lot, and they got on the road.

Sophie checked her phone. "Freitan texted me that she's deep into it with the family murder case and can't respond to pick up Webb and Rayme. She is sending a couple of uniforms out to Travelers' Rest to arrest them."

"That will have to be good enough. Hope Bonnie and Clyde haven't skedaddled by the time the officers arrive."

"Bonnie and Clyde?"

"Famous male and female outlaw team of the early twentieth century."

Sophie sneaked a glance at Jake. A slight smile curved his mouth, and he flexed his hands on the wheel. He radiated a sense of satisfaction. Clearly the contretemps at the camp had energized him. One of his knuckles was bruised from knocking Webb around, and Sophie's hand felt a little sore, too.

"Speaking of Bonnie and Clyde." She cleared her throat. "We

make a good team, too."

"Agreed." Jake reached over and lifted her hand to his lips, giving her scraped knuckles a quick kiss, surprising her. "Bonnie and Clyde were more than partners—they were lovers."

Sophie pulled her hand away. "You are probably right that we should not fraternize."

"Fraternize? I love your nineteen fifties vocab. For the record, I'm all about effective partnerships--in and out of the bedroom."

"How are we talking about this again?" Sophie threw her hands up. "Let's focus on the case. I want to see Julie's bracelet."

Jake dug the delicate chain with its butterfly charm out of his pocket and handed it to her. "Do you think we should call the parents with this progress report?"

Sophie examined it. "Not yet. But we should update Bix on our headway." Sophie took out her phone and tried to get a signal. "Can't pick up anything out here." She looked around at the surrounding jungle, dripping after a recent deluge. "It's strange how intermittent the signal is. We were able to reach Hilo PD at the encampment."

They drove on in silence, re-connecting with the main highway and heading toward the area where the couple had robbed and abandoned Julie Weathersby, midway between Hilo and Volcanoes National Park.

Outside the Park, they pulled over and grabbed a quick bite to eat at a convenience store/coffee shop.

After lunch, Jake pointed to a row of rental cabins set off the road in a forest of enormous tree ferns. "This is a central area to our investigation zone. I think I'll reserve one of these for tonight." He headed off toward the office, pulling out his wallet.

Sophie fed the dogs from a bag of dry kibble and gave them water while Jake was gone. She glanced over at the cabins. *They looked awfully romantic.*

Sophie flashed to spending an unforgettable weekend with Connor in an oceanfront cottage on Maui. They had seldom left the bedroom, but the ambience of the Hana Hotel's gracious grounds and beautiful infinity pool had lent even more romance to their paradise getaway.

No. Sophie shook her head, banishing the nostalgia. *She was done with Connor.* Done with thinking about hours in bed with a handsome man she'd thought she loved.

Jake took that moment to return. Sophie glared at him.

"What?" He lifted his hands in a surrender gesture. "What did I do?"

"There better be two bedrooms in that cabin."

"Of course. I was the one to turn *you* down, remember?"

Unfortunately, she did remember.

They got on the road again, and ten minutes outside of the park area, turned onto a side road heading deep into the jungle, where Webb and Rayme had said they'd abandoned Julie after robbing her.

Overarching *albizia* trees, thick with dangling vines, almost blotted out the sun, which had vanished as clouds rolled in. A sudden wind whipped over the trees, and a torrent of rain broke over the Jeep. Jake pulled the vehicle over and the two of them scrambled to get the detachable cover up. Finally, the vehicle was sealed. With rain beating down on the soft top, the interior smelled terribly of wet dog as Ginger and Tank wound themselves into a doggy pretzel on the back seat, their mournful eyes complaining of the damp.

"I hope it's not far," Sophie said. "I could really use a hot shower." Rain had soaked her to the skin, and she shivered in spite of the humid warmth. Jake cranked up the Jeep's inadequate heater. Sophie gestured to the dogs, on the back seat in a comfortable pile, their heads close together. "So sweet. I'm so glad you thought to rescue Tank."

"Poor Tank doesn't seem like he's had a break in a while." Jake rubbed his nose. "But he sure does stink."

Sophie leaned forward to peer into the gloom as the windshield wipers, going full speed, barely seemed to keep up with the water streaming down.

"I see why this area is called a rain forest." Sophie spotted the mile marker where Webb and Rayme claimed they had let Julie Weathersby out. "There! They said she ran away into the jungle as soon as they opened the door of the car."

Jake navigated over to the side of the road. They sat, waiting for the rain to lighten up, and eventually it did. Ginger whined to be let out, and they walked back and forth near the mile marker sign as Sophie searched for any hint of Julie's presence. With the recent rainfall and the intervening hours, there was nothing to see.

Ginger squatted, doing her business on a rock near the signpost, and then gave a sudden bark. She yanked the leash right out of Sophie's hand and charged into the deep brush, jumping over a roadside ditch. Sophie rolled her eyes. *Here we go again.* "Ginger! Come back!"

Sophie jumped the overgrown ditch and ran after her dog, feeling a familiar discomfort in her belly as she remembered that the last time Ginger had acted like this, they had found a massacred family.

Sophie tripped over something and drew to a halt because Ginger had stopped and was waving her tail.

The pack lying on the ground was a serious hiker's model with a carbon-fiber frame, and the compartment done in camouflage greens. Ginger nosed around the pack, sniffing thoroughly. *This was Julie's pack!* Sophie recognized it from the photo they'd been showing around. Making a visual survey of the area, she spotted Julie's boots tossed aside, and a scatter of discarded clothing.

This could be a crime scene.

Sophie stood very still. "Come, Ginger."

The dog finally came. She caught the Lab's leash and held it close.

The story told by this scene did not match the couple's description of abandoning the girl after just taking her cash and jewelry. Wherever Julie was now, she was naked and unshod—and that was not a good sign.

Sophie tightened her grip on the leash, afraid to let go—*would the next thing Ginger found be Julie's body?*

CHAPTER FOURTEEN

JAKE CRASHED through the deep underbrush and ferns that were covering a rough lava and dirt landscape, following Sophie's headlong flight into the jungle. "Sophie!"

"Here, Jake!"

He reached her at last. "That damn dog of yours . . ." His voice trailed off as Sophie pointed to the backpack, discarded boots and scattered clothing. The scene told a mute tale of struggle.

"Shit." Jake looked up and met Sophie's gaze. Her eyes were wide, her mouth pinched. The color had drained from her face, leaving her skin sallow and the scar on her cheek, a vivid line. *She thought the worst.*

"Maybe Julie got away." Jake didn't sound convinced, even to himself. "Maybe she's been kidnapped. They're holding her somewhere, tooling her parents. We shouldn't touch anything. Do you have a signal? We need to call Freitan."

Sophie had let go of the dog's leash, and she was watching Ginger still nosing around the discarded items. "I think if there were a body nearby, Ginger would be looking for it. But the trail seems to stop here." She took out her phone and held it up. "Excellent. I have three bars."

She made the call to Freitan as Jake photographed the site thoroughly, dividing the area into a grid and taking photos up and down until they had enough for a composite. "I'll update Bix while we wait for the detectives," he said, when Sophie told him Freitan and her partner were on their way.

They made their way back to the Jeep, careful not to trample the area or obscure any possible tracks or other evidence. Once at the Jeep, Jake detailed the progress to their superior at Security Solutions. "I don't know if it's time for an update to the parents. I will leave that to your judgment," he told his superior.

"Great," Bix said dryly. "You know how I love breaking this kind of news to families."

"Rank hath its privileges," Jake said, and hung up.

While they waited in the Jeep, Jake made notes on his small work laptop, logging the stages of their investigation as far as location time and detail. Sophie had her laptop out, too. She typed at a ridiculous speed.

"I need to find a way to use DAVID. Julie could be part of this disappearance pattern." Sophie's voice was low and firm.

"This couple could have been preying on people for a while now. There's no telling what the cops will turn up when they tear that little hovel apart at Travelers' Rest," Jake said. "I took them just for opportunistic predators supporting a drug habit, but they could be much more than that. Who knows how long they've been operating in the area, and what they've been up to."

"We have to find out." Sophie glanced up. "If we could track their movements around the island, we might be able to put together a picture of the people who've gone missing, and figure out a profile. See if there are patterns that intersect."

"But you need access to the police database to search all the missing persons and a secure uplink to use that program," Jake finished. "I think you should talk to the detectives about your theory."

Sophie nodded her head. "Hopefully, they will be open to working with us."

Us.

Jake liked the sound of that.

CHAPTER FIFTEEN

KAMANI FREITAN LOOKED tired to Sophie. Dark circles under her eyes looked bruised, and her thick black hair straggled out of its braid as if she had slept on it. She stood beside Sophie, her partner in her shadow, and glanced around the area at Julie's belongings. "Think this might be a homicide?"

"Could be just a kidnapping," Jake was avoiding eye contact with the detective. Sophie noted the rigidity of his shoulders, the tightness of his voice.. "These are definitely her things, and we have evidence linking her to Rayme and Webb." He gestured with his chin to Sophie. "Show her the chain."

Sophie slid the slender gold charm bracelet out of her pocket and dropped it into Freitan's extended hand. "We took this item of Julie's off Holly Rayme not long ago."

"Rayme and Webb said they got to know her, took her to Volcano, and rolled her for her money and jewelry. They claim they let her out of their car at this mile marker. Uninjured, with her clothing and her backpack. We had no reason to doubt their story at the time," Jake concluded.

Freitan's partner, Detective Wong, surveyed the area. "We should photograph this, and then take the items into evidence."

"Yeah. Our officers picked up Rayme and Webb; we can interview those two down at the station. Since we're being stonewalled on the family body dump case." Freitan's full mouth tightened into an irritated line.

This was her chance. Sophie cleared her throat. "I have a theory. I would like to be able to use your secure Internet connections at the station to run my idea through some software I possess. My theory has to do with these missing persons cases."

Freitan had sharp dark eyes that reminded Sophie of a mynah bird. "What's this theory?"

"I can't tell you until I have a chance to assemble numbers and run statistical analyses on some data I need to put together." Sophie met the woman's gaze squarely. "I promise I will share any findings I get with you. But I need a hack-proof place to work that's cool and dry. This environment kills computers." Sophie gestured to their damp and dripping surroundings.

Freitan gave a brief nod. "I ran background on you. You were quite the tech agent in the FBI. You will need to sign confidentiality agreements, but I'm down with that."

Wong nodded as well. "We will have to run it by our station chief, but I don't anticipate a problem. You two have been straight up with us and brought us good leads."

Relief brought a smile to Sophie's face. She couldn't wait to get DAVID burrowing for missing persons data. "Terrific. You won't regret this. When can we get started?"

Freitan tipped her head back to survey the sullen clouds, prematurely darkening the area. "Tomorrow. We have a lot of ground to cover, dealing with this scene and interviewing Webb and Rayme. And we'll still need an okay for you to use the facility. Wong and I will be in touch." Freitan ran an assessing glance over Jake, his black combat clothing smeared with leaves and mud. "You're filthy, Jake. You need a good scrub in a hot shower, my man. Take two, baby, and I'll see you in the morning."

Jake glared, then stomped away through the brush toward the

Jeep, the back of his neck reddening. "Kamani! Rude!" Wong smacked Freitan's arm.

"What? Dunn's a dirty boy who needs a good rubdown," Freitan laughed, unrepentant. "I wouldn't mind hitting that."

Freitan was never going to get anywhere needling Jake that way, and he deserved a little inappropriate teasing after all he'd put Sophie through early in their working relationship. Still, she felt protective. "That kind of speech is inappropriate, Detective," Sophie said. "You wouldn't like a male officer to engage in sexual innuendoes with you, would you?"

"And you don't think I deal with that kind of shit talk every day from the guys?" Freitan tossed her head defiantly. "I'm just getting in a few licks for our team." Her grin was toothy and feral. "So to speak."

Sophie shook her head and followed Jake at a slower pace, leaving the detectives to photograph the site and collect the evidence. She felt exhausted but wired.

What would they do in that cabin all evening until tomorrow?

CHAPTER SIXTEEN

JAKE TURNED the wheel of the Jeep, guiding the vehicle into the Volcanoes National Park through an entrance nestled between beautiful lava stone entry portals. He glanced at Sophie. "Do you mind taking a run along the rim of the crater? We have a few hours of daylight left."

Sophie's smile warmed him. "You must have read my mind. I need to discharge some energy. Get the kinks out, as Marcella would say."

Jake nodded. Relief that she so clearly understood allowed his tight jaw to loosen.

He paid their park entrance fee and drove to a parking lot near the Volcano House Inn and Restaurant. That venerable old establishment perched on the rim of the caldera, a historic barnacle on the living organism that was Kilauea volcano. Sophie took running shoes out of her backpack after they parked. "I think the dogs will be glad of this too."

"Yeah. We get to see how Tank does on a leash."

Soon they were jogging along the wandering path that circumnavigated the edge of Kilauea Volcano. The dogs were perfectly behaved on their leashes, and Jake felt the frustration and tension of their challenging day drop away as they ran.

The views from the edge were stunning. The caldera was as austere as an asteroid and just as foreign, sweeping out below them hundreds of feet, a cliff ending at the flat black field that had once been liquid stone. The active vent of Halema'uma'u gushed sulfurous steam, looking like a giant campfire set on the barren surface of the moon.

Sophie took the lead, her athletic body moving easily along the trail. Jake glimpsed those sexy tattoos on the insides of her arms, but regrettably, the ones on her legs were hidden by nylon pants.

They ran for miles, until the dogs were panting with tiredness and sunset was a glowing coal in the west.

Eventually, they returned to the Jeep and fed and watered the dogs beside the vehicle. Jake cocked his head as he met Sophie's eye and pointed. One of the frequent rainbows of the area caught the last of the sunset's light, landing on nearby rocks. "Must be a pot of gold somewhere around here."

Sophie scrunched her brow. "Pot of gold? This must be one of those cultural things."

"Indeed it is. An old Irish legend is that at the end of a rainbow, there's a pot of gold guarded by leprechauns. Wee folk. Related to fairies."

"A common enough conceit. Almost every culture has some version of magic and . . . tiny people." Sophie was cute when she groped for words.

"Never say leprechauns are common in the presence of an Irishman." Teasing, Jake hooked an arm around Sophie's neck to give her cropped head a knuckle rub. Sophie stiffened in surprise. She tossed his arm off as she spun to confront him, eyes wide with surprise and apprehension.

Jake felt a stab of pain to his chest that he had activated that old fear in her. He held his hands up, palms out. "I'm sorry. I was only playing."

Sophie's gaze softened. She smiled. "Thor save me from a large man with a sweaty armpit anywhere near my face."

"Thor save you?" Jake got into the Jeep as she secured the dogs.

"I've decided to rotate my insults among all the known deities."

Jake laughed and fired up the Jeep.

They drove out of the park toward the cabin where they'd be staying. He forced himself away from imagining how he'd like to fill the hours alone with her in the dark.

JAKE DROVE Sophie to Hilo the next morning. They'd had fish tacos at Volcano Village after their run, then a platonic evening working quietly on their laptops and early bed. Freitan had called and given the okay for Sophie to come into Hilo to work at the computer lab at the station, and Jake could tell by Sophie's tense silence that she was dying to get to it.

Last night in the cabin had been torture, knowing that Sophie was sleeping naked in the room next to him, with nothing but a thin wall and an unlocked plywood door separating them. He hadn't gotten any rest until Tank got up on the bed with him, curling up at his feet with a warm comforting weight. Ginger was similarly keeping Sophie company. Something about the situation with the dogs had finally given Jake the peace to sleep.

He glanced at her profile. "I'll take Tank to the Humane Society while you work."

She was still looking at the dogs. "What if they don't find a home for Tank? What if no one wants him? Tank looks rather . . . scary."

Jake swallowed. "They get put down."

"Put down? You mean killed?" Sophie glared at him. "What's humane about that?"

Jake cleared his throat. "I guess . . . it's humane the way they do it. The animals get a shot. Never feel a thing."

"No. Unacceptable."

Jake felt bad about it too, a queasiness roiling his gut as he thought about filling out a form surrendering Tank and leaving him in a cage. "He's not technically our dog. We rescued him from a bad home."

"Only to put him in a place where he'll be killed if he isn't adopted? Through no fault of his own?" Sophie snorted. "I'll keep him."

"Right. Because you're in a position to take care of two dogs."

She made no response to this, and he glanced over. Her eyes were downcast, her mouth pulled down. Even sad, Sophie's mouth looked kissable. "I should go back to Oahu and quit this attempt to hike around. Then I could keep both dogs. But I'm not ready to. I want to keep exploring for a while."

Jake sighed. "You hardly had time to do much of that this time."

"I've been able to see a lot of interesting back roads, got to see the lava hit the ocean, and I've run on the rim of the crater, thanks to you. But you are right. Ginger is more than enough for me to deal with while hiking and camping." She looked regretfully into the back seat. "She seems so happy with him."

"I'm sorry. I don't want to give him up either." Jake shook his head. "I just don't know what else to do."

They reached the station, and Sophie's phone dinged. She pulled it out of her pocket and held it up. "It's the contact who knows something about the missing persons again. I think we should meet whoever it is when I'm done here. I don't know how long it will take, but I will likely need a break at around two p.m. Will that be an okay time for you to pick me up?"

"Fine. I'll deal with the dog situation and keep an eye on Ginger. I'll be back for you at two."

"Sure you don't want to come in and greet Detective Freitan with me? I'm confident she will want to see you—preferably without clothing." Her eyes sparkled playfully at him. "I cannot help enjoying this a bit after how you used to harass me."

"And if you were half as uncomfortable as I am, then I apologize again for the teasing," Jake said. "Freitan is a piece of work."

"The same has been said about you." Sophie picked up the small daypack containing her laptop. She petted Tank's head. "Goodbye, my friend. I hope you quickly find a new home." She dug into the outside pocket of her pack and pulled out a fistful of cash, tucking it into Jake's pants pocket. "Here's some extra money to pay for him to be there longer. Without being put down."

"I will talk to them. Make sure everything that can be done for him is done."

"I know you will." She shut the door with a bang. "I still hate it."

Tank whined sadly as if understanding exactly what was going on. All three of them watched Sophie walk into the station's utilitarian storefront doorway, and disappear inside.

Jake sighed and put the Jeep in gear. "Might as well get this over with."

CHAPTER SEVENTEEN

SOPHIE unslung her backpack in the quiet computer lab of the South Hilo Police Department. She looked around at a row of aged desktops that made up the station's tech workspace. "These appear to be at least ten years old."

"That's right." Kamani Freitan had had a shower but didn't look any more rested than yesterday. She rubbed bloodshot eyes. "Good thing you brought your own equipment." She pointed to a coil of blue internet cable. "That's what you really came for."

"Exactly." Sophie unrolled the cable and plugged it into her laptop. "Anything new on the Julie Weathersby situation? Did Webb and Rayme give you any pertinent information?" She opened her laptop at an empty workstation on the long table.

"They both stuck to the story that they dropped Weathersby off on the side of the road. Wong and I put them in a cell overnight to think about things. When the officers searched their squat out in Oceanview, they didn't find anything that clearly belonged to Weathersby, though. There were some items that seemed like they might have been stolen from tourists, though. Expensive sunglasses. Phones. Some camera gear." Freitan shook her head. "Those two are nasty."

"I agree. I look forward to being able to determine if they might be associated with other missing persons." Sophie didn't want to describe how DAVID worked. Permission for her software to rifle through the police department's databases was not going to be given, no matter how many confidentiality agreements she signed. She'd have to disguise how she obtained any data she procured through DAVID's searches when she presented her findings to the detectives.

Freitan departed. Sophie plugged in headphones. She queued up some of her favorite classical music, cracked her knuckles, and dove into the wired world.

DAVID easily penetrated the police department firewalls, and soon she was surfing through reams of data on the missing persons situation on the Big Island.

There were too many cases. Sophie set the parameters for a time frame within the last five years. She input filters screening out cases that had been solved due to runaways, kidnappings, misunderstandings, and more.

She needed to know what bodies were turning up, and being matched to missing people. She started a new search on unidentified bodies. These turned out to be few and far between, though she was able to eliminate another layer of disappearances by reconciling them with recovered corpses.

She still ended up with close to a hundred people who had gone missing in the last five years.

Sophie shivered, looking at the number.

But it didn't have to be a serial. This area attracted people who wanted to disappear. Perhaps some were just using the Big Island as a launching pad to the rest of their lives, as she was. In addition, there was a booming underground drug trade here that caught many in its undertow.

She needed to find a recognizable trend. She introduced filters and keywords screening for age, marital status, ethnicity, socioeconomic status.

Patterns began appearing, emerging like snowflakes only to melt under the scrutiny of her analysis.

Someone touched her on the shoulder. Sophie jumped, yanking her headphones off and thrusting back in her chair.

Wong stepped back, his square face earnest. "Whoa. Didn't mean to startle you."

"I'm sorry. I get so deep in concentration that I lose track of where I am," Sophie said.

Indeed, her body felt stiff and her muscles had locked up. She glanced at the clock on the far wall. Two hours had passed. She had only two more before Jake returned. Her gaze dropped to her phone, just as it dinged. *"Want me to bring some lunch?"* Jake had included a photo of a sandwich with layers of ingredients. *"Never mind. I got you a BLT."*

"Freitan sent me to check on you. See if you had anything to share, or needed anything." Wong eyed her laptop's screen curiously.

Sophie closed the unit. "Unfortunately, I am not ready to share any data yet. I only have a few more hours to work here today before my partner and I have an appointment." It felt strange to refer to a meeting with an unknown confidential informant in a community park by such a formal title. "I will let you both know as soon as I have anything of interest."

Wong leaned his hip against the table. "I'm not sure what you're looking for. Something to do with missing persons, you said?"

Sophie stood up and stretched her arms overhead, thankful she always wore easy-movement clothing. She hinged at the waist and set her palms on the floor, stretching her hamstrings and back.

"Yes. I'm running statistics on the numbers and situations related to missing persons cases on the Big Island. This was sparked by our investigation into Julie Weathersby's disappearance and then discovering that there are so many lost in a relatively small area." Sophie straightened up and eyed Wong, taking his measure. The short, wiry Hawaiian Chinese detective had the kind of toned-down personality that didn't get much attention in the shadow of his flamboyant partner. That didn't mean that Wong wasn't a sharp investigator; Sophie had already noticed how observant he was, and what a good foil for

Freitan. Sophie had sometimes experienced that the quiet investigators were the ones who really got results. "Still waters run deep," Marcella would say, a colloquialism that made sense.

"I'm glad someone is taking the time to look at the big picture," Wong said, meeting her gaze with intelligent dark eyes. "We are always so busy chasing each case that I have often worried we are losing sight of the forest for the trees."

That was a good saying too. Sophie nodded. "Focusing on the sand grains rather than the beach."

"Right. We're going to get some lunch. Do you want to come?"

"No, my partner is bringing me a sandwich, I believe. I have to get all I can done before that meeting this afternoon. But I look forward to a . . . rain check." She was gratified that she had come up with the phrase, though that one made little sense at all. She needed to Google its origin. Wong turned to leave, and she touched his elbow. "Is there anything you can tell me about the body dump I found? About that family?"

Wong's expression went serious as his brows lowered and lips folded together. "The family was in Witness Protection under the cover name of Jones. They had hiked out to watch the lava at Kalapana much as you did—witnesses reported seeing them at the active lava site where you told us you spent the night. Somehow the killer coerced the family into walking to the *kipuka,* where they were executed. The Marshals think it was a professional hired by the organized crime outfit they were hiding from. We have uncovered photos and video of their execution being circulated on the dark web and being used as a lesson of what happens if you go against this outfit."

Sophie's pulse picked up. "Who in your department knows how to search the dark web?"

Wong had a dimple when he smiled a certain way. "Me."

Sophie frowned. "Have you been able to track the source of the video?"

"Anonymous upload. Multiple VPNs masking the original entry point." The spark died in Wong's eye. "I don't think we're going to solve this case. The father was going to be giving testimony to a grand jury; that's all the Marshal on their case would give us. It's a real blow to have lost that testimony. WITSEC in Hawaii is freaking out, because this is the latest in a series of incursions and leaks that have resulted in the loss of valuable witnesses."

"I wonder if some of the missing persons I'm looking at are WITSEC," Sophie said thoughtfully, tapping her lips with a finger.

"Quite possible. They won't tell us if they are, and we'll never get that list. Local PD is always seen as too permeable for that kind of top level intel."

Sophie was more impressed with Wong by the moment. "Thank you for telling me. I'm sorry this is the situation. I wish I could help."

"I wish you could, too. And I'm sorry you had to find that family on your vacation." Wong made air quotes as he gestured towards her laptop.

"There are things I care about much more than a vacation. Justice for those who need it is one of them."

Wong gave a brief nod and exited.

Sophie sat down, her mind whirring with the implications.

This was the perfect case for the Ghost. Sophie did not have the time or ability in her current situation to burrow into the WITSEC database and organization to uncover the leak and the mobsters that were taking advantage of it. *But Connor would love that opportunity.*

Saying the word "justice" aloud reminded her of Connor so clearly. His ocean-colored eyes. His disciplined body. His incredible musical ability. His genius behind a computer. *His dedication to reaching those who couldn't be reached by the law.*

Before she could second-guess herself further, Sophie dug the square weight of the external hard drive that contained the Ghost software out of the bottom of her bag. Connor had given her a copy of the software he used in his vigilantism, doubtless trying to lure her into being his partner on his mission. But it just wasn't her style or passion to set up clandestine communication manipulations that resulted in consequences for untouchable criminals. That didn't mean that she couldn't appreciate the function that the Ghost performed, even respect the necessity of it in the grand scheme of things.

Sophie saved her current results to the Cloud, shut down DAVID, and plugged the Ghost software hard drive into her laptop.

She opened the program, her fingers tripping as they typed in the password, *I*love*you*Sophie* that Connor had personalized the portal with.

"Talk about awkward," Marcella's voice said in her head. "He knew what he was doing when he programmed that password."

Sophie vividly remembered the hours spent trying to crack the code to get into the program and her initial disappointment that he hadn't left her a clue or message through that process. It turned out he had, and in Connor's usual way, it was bolder than anything she would have guessed.

Using the Ghost's search function, she imported the Hilo PD's case information from the Jones body dump and downloaded a saved chunk of the missing persons data as well. She opened a chat box and sent a note to Connor:

"I came across this body dump on the Big Island; a WITSEC family, executed by pros. Hilo PD has been shut out of the case, including the leak in Witness Protection that has led not only to this family's execution, but to the loss of other valuable witnesses. A video of this family's execution is circulating on the dark web and being used to intimidate. I don't have time or resources to find out more, but I thought the Ghost might take an interest."

Sophie's fingers paused. She stared at the message window, struggling with the secret hope that Connor was online. His pingback beacon on the software would have alerted him that she was in his program, and if he was active, he would write her back.

Several moments passed. No response.

"Son of a disease-ridden water buffalo," Sophie cursed softly. She closed the chat window.

"I take it your research is not going well." Jake had appeared at her elbow like a large, muscular djinn.

Sophie slammed the laptop shut and removed her headphones. "Hello, partner. You should alert me to your presence."

"I knocked, but you were in another world." Jake set a bag, stained with grease, beside her computer. "You didn't tell me what you wanted, so I took my best guess."

"Thank you, Jake." Sophie opened the bag and peeked inside. She raised her eyebrows in question. "I appreciated the photo. But what is it?"

"It's a BLT. Bacon, lettuce, and tomato. And some homemade taro chips." He reached into the bag and produced a thick purple slice of taro, staple food of the Hawaiian diet. Boiled, sliced and fried, the starchy tuber was delicious—Sophie had tasted it served that way in Honolulu.

Sophie took the chip. "Mine. Thank you."

"Fortunately, I brought my own." Jake held up his own bag. "I'm sure this isn't where they want us eating, but forgiveness is easier than permission." He sat beside her and pulled out a wrapped sandwich. He produced bottles of iced tea, and soon they were lunching in companionable silence.

"What did you find?" Jake eventually asked. His mouth was full, so his words were a little hard to understand.

Sophie swallowed her bite with a gulp of ice tea and answered. "Too much. Too many. I think there's something going on, but I need a lot longer to work through the different variables." Holding up a taro chip, she pointed it at him. "Wong came by. That man has a lot more going on than initially appears. He has computer skills."

Jake clutched his chest theatrically. "Oh! The easiest way to Sophie Ang's heart has been revealed. And here I was, trying the old-fashioned way of getting to her through her stomach."

Sophie's brows scrunched. "I do not understand."

"Never mind. Fill me in on these mysterious skills of which you speak."

"Well, he told me that the Jones family, the body dump I discovered, was in the WITSEC program. He confirmed that there's a possible leak in that program, and that photos and video of the family's execution are being used to coerce other witnesses. He discovered this fact himself online, surfing the dark web."

Jake finished his sandwich, as usual a fast eater. He wiped his hands on a napkin. "You are thinking of hacking WITSEC and trying to track that case?"

"No." Sophie was still on the first half of her sandwich. She dabbed her lips with a napkin. "I do not have time, resources, or the protected online access I'd need to do such an investigation, let alone an agency willing to back me by acting on any intel I might uncover."

"But you know someone who does."

Sophie met Jake's gaze. His eyes were a darker gray than usual, the blue in them bruised-looking. *Something was bothering him.* She looked down at her sandwich and took a bite, refusing to answer.

They'd never discussed the Ghost and his association with Security Solutions, let alone Sophie's personal connection to the cyber vigilante. Unless Bix had told him about the FBI probe into Sheldon Hamilton at the agency, he wouldn't know about any of it.

As if reading her mind, Jake pushed back the rolling office chair he sat on and extended his black-clad legs, stacking combat-booted feet on the edge of the desk. "I think it's time we discussed the Ghost."

CHAPTER EIGHTEEN

JAKE WOVE his fingers together and rested them on his stomach, fixing his gaze on Sophie. She set the uneaten half of her sandwich down and picked up her bottled tea. Her eyes flicked to the computer. "I have some more filters to run before we go," she said, ignoring his prior statement.

He wasn't giving up so easily.

"And I said it was time we talked about the Ghost." He wanted to know what she knew about that slippery cyber vigilante Bix had told him was allegedly associated with Security Solutions. "The FBI's trying to make a case against our CEO, Sheldon Hamilton," Bix had told him before he left Oahu for the Big Island. "But they can't get anything to stick. And they won't. Hamilton's nose is clean."

Bix had brushed off the rest of Jake's questions. "I only told you so you won't be surprised if you get questioned by one of Sophie's former teammates. And she knows all about this."

That Sophie knew about the Ghost and had never said a word rankled Jake. *He hated secrets.*

Sophie raised her eyes to his. "Please, Jake. Don't ask me about this. I can't talk about it."

The naked appeal in her gaze disarmed him. *Such a warm amber brown, and those lashes!* Her eyes were a damn superpower.

"Fine," he said gruffly. "Since you don't trust me."

"I trust you. I just . . . don't want you to be hurt. And the less you know about this particular subject, the better for you." She stood up abruptly. "I won't get anything more done here, today. Let's go. We can case the area where we're meeting the informant first, which is good practice."

Jake dropped his booted feet to the ground, puzzling over her words as Sophie rolled up the internet cable and stowed it. "How would I be hurt by anything to do with that cyber vigilante?"

Sophie folded her lips together tightly. "I think I misused a figure of speech. I meant that . . . you should not be responsible for any more knowledge, in case you are questioned."

"Ah-ha. So, you do know something."

Sophie stowed the laptop in her backpack and slung it on. "Let's go." She headed for the door.

Jake picked up their discarded lunch. She had only eaten half her sandwich and chips. *He was going to make her finish the rest.*

They reached the Jeep. Jake beeped it open to the happy greeting barks of the dogs, and set the lunch bag inside on the dash.

Sophie opened her door and her face lit up. "Jake! Tank is still here!"

"I couldn't do it." Jake's ears were hot with embarrassment. "I took him to the Humane Society and started filling out the paperwork, but one look at those cages . . . I just couldn't do it."

Sophie ran around the front of the Jeep and embraced him. She wrapped her arms around him, pulled his head down, and kissed him.

Surprise had him standing stiffly, but Jake recovered quickly, kissing her back, squashing her against the side of the Jeep as pent-up hunger took over. She was making a little humming noise in her throat as she wound around him, not put off by his clumsy enthusiasm. Their mouths fused, their hands roamed, and his brain shut down as one of her legs came up, wrapping around his hip. *God, she tasted good . . .*

"So that's how it is, eh?" Freitan's voice, heavy with amusement, came from behind Jake. "Can't say I blame you, but the parking lot of Hilo Police Department might not be the most private venue for what you got goin' on."

Jake buried his face in Sophie's neck, breathing heavily, imagining that devil-woman dancing a jig in hell. "Dammit." *Maybe Freitan would just go away.*

Sophie shoved at his chest, cursing in Chinese or Thai or something. He let go, keeping his back turned to Freitan so she couldn't mock the action he had going on at the front of his pants. Sophie went around and opened the Jeep's door as Jake kept his back to the detectives, simmering with temper and frustration.

"Sorry for the cock block." Freitan laughed harshly.

"Kamani, leave them alone." Wong's voice, coming to the rescue. Jake heard the sound of their vehicle beep open. The two bickered.

Jake shoved his hands through his hair, calming himself, tugging his shirt down, setting himself to rights physically and mentally as their car pulled away.

"Tank, you beautiful boy. I'm so glad you're still here." Sophie was already inside the Jeep talking to the dogs. Jake turned around when he was sure he was decent, and it was just in time to see her feed the other half of her sandwich to the dogs.

"I brought that so you could eat it. Not them," Jake scolded. He had himself back under control, but all he could think about was getting his hands on her again.

"I'm sorry about kissing you. We appeared very unprofessional." Sophie wouldn't look at him as she turned in her seat to face forward, and buckled in. "We should hurry. We'll be late."

"I'm just sorry Freitan interrupted us." Jake fired up the Jeep. "Though we could have picked a better place to make out." His lips felt sore in a good way when he smiled at her. "We still can."

"I think that was quite enough of that," Sophie said primly. She worked her phone with her thumbs. "I am confirming our meet with the informant."

Jake glanced into the back seat. Tank thrust his big square head forward to touch his shoulder. "Thanks, buddy. You got her to give me a kiss." The big dog woofed in reply.

Forty minutes later, they pulled up in a nondescript community park with a weather-beaten jungle gym, cinderblock bathrooms, and a patchy soccer field ringed by palms. Jake took his weapon out of his pack. "Think we should be strapped for this."

"Yes." Sophie had also taken out her Glock. Jake checked his weapon, watching out of the corner of his eye as she expelled the clip, checked the number of rounds, and rammed it back in, stowing it in a side pocket of her nylon cargo pants. They got out of the Jeep. "We're half an hour early. Let's let the dogs run loose since no one's around," Sophie said.

"Good idea. They've been very patient in the car." Jake opened his door. Tank barreled out, running over to investigate the row of trash cans by the bathrooms, while Ginger galloped off to fetch a stick. Jake tried not to be too obvious as he watched Sophie do some yoga stretches, but the shape of her butt was too distracting. He turned to grab Ginger's stick and threw it for the energetic Lab. She hurtled after it, soon joined by Tank. The dogs tussled playfully, and eventually, Tank got the stick and brought it to Jake.

"He seems to know his master." Sophie came to stand beside him.

"I can't keep him. I travel too much. But I can work on finding a real home for him."

"My father might be able to watch him while you do," Sophie said. "He's in Honolulu for a month or so."

"That would be great." Jake threw the stick again, feeling his belly tighten with regret. He really did wish he could keep the dog. Jake whistled for the dogs. Both of them came, thundering at him like charging horses. He ushered them into the back of the Jeep and filled the water bowl from Sophie's backpack from a jug he'd picked up at a convenience store.

Sophie stiffened. "We have incoming." A large black truck was headed their way, coming down the feeder road.

"What did you tell the informant about us?"

"Me and my boyfriend are looking for your missing cousin, Julie Weathersby," Sophie said. "We're rich."

"Rich boyfriend. I like the sound of that," Jake drawled. Sophie kept her gaze studiously on the vehicle as it approached and parked beside them.

CHAPTER NINETEEN

SOPHIE ASSESSED the Honda Ridgeline extended cab, noting the extra chrome and silver paint designs on the side and memorizing the license plate. The informant seated inside was young, a Caucasian of average height and doughy build, with pale skin that didn't look like it had seen much of the Hawaii sun. He wore a billed hat emblazoned with Xbox, and he didn't get out of his truck.

She approached, going with their usual routine of her out in front and Jake as backup. The dogs barked loudly in the Jeep, lending to a feeling of authenticity that they were a resident couple.

"Hello. Are you Sandy?" the young man asked.

Sophie had given him her false identity name of Sandy Mason, and she nodded. "Yes. I'm Sandy, and this is my boyfriend, Jack."

The informant's gaze darted nervously around the park, coming back to rest on Jake's superior biceps with a look of apprehension. "I go by Cypher."

Sophie suppressed a smile at the moniker. "Well, as I told you in my text, Jack's cousin, Julie Weathersby, is missing. She was camping around the island, and supposed to meet up with us in Hilo at the end of her trip. That was over a week ago. Her parents are worried. I saw your poster at the store and thought we'd reach out since the police don't seem to have any leads."

"Sandy's got it right." It wasn't strictly necessary for Jake to wrap a possessive arm around Sophie's waist, but she let it stay there for the moment as he went on. "Julie is super responsible. She wouldn't just run off." He took out his phone, and scrolled to her photo. "Here is what she looks like. In case you have seen her, or even the missing person report that was filed."

Cypher took the phone, looked at the photo, and nodded. "Yeah. I added her to the database, and speculated she disappeared from this part of the island based on her last known location, which was in Volcanoes National Park."

"What database?" Sophie's attention was pricked, but she softened her voice as Cypher quickly handed the phone back in response to her tone. "Can we sit down in your truck and get comfortable so we can talk privately?"

He nodded reluctantly and got out to open the driver's side seat of his extended cab for her. Jake got into the passenger side, and they all settled themselves.

Cypher took out a laptop, and Sophie's interest piqued further. "I think there might be a kidnapper at work," the young man said. "Only he doesn't give back the victims."

Sophie's brows drew together. "What makes you think so?"

"Many of the people that disappear have assets. They aren't rich, necessarily, but a lot of the victims actually have some means." Cypher's eyes flicked over Jake. "For instance, I'm guessing you and your cousin aren't poor."

"We get by." Jake frowned. "But my aunt and uncle would have said something if they had gotten a ransom demand."

"The interesting thing about these demands is that they seem to be unfulfilled." Cypher was studying his laptop. "The families pay the modest ransoms, but the missing are never returned. I'm tracking the concerns, and I've taken it on myself to warn people."

A tingle of alertness lifted the hairs on Sophie's arms. There was a shine of perspiration above Cypher's lip. The young man was nervous, hiding something.

She didn't dare look at Jake. A secondary predator role of taking money from family members might fit his profile perfectly.

Cypher was setting them up. He was checking them out as a target of extortion money, and he'd decided they weren't good candidates. Now he was warning them away.

Sophie reached over and clutched Jake's arm in mock distress. "This is just so much to take in. I think we should really go to the police with this news."

"Hush, darling." Jake patted her hand. His voice was warm with supportive comfort. He was reveling in his role, and she dared not glance at him and see the humorous glint in his eyes or she'd lose her composure. "It's not up to us to solve this, honey. We will take everything we learn back to the cops, of course, but now we have this nice young man helping us, too."

Cypher smiled. His teeth were not brushed very often. "Yeah, quite a disturbing situation might be going on here."

Sophie blinked her eyes, as if confused, leaning forward from the back seat. "How do you know all this?"

"I thought you would never ask." Cypher scrolled to a website and expanded the view for them to see. "This is a missing persons posting on the Big Island bulletin board website where parents and families weigh in on the investigations."

Sophie recognized the site as one of the ones that DAVID had cross-checked with police records. She was eager to see how his data analysis stacked up to the preliminary findings DAVID had compiled. *But would he share?*

She took out her own phone to pull it up, but couldn't get any reception. She frowned at Cypher. "How are you getting any Internet out here?"

"I use a sat phone. Only way to deal with the spotty reception. Got a hotspot set up. But you can look at my laptop for now," he said magnanimously. Sophie leaned over the young man's shoulder to look through the rows of posts.

There were many more pictures of each missing victim than the ones she recognized from the police department database. Heartbreaking personal stories, rants about the lack of response from the police department, and a series of highlighted letters, complaining that they had been contacted for ransom, and, once paid, had never heard from the extortionist again.

"So, what's your skin in this game?' Jake said. "What do you get out of it?"

"I'm just a concerned citizen living in a dangerous community. Trying to help by warning victims' families."

"Then I'm sure you won't mind coming down to the station in Hilo with us, and making a statement to that effect," Sophie said, as Jake reached over and plucked the truck's keys out of the ignition. "Being the good citizen that you are." Sophie pointed her Glock at Cypher's ribs. "We're taking you in. Let's go."

"Sure you got him handled, babe?" Jake bounced his brows as Cypher groaned, closing his laptop.

"This young man will be driving straight to Hilo PD to make his statement. I'm sure he won't give me a minute of trouble, *babe*."

Jake's teeth flashed in a grin as he got out of the truck, slamming the door. "I'm right behind you in the Jeep, Cypher, so don't give my girlfriend any crap."

Cypher banged his head on the steering wheel as Jake got into the Jeep, preparing to follow them. "I knew I shouldn't have let you guys get in the truck."

Sophie kept the gun on Cypher, dug into his ribs, for the forty-minute drive back to Hilo. Freitan and Wong were not back from wherever they'd gone, but the intake officer checked their permits to carry and their IDs, and they settled Cypher in the waiting area.

The minute Sophie's gun was stowed, the young man made a run for the glass doors. Jake seemed to enjoy wrestling Cypher back inside and making him sit.

Freitan and Wong returned. "What did you chase out of the bushes?" Freitan asked.

"This young man knows all about shaking down the families of missing persons," Jake said.

The two detectives took charge of the witness, after a brief conference with Jake and Sophie. "You should go to his residence. Search for evidence related to the victims," Sophie urged.

"He's lawyered up already, so it's going to be a process." Freitan had a vein in her neck that pulsed when she was annoyed. "His weird scam of warning people might not be enough to get a search warrant on his home."

Sophie frowned. "Perhaps . . . his address fell somewhere and we saw it and took matters into our own hands."

"Unscrupulous private investigators that we are," Jake filled in.

"That would never happen around here," Freitan swiveled her monitor so they could read Cypher's address. She stood, and walked off toward the interview room where Wong already waited with the witness.

"Cypher" was named Paul Chernobiac, and he lived at 1140 Ocean View Terrace.

Sophie plugged the address into the GPS on her phone, grateful to have a signal. "Let's go." They hurried out of the building.

The day was waning. Sunset was upon them, a glorious molten red that reminded Sophie of the lava flows. She glanced at Jake as they got into the Jeep. "I hope we have time to make it out there before dark."

CHAPTER TWENTY

JAKE RESIGNED himself to doing the long drive again. According to the GPS, Ocean View Terrace was located well off the beaten track on the other side of Volcanoes Park. They needed to try to hit this house while Paul Chernobiac, a.k.a. "Cypher," was being interviewed. Jake was glad Sophie had downloaded and saved the map with the location as they drove an hour back in the direction they had come.

The sunset was a spectacular streaking of reds, yellows, and purples over the sky from the ocean to the west. Sophie sat quietly, her gaze out the window, her hands folded in her lap. The dogs snored peacefully in the back.

How could he move things forward between them? *Chicks loved hashing over that shit.* "Should we talk about what's been happening?"

"With the case?"

"No. With us. You and me."

Sophie glanced at him. "No."

Her answer hurt, but he tried to sound humorous. "You're the only woman I've ever met who never wants to talk about a relationship and where it's going."

She leaned even further away. "I'm not like other women."

"You can say that again." Jake winced. He was mucking it up. *Stop talking now!*

Sophie scrunched her nose. "Why would I say that again?"

"I never realized how many expressions and idioms there were in the English language until I began explaining them to you all the time."

Sophie's cell phone rang. She took it out of her pocket. Her mouth made a little O. "It's Alika."

Jealousy felt like a punch to the solar plexus, but Sophie had told him that jealousy was a turn-off after her homicidal bastard ex-husband. Jake smiled with difficulty. "Tell your helicopter buddy hi from me."

Sophie rolled her eyes, and Jake laughed. That they could even kind of joke about it felt good.

She answered the phone. Jake could hear their conversation. "Sophie. How's it going on the Big Island?" Alika had a nice phone voice. "I miss you."

Jake never sounded good on the phone—too abrupt and too loud.

Damn the man and his slick manners, sweet chopper and those armband tribal tats . . . maybe Jake should get some. Barbed wire around his biceps, or some shit. But Sophie wouldn't be impressed with that. It would have to have *meaning.* And other than his Special Forces unit, he had never cared about symbols enough to put them on his body.

"Well, actually I haven't been able to do much of what I planned," Sophie said. "I found a body dump on my second day hiking, and then was drawn into an investigation right after that."

"You're kidding!"

"Unfortunately, no. I am not."

When was it that he had come to love even her pedantic speech patterns?

"Alika, Jake and I are working a case for Security Solutions.

Searching for a missing young woman, and we're driving to do a recon of something related to the case. I should go."

A pause. Then, "Jake is with you?" Alika didn't sound happy.

Jake leaned over and spoke into the phone. "Howzit hanging, Alika? I'm working with Sophie twenty-four seven. We're even sharing a motel room. Catch you later, pal."

Sophie scowled at him and lifted the phone tight to her ear. She turned away to face the window. "I'll call when I can speak privately, Alika," Sophie said softly. She murmured something he couldn't catch, and ended the call. She slid her phone back into her pocket and turned to him. "Don't be obnoxious, Jake."

Jake rolled his shoulders. "Can't help my natural charm."

The headlights caught a reflective sign marking the turn off, and Sophie pointed. "There!" Soon they were bouncing along a rutted, unlit road.

Jake tightened his hands on the wheel. "I want to park away from the house. We need to drive by it, identify it, park with our lights off and go in dark."

Sophie nodded. They drove slowly as Jake strained to see between the thick bushes that screened the driveway coming off of the narrow road. "I don't see any mailboxes or other number identification," Sophie said. "but the GPS says we have arrived."

Jake pulled the Jeep over deep onto the shoulder. Sophie took a bag of kibble out of her backpack and shared it into small piles on the back seat, leaving a fresh bowl of water for the dogs on the floor. The two animals seemed perfectly content to eat their dinner and relax together.

Jake produced a small, high beam flashlight as Sophie checked her weapon, stowed it in her cargo pocket, and produced a similar light. Jake locked the Jeep, and they headed up the road toward Chernobiac's driveway.

Jake signaled that he would take the lead as they turned off the main road, and he was gratified when Sophie did not argue, merely falling into his shadow as they worked their way stealthily toward the house. As soon as they reached a clear area in front of the dwelling, motion detecting lights bloomed on.

Jake took cover behind a tree, and Sophie stayed glued to his side. "Let's see what happens now."

Jake assessed the simple wooden house, just another of so many built on the Big Island made from standard kits shipped to Hawaii. A lamp burned in an upstairs window, implying someone was home. An untrimmed yard surrounded the place, and a showy Honda street rod gleamed in an open garage on one side of the house. Jake pointed. "Seems like a pretty nice ride for a gamer dude of Chernobiac's age," he whispered.

"His truck was too expensive as well." Sophie's breath stirred the hairs near Jake's ear and brought up goose bumps on his skin. Her body warmed his back.

No movement from the house. Eventually the light went off.

"I don't think anyone is home, though that sensor light will out us," Jake whispered. "But we can always pretend we're a stranded couple in distress." Jake reached back to take Sophie's hand. Her fingers felt warm, slim and strong, just like the rest of her.

A rush of endorphins flooded Jake's system.

He stood poised at the brink of danger, lawbreaking for a good cause, the woman he loved at his back, and a couple of good dogs waiting for his return.

He was a simple man, and he knew it. Jake shut his eyes for just a second, overwhelmed. *So this was what happiness felt like.* "Let's do this."

CHAPTER TWENTY-ONE

Sophie held Jake's hand and reached her other one into her cargo pocket, her fingers curling around the cool pebbled grip of her Glock. The weapon felt comforting as she ran on bent knees in Jake's body shadow, the sensor light striking them with illumination. They reached the cover of the carport, and another beam bloomed, lighting up the back door above wooden steps rising out of the carport's cement floor.

Jake led and they sidled along the wall to the back door, scanning for any movement. Nothing broke the silence of the night but the high-pitched calling of coqui frogs from the trees in the surrounding area.

Jake tried the back door handle. "Locked."

Sophie felt quickly around the door jamb and under the mat, and smiled as she held up a spare key.

"I didn't think Cypher looked that bright, and now I know he isn't," Jake said.

Sophie unlocked the door. She stepped inside and they left it ajar, alert as they entered for any dog or other occupant. Jake signaled for them to spread out and check the house, and she went one way as he went another. They moved quickly through the rooms to check that they were clear, reconnecting in the living room.

Sophie swung in a circle, assessing. The house was decorated with mismatched castoffs. A big screen TV took up one wall in the living room, which was fronted by a lounger with built in cup holders and a heated massage feature. Pizza boxes and takeout containers, crusty with dried leftovers, littered a coffee table.

"What are we looking for exactly?" Sophie frowned.

"Anything tying Chernobiac to the disappearances. I don't know what that would be, but hopefully, we will recognize it when we see it."

"He's a gamer. Anything relevant will be on his computer, most likely." She turned and headed for a set of stairs at the back of the building leading to the second floor. She found his computer station in a bedroom that contained nothing but the desk with his monitor and a rumpled queen-sized bed. Sophie unslung her small rucksack and dug in it for the write blocker program. She sat down and plugged it into the computer's back port to copy Chernobiac's hard drive. She accessed her codebreaker software on a stick drive and was working on decrypting Chernobiac's security code when Jake rejoined her.

He held up a lumpy black plastic bag. His bulging biceps told Sophie that it was heavy. "Guess what I found in the linen closet? I think we just hit pay dirt. Literally."

"I need a moment." Sophie cracked the encryption and activated the write blocker. The software would make a complete copy of Chernobiac's hard drive, but it needed fifteen minutes or more to run, depending on how much data he had. She swiveled Chernobiac's office chair and turned back to Jake.

Her partner had set the bulky bag on the bed and untied the knot securing it. Inside, stacks of rubber-banded cash were piled like so many pairs of socks. "I'd be very interested to find out what Cypher says he did to earn all this cash." Jake's eyes seemed to glow with excitement. Sophie could smell it on him, a potent cologne.

"I'll take pictures of this money, but by the time Freitan and Wong get a warrant to search the place, I feel confident that the cash will be gone."

"Not if you text them a photo," Jake said. "They'll move heaven and earth to find out where this much dinero came from."

Sophie photographed the bag of money and texted it to Freitan. She included a line of explanation: *"Found this in subject's linen closet. You might want to get a search warrant for the premises."*

"On it. Holding subject for 24 hours." A smiley face followed. *"Good job, you sexy beasts!"*

Sophie decided not to mention Freitan's joke to her partner. "They are holding Cypher for twenty-four hours. I need time for the write blocker to clone his hard drive. You might as well be thorough and search the rest of the house."

Sophie turned back to address Cypher's computer. She flexed her fingers over his keyboard. The keys were unpleasantly sticky.

She would be able to surf through the contents of the young man's computer at leisure later on. To keep updated, she planted a keystroke logger program that would advise her of any new activity and send it to her in a coded message.

"I'm surprised he's so lax with his security," Jake said. He had returned the bag of cash to its hiding place. "You'd think the guy would be more careful with his remote location and no visible security system. I hope there's not something we overlooked."

"Why don't you check?" Sophie peered at the computer screen. "The write blocker still needs another ten minutes. He has a lot of data on this unit."

Jake disappeared. Sophie nipped into Cypher's online activity, just to see what she could see.

As she had suspected, he was the one operating the missing persons website, though he had chosen an avatar of a blonde soccer mom to be his public admin profile. Chernobiac's operation was crude, but clearly working well if that bag of cash and his cars were any indication . . .

Jake reappeared in the doorway. "We've got to go. He has a secret alarm system, and we tripped a silent alarm. I'm guessing we have minutes to move before someone gets here."

Sophie stared at the write blocker, willing it to work faster, but it was only fifty percent done. *That would have to be good enough.* She closed the program, ejected the drive, and exited his rig, shutting it down manually. She used the edge of her shirt to wipe down the keyboard and desk nearby. Jake was already doing the same with a paper towel on the other areas they'd touched.

"Stay off the road in case someone comes," Jake said. Minutes later, they were running through the woods beside the driveway, headed back to the Jeep.

A big black SUV with mirror tinting on the windows barreled silently past them, lights off, heading toward the house. They'd left the way they came in, locking the back door, but the sensor light in the garage was still on. The responders would know someone had been there.

"I don't think those are cops. Maybe private security." Jake had pulled his weapon, and he reached for her hand.

His hand served no useful function so Sophie ignored it, palming her Glock as well. "How far off the road did you park the Jeep? I didn't pay attention."

"Not very far. Hopefully they went by too fast to notice it. I wish I'd hidden it better. That SUV has a gangster vibe." Jake beeped open the Jeep. They jumped in, firing up the engine, as the dogs woofed a greeting.

Sophie gritted her teeth and Ginger gave a startled yelp, as Jake floored it, peeling out onto the road,. They roared down the potholed road, catching air on the dips due to the Jeep's stiff suspension. Sophie clung to the door handle as they took a curve too fast, throwing her against the window.

Jake hung a left once they reached the main highway, continuing to break speed limits for a few more miles. He hung a left onto a tiny side road, and backed the Jeep in under some trees so they could watch the highway. He turned off the lights.

Darkness settled over them, marked by the dogs' panting.

They were rewarded a few minutes later by the sight of the big black SUV streaking back toward Hilo. Jake craned to look after it. "Did you get a plate number?"

"No. They were moving too fast. Not that any plate on that SUV would go back to anything real." Sophie's heart rate was finally settling. "Speaking of, maybe we should obscure our number, too, in case they took it down when they passed us near the house."

Sophie got out of the vehicle, scooped a couple of handfuls of handy mud from a nearby puddle, and rubbed the slurry over the rental's license plates. She got back in the car and poured some of the dogs' water over her hands. "I can't wait to get a shower at the cabin."

They drove at a much more sedate pace back toward Volcanoes National Park, just a couple of tourists in a rental Jeep. There was no telling whether that SUV was pulling the same trick they had done, and hurrying would draw attention.

Sophie liked it that Jake knew this, that he knew how to shake a tail, that he'd thought of staying off the road when they left the house. They worked so well together that they hardly needed to talk about what they were doing.

What she didn't want to think about was another night, tossing and turning on the other side of a wall so thin that she could hear him tossing and turning, too.

CHAPTER TWENTY-TWO

S<small>OPHIE SET</small> up her laptop to download and view what she had been able to capture of Cypher's hard drive. Both dogs were up on her bed, snuggled together.

Showering off the sweat and dirt she'd picked up during the day had felt amazing, even in the tepid water and low pressure of the cabin's inadequate shower. Sitting down in front of the computer, she felt clean and restless in fresh clothing, a towel on her head turban style.

She tried not to listen to the rush of water as Jake showered, wrestling with a mental picture of his ripped body under the stream of water, his soapy hands sliding over all those muscles . . .

She needed to focus on the data reports she was compiling on DAVID's searches through the missing persons information. *Needed. To. Focus.*

The water shut off in the bathroom.

No, he wasn't toweling off in the bathroom, filling the whole tiny closet of a space with his yummy lemony aftershave and man smell. No, he wasn't rubbing his hair and brushing his teeth, and wrapping a towel around his waist and coming out and . . .

"Whatcha' doin'?" Jake's voice from the doorway made Sophie jump.

She turned.

Yes, there he was, leaning on one elbow in the doorway, with the towel wrapped around his waist and nothing on "but his birthday suit and sexy mojo," Marcella's voice supplied in her mind.

"Uh." Sophie's tongue felt thick. *Off men! Totally. Forever!*

"All work and no play makes Sophie . . . Sophie." Jake ambled over and leaned over her shoulder to look at the screen. His smell surrounded her. His voice was a low rumble that scraped along her nerves. "Looks like a lot of statistics. Stats are so sexy."

"*Son of a yak!* Put your clothing on, Jacob Sean Overstreet Dunn! You told me no partners with benefits!" Sophie leaned away, flapping her hands at him. "I am resisting. Resisting!"

Jake straightened up and laughed. Laughed and laughed, leaning backward. *Those abs!* Sophie watched the towel in fascination as it loosened, slithering toward the floor. He caught it at the last moment. "You are so damn cute I can't stand it," he finally said. "And you called me by my full name."

"Son of a yak?" Sophie felt a smile tugging her lips. "It sounds better in Thai."

"Is that what you said? No, I meant the other thing you called me." He squatted. Now he was near her waist. Her whole body felt warm and tingly. She couldn't look away from his eyes. *Gray never looked so hot.* "My. Full. Name. Say it again." He swiveled the cheap chair to face him. Her vision was filled with him, her senses overwhelmed.

"Jacob Sean Overstreet Dunn," she whispered. "Jake."

"Partners with benefits it is. I can't take this anymore." Jake pulled her into his arms for the kiss she'd been craving since the last one.

This time, "yes" was the word she cried aloud, again and again.

CHAPTER TWENTY-THREE

THE NEXT MORNING Sophie sat down at her laptop, doing what she should've been doing last night instead of what she had ended up doing. The screen's blue glow fell over her hands. She stared at them blankly.

She could still feel the solid warmth of Jake's body impressed on her fingers.

Sophie couldn't help glancing over at the bed. The dogs, ousted, lay on the braided rug under the window. Jake sprawled across the full-sized mattress, taking up the whole thing. Her gaze traveled over him, lying face down and gloriously nude, the sheets tangled at the foot of the bed. *Turns out he liked to sleep naked, too.*

She felt really good this morning. Weak in the knees, loose in the joints, with happy aches in between.

She'd now had two lovers.

She didn't count Assan Ang. He had been . . . something else. A long, dark, closed chapter.

Whatever might happen in the future because of being with Jake, she wasn't sorry. They'd both needed the release after the events of the day. And having sex with him didn't mean she was ready to be in a relationship. Nothing had changed about that. Jake was the one who had agreed to her terms and walked through the door. Literally.

Jake rolled over, his breathing slow and deep, one arm reaching across her side of the bed, his fingers spread. *Even asleep, he was looking for her.* And damn, it had been as good as she imagined. Jake was a thoughtful and energetic lover, and had been determined that she would enjoy the experience.

He was nothing if not single-minded about his goals.

Tenderness bloomed, watching him, and she sucked in a breath, biting down on her lip, shutting off the emotion. He was sure to think that they were "together" now. *And they weren't.*

Sophie made a cup of hot tea in the hotel carafe and refocused on the cache of data she had extracted from DAVID. She needed to get back to the computer room at Hilo PD so she could finish some of the pattern analysis she had been running.

The cabin didn't have Wi-Fi, so her temptation to get into DAVID was stonewalled—but at some point, her email had kicked in, and she was able to look at her messages.

A message from the Ghost's signature chat box awaited her.

Sophie felt a twinge as she clicked on it, unsure if her feeling was apprehension or something else.

"Thanks for the referral to this WITSEC situation, Sophie. I take it as a vote of confidence. I'll get to work on this, and you can expect to hear back from me in a couple of days. It's good to be in touch."

Nothing more, thank the great Thor.

She was relieved.

Morning bloomed outside the windows, and there was work to do. She walked over and shook Jake's shoulder, using one of Marcella's phrases. "Rise and shine, lazybones."

She wasn't prepared for how quickly he reacted, grabbing her wrist and pulling her down and across him. He nuzzled her neck, and his bristly beard sent shivers down her bare skin. "I wondered if I dreamed last night. But here you are, naked in my room . . ."

"It's *my* room. And . . . thank you for the good times, but we have to get to work." Sophie extracted herself and walked with dignity to the bathroom. She locked the door so he wouldn't join her, and took extra time washing up.

Jake needed to get the message that they'd had a "one and done," as Marcella called it. She couldn't let him get too attached.

THE DRIVE to Hilo Station was silent and uncomfortable. Jake kept yawning, great stretches of his jaws. Sophie would have offered to drive, but she knew he'd decline.

"I need food," Jake said. "I'm depleted from my exertions yesterday."

Sophie ignored his wink. "I'm amenable to a stop for breakfast." She looked at the dogs, who had perked up at the mention of food. "We can order something for the dogs, too. I'm out of kibble."

Sophie's phone beeped with an incoming text, and she took it out of her pocket.

An unknown number showed. *"Come to Hilo Bay Park at noon. I have important information about your mother."*

Sophie's belly clenched. Her mother?

As far as Sophie knew, Pim Wat Smithson was institutionalized in Thailand in an exclusive mental hospital, where she had been installed after her most recent suicide attempt. Her aunt, who kept her informed, had sent monthly progress reports on her mother's almost catatonic depressive state.

The phone dinged again. *"Come alone. Ditch that man with you. And tell no one."*

CHAPTER TWENTY-FOUR

JAKE GLANCED over to see that Sophie had withdrawn from him completely. She'd folded her body tightly into her seat and now she stared out the window, holding her phone pressed close. Who had sent her a text she was all but cradling? Was it Alika?

Something had been going on with those two on Kaua'i, he'd bet money on it. Jake squelched his possessive feelings yet again. At least he'd been able to get her all to himself on this trip, away from that gym rat businessman with his chopper and fancy houses.

Sophie had resisted his overtures this morning, and he wasn't even surprised; what surprised him was how much it hurt even though he'd prepared for it.

She didn't want to be with him. He knew that, and he'd wanted her too much last night to care.

He'd back off, go as slow as she needed to. *He wasn't the one with wounds and scars.* Yeah, he'd fallen for a few women in his time and thought his heart was broken—Tina, who'd cheated on him while he was in Afghanistan, and Debbie who'd refused a ring he'd impulsively offered on one of his leaves—but not a shadow of the suffering Sophie'd experienced. It was understandable that she didn't want to get into anything after what she'd been through. That psycho husband of hers and five years of abuse. Then she finally dates Alika, and he gets beat to shit. Then her next boyfriend Todd Remarkian gets killed. So even with Assan Ang finally out of the picture, it was no wonder she was afraid to trust that anything good could happen to her.

He'd have to trust enough for both of them.

But at least he had been able to get her to come unglued—several times, in fact. He suppressed a grin—the memory would have to keep him warm until he could get her into bed again.

They ate a silent breakfast in a café at the edge of Hilo, and fed the dogs. Jake busied himself with the local paper, searching for news about missing persons, while Sophie obsessively worked her phone.

At the station, Sophie was all business with Freitan and Wong when they met the detectives in their cubicle.

"We think Chernobiac has partners. We couldn't call you to update last night due to a lack of phone reception, but his house had a silent alarm we tripped. The responders were not law enforcement, nor any normal security company that we could tell. Their vehicle was an unmarked black Escalade, and they pursued us aggressively."

Freitan nodded. "Yep. Chernobiac has been making veiled threats that we better let him go, or else. I keep saying, or else what? But he hasn't said. We did get a search warrant for his house, and with your intel, will take a back-up unit with us when we go. We're leaving in half an hour."

"We can help. Save you some time by pointing out where we found the money and other items." Jake was calm and assertive with Freitan. "We'd like to ride along."

Freitan gave Jake a once over. "You look a little ragged, my friend. Tough time sleeping?"

"Wouldn't impair my performance, if that's what you're implying," Jake said. He needed to get a level playing field with this woman, but still hadn't been able to.

Sophie cleared her throat. "Jake can go with you. I want to spend the morning working in the computer lab. I'm going to be ready to pull together the missing persons research analysis if I have a few more hours to work, and the dogs shouldn't be left in the car all day again. I'll take them for a run at the park."

Freitan glanced back at Jake. "All right then, Soldier Boy. Meet us at our vehicle in twenty. I'll bring an extra vest for you." She walked off with Wong in tow.

Jake turned to Sophie. Her face had that neutral, blank look he hated. *She had shut down toward him.* The wise course was to accept that, and retreat. Come back to fight another day. He smacked his thighs and stood. "Sounds like we have a plan. I'll help you get the dogs situated."

They tied both animals under a shady tree behind the building near the dumpsters and gave them water. Sophie held her hand out for the keys. "I want to run to the store and get food for them later. I'd like to use the Jeep."

"Just don't get in an accident. You're not on the paperwork," Jake said.

Sophie tightened her lips in annoyance at the reminder, but nodded.

He handed her the keys. "See you later."

He made himself walk to meet Freitan and Wong without looking back. Hopefully, Freitan would behave herself. The thought of a whole day trapped with that woman made him clench his jaw.

"Never give up, never surrender," he muttered. His mantra had worked in Special Forces, and it could work to deal with Freitan.

CHAPTER TWENTY-FIVE

SOPHIE ALERTED mountainous Officer Tito on duty at the watch desk that they had tied their dogs out in back, and asked that if any of the officers headed that way could give them a little attention. Tito set his Sudoku tablet aside, winking broadly at Sophie. "I'll pass it on. Now they'll be doing nothing but smoke breaks out back."

"My partner and I appreciate it. The dogs got used to being with us all the time and now we both have to leave them alone. I'll be in the computer lab if anyone needs me." Sophie surrendered her weapon and, carrying her laptop, headed for the back.

As usual, no one was in the lab. The place would be much more useful if the equipment were updated, but Sophie understood the limitations of local budgets. She parked herself at her usual opening between computers, unrolled the Internet cable, plugged it into her laptop, and put on her Bose headphones. Beethoven thundering in her ears, Sophie settled in to some serious data surfing.

The timer she had set on the laptop beeped at eleven a.m., and Sophie startled out of a wired-in trance, checking the wall clock reflexively. It was time to get down to the park and surveille the meeting area her mysterious contact had directed her to.

Only a few people had her latest burner number. Anyone else

who had it either had highly superior tracking abilities (like the Ghost) or had obtained the number from one of the few, which automatically meant this was someone she should speak to.

Was this message from Connor? Did he have information about her mother? Was she ready to see him again?

She *did* want to speak to anyone who had any knowledge of her mother . . . but only Connor, or her father, would be at all likely to have any such knowledge.

No way to find out but to go.

Packing up, Sophie considered why she hadn't told Jake about this meeting.

She didn't talk about her family. In some ways, it was really that simple. Her father was a very private man with a public, high responsibility job as an ambassador. The Smithsons told no one their business, and that went for her mother's well-connected family as well. And later, she'd married a gangster. Secrecy was an ingrained habit, and anything to do with her mother was not for anyone but family to know.

Pim Wat's perfect oval face appeared in Sophie's memory. Her mother's drooping mouth and shadowed eyes were Sophie's most familiar impressions of her. But Sophie hadn't actually seen her in nine years.

Her mother had attended her wedding in Thailand, of course, having helped broker the arrangements that married Sophie to Assan Ang. Sophie hadn't known then that it would be a year later before Assan, pressured by her father, had allowed one visit home to Thailand when Sophie was twenty. In the entire week they'd visited, he had never let Sophie out of his sight to have a private moment with her mother. Her father, divorced for many years from her mother by then, was between postings in the United States.

Sophie still remembered trying to get her mother alone to tell her about Assan's abuse. In spite of her pleading eyes and anxious plucking at her mother's sleeve, Pim Wat had been indifferent, closed in on herself, and had made no effort to respond to Sophie's frantic whispers that they needed to speak alone.

Sophie hadn't seen her mother since. It was strange to realize it had been so long.

Faced with this mysterious message, she realized that part of her was waiting, braced to hear the news that her mother had died.

And maybe she had. Maybe that's what this was about: someone wanted to meet her in person to tell her that Pim Wat had died.

Her body disengaged from her mind, moving on autopilot, Sophie left the station, loaded the dogs in the Jeep, set the GPS for Hilo Bay downtown, and drove through brisk midday traffic to the waterfront park.

The sun was bright on the ruffled waters of the bay. A jetty jutted into the horseshoe of water, and a little old man walked along it, jigging with a bamboo fishing pole. Neatly trimmed palm trees swayed in a light breeze. Mynah birds, their bright yellow beaks contrasting with dark plumage, hopped and foraged on a vast, velvety lawn bisected by concrete walking trails and benches for sitting.

Sophie was already dressed for action in a pair of nylon running pants, athletic shoes, a sports bra and tank top. She drank some water, put the dogs on their leashes, and set off at a brisk jog at eleven fifteen a.m.

She circumnavigated the park, billed hat pulled low and eyes moving, searching for anything out of place or familiar; anything that would give her a clue about what to expect.

Tank was not used to being on a leash, and kept charging off to try to chase mynah birds or a spare frisbee. Controlling the two unruly dogs kept Sophie more than busy, but she hoped that made her look like just another local girl out for a run with her badly behaved pets.

She saw nothing that seemed out of place. Besides the old fisherman on the jetty, young families with children clustered around a central play structure. An old woman sat on one of the benches with a newspaper open in front of her. A lone exerciser did squats and lunges near a pull up bar, and a pair of tourists walked hand-in-hand.

Tank made a particularly egregious bolt for freedom and dragged Sophie, stumbling, off of the concrete walk. Ginger took advantage of the revolt to tangle her leash with Tank's.

"Nine headed hydra from hell!" Sophie exclaimed, wrestling the frolicking dogs. *"Foul-smelling offspring of Bastet!"*

"Your language has certainly gotten more colorful over the years," came a voice from the nearby bench.

The tone was dryly ironic.

The language was perfectly enunciated Thai.

The voice was her mother's.

CHAPTER TWENTY-SIX

THE TROUBLE with going on a police raid was that Jake, as a civilian, had to stay behind.

He sat in the armored, bulletproof SUV parked in the driveway of Chernobiac's house, grinding his teeth, and metaphorically twiddling his thumbs—which meant cleaning his gun.

He had spent the drive to Ocean View Terrace drawing an interior schematic of the floor plan of the house as he had memorized it, notating the whereabouts of Chernobiac's stash behind the laundry hamper in the linen closet. His crude map had been plucked from his fingers as they drove up to the dwelling.

Freitan gave him a predatory smirk, waggling the map. "Sit tight, honeybuns. We'll be back soon enough to have you for lunch."

Did the woman ever say anything that wasn't sexist or condescending? Humiliated and seething, Jake watched as the detectives retrieved the key from the place where he had described it and entered the house. They were back in less than ten minutes, just as he put away his weapon.

Freitan's brow was puckered in an angry frown. Wong shook his head at Jake as they reached the vehicle.

"Cash is gone. No signs of forced entry. I think you were right;

this guy had partners. They must've picked up the money when they chased you guys off."

Freitan threw herself into the front seat. "We still have to go back in for a deeper search, looking for anything pertaining to the missing persons. Maybe we'll get lucky, and Chernobiac kept some kind of record or souvenirs from the victims. You can help, now that we know the place is clear. Wouldn't want to endanger a civilian." She handed Jake a pair of latex gloves. "Glove up." She bounced her brows. "We might need to go in deep."

Jake rolled his eyes. She was ridiculous, and any sort of response just made her worse.

He followed the detectives back into the house, trying to put himself in the mind of that squirrely, pudgy little gamer. *Where did a gamer keep his treasures?*

Where his most prized possession was. So he could keep an eye on it; be close to it.

Jake headed straight upstairs to the computer area in Chernobiac's bedroom. The young man had two computer rigs parked below a simple table used as a desk. Jake moved the chair out and crawled underneath. He took his own rolled-up fabric tool kit out of a cargo pocket. Inside was an all-purpose utility tool, a set of lock picks, and a graduated row of Phillips head screwdrivers. Jake chose one of the smallest of the screwdrivers and went to work on the back of the computers.

The first was filled with nothing but what he expected: the innards of a computer. Wires, a fan, several stacked hard drives wired together.

Jake screwed the back on and went to the next one.

"Nice view." Freitan's voice from behind Jake made him recoil and bang his head on the bottom of the desk. He swore ripely.

"Nice cussing there, Soldier Boy. Good idea, checking in his computers." She squatted next to Jake at the corner of the desk. "We're on the same team, you know."

Jake rubbed the top of his head. "I'm trying to remember that. You're not making it easy."

"I'm just a girl who knows what she wants."

Jake could feel Freitan looking at his body. Down on his hands and knees, trying to unscrew a computer from a weird angle, his ass in the air, Jake felt vulnerable. *Shit.* He was never making an inappropriate crack about a woman's body again; it sucked to be seen as a piece of meat.

Jake focused on the tiny screws. The back came off, and he peered inside. "I think we just hit gold, Detective."

CHAPTER TWENTY-SEVEN

SOPHIE'S BODY FROZE. Her mouth fell ajar and her eyes were wide as she turned to face her mother. Tank and Ginger dragged her toward this new person for enthusiastic greetings, and that gave Sophie a moment to recover her composure.

Pim Wat was hidden under bulky layers: a conical straw sun hat, a long khaki parka, loose, wide-legged pants. Her shoes were orthopedic, and though her face was still beautiful and unlined, a sense of age was conveyed by hunched posture and the way her gloved hands gripped the knob of a bamboo cane.

"Mother. What are you doing here?"

"You are the only one with a right to call me that." Pim Wat gave a brisk nod. Her voice was commanding. "Deal with those unmannerly animals, Malee, and come sit with me."

She must be dreaming this. She'd wake up in the morning and shake her head over the whole ridiculous scenario she'd imagined—but no, it was too complete, right down to the details like the fact that only her mother called Sophie by her Thai middle name.

Sophie tied the dog's leashes around a nearby metal pole. She took out the collapsible watering bowl from her jacket and opened it, pouring water from her canteen into the bowl. She left the dogs lapping thirstily and went to sit beside her mother, near the edge of the bench.

Pim Wat had set aside her cane. She kept her gaze on the newspaper she held. "We cannot appear to be conversing."

"Why not?" The shock of disbelief was giving way to anger as Sophie leaned over the bench, beside her mother, stretching her calves. "What the hell is going on? Aren't you supposed to be in the hospital?" Sophie's Thai was rusty, and emotion made her trip over the words, her tongue tangling on the smooth vowels she hadn't had occasion to speak in so long.

"You must not let your feelings rule you."

"You are one to talk, Mother. Your feelings ruled you all of my life."

"That is what I let you believe."

A deep shiver passed over Sophie. She pressed her hand over her chest, feeling her heart lurch. "I do not know what you mean."

"I'm not who you think I am."

Sophie pressed harder against her heart, because it was galloping now. She couldn't look at the petite figure beside her on the bench. What was her mother trying to tell her? She focused on the only thing that made any sense. "Why now, Mother?"

"Because this is the first time I could find you and get you alone. Everything that I planned with Assan Ang went so badly wrong."

"You planned my suffering?" Sophie wrapped her hands around her waist as she turned on the bench. "You gave me to him. You, Mother."

"I know. I am sorry for how it turned out. But there was nothing to be done. I couldn't get to you, once he had you. Then you fled and joined the FBI, and during that time I was . . . unavailable."

Sophie focused on breathing, willing her logical mind to take over and sort through the confusion of jumbled emotions. "Perhaps it would be best if you just told me what you came to tell me."

"That's my Sophie. You were always such a good girl."

Sophie tightened her arms around herself. Yes. *Good girl.* That's

136

what she had always tried to be for her mother, so she didn't cause more distress, so she didn't send her mother into a downward spiral.

So her mother didn't kill herself because of something Sophie had done.

The dark, unspoken threat of suicide had hung there, a guillotine over Frank and Sophie's heads. She'd been relieved to be sent to boarding school.

Sophie waited. Pim Wat would tell her what she wanted in her own good time. Her mother was not someone who could be rushed.

"I married your father for political reasons. It wasn't my choice."

Sophie wasn't surprised. In the way of children, she had always known her mother didn't love her father. But her father had tried hard to make both the cross-cultural differences and her mother's illness work. "But Dad loved you. He really wanted us to be together."

"Yes. Frank was very idealistic." The word rolled off Pim Wat's tongue like it tasted bad. "I had other priorities, the good of our family chief among them."

Pim Wat referred to Sophie's wealthy, royalty-related Thai relatives. Other than her aunt, Pim Wat's younger sister, Sophie wasn't close to any of the host of powerful uncles and scheming cousins she had left behind in Thailand.

She went on. "I was supposed to stay married to your father. Travel with him. Gather information for our government."

Her mother had been a spy?

Sophie was reeling, but she focused on what she most needed answers for. "But I don't remember that happening. You were always home. Separate from Dad and his job functions, except for those big social events."

"I was not up to the task physically or emotionally. Alas."

"So, your depression was real."

"It was, particularly after you were born. I was not suited to be a mother." The cold precision of Pim Wat's words made Sophie's heart lurch, again. "So we had to adopt a new plan. My brothers sanctioned our divorce. We allowed your father to think you were his, that he controlled what happened to you, by sending you to that boarding school in Geneva to be westernized. But I found a use for you, eventually. We needed an alliance with Hong Kong. Assan Ang was the key to increased commerce between Hong Kong and Thailand." Pim Wat set aside the newspaper. She sighed, fiddling with her cane. Sophie sneaked a glance. Her mother's face was smooth, her skin a glowing honey color. Her hands, holding the cane, were gloved in silk. Those hands had never worked a day of manual labor in their life. "I thought Assan would be good for you. An older man, suave and experienced. He would protect you, and show you the world. Take care of you. I did not know what he was." For the first time, real regret colored her mother's voice.

"Maybe I didn't need or want to be taken care of, Mother. Maybe I wanted to grow into who I was and be loved for who I was." Sophie's voice sounded husky, filled with sorrow. She cleared her throat. "I have fought hard for that."

"You have been in America too long. All of these ideas about self this and self that . . . So much pop psychology. What matters is family. Security. Belonging."

"And you have provided none of those things for me, Mother."

Sophie turned completely away from Pim Wat, and now faced the dogs. A long moment passed. The newspaper rustled behind Sophie as she stared blindly at the animals.

Tank and Ginger lay close, their legs entwined, licking each other's faces.

She flashed to the men in her life, each of them so different, each of them nurturing some part of her. Alika, with his total acceptance and unconditional support, always challenging her to be her best. Jake with his intensity, energy and passion, spurring her into danger and risk, but caring for and protecting her too. *And Connor.* Connor, who was the most like her, as she was coming to know herself: dedicated, perfectionistic, a man whose disciplined body expressed his aesthetic, a brilliant loner who lived by his own rules and had chosen her alone to trust.

Would she ever be able to choose one of them, and settle into a quiet, contented life?

Pim Wat spoke again. "I thought to presume upon the duty of a daughter to her mother. But I see that the years have stolen our connection. So, I speak to you now on behalf of your government. You are needed by your country to help defend against criminals who are attacking us from within the cyber world."

"I do not know what you are even talking about, Mother." Sophie frowned. "Are you offering me a job?"

"I'm asking you to join the Yām Khûmkạn, an ancient organization that protects the royal family of Thailand. We have been in place for millennia, and we need your skills."

CHAPTER TWENTY-EIGHT

JAKE EXTRACTED a small cache of jewelry items with a gloved hand, handing each piece to Freitan. A gold key ring, a man's diamond wedding ring, a platinum ankle bracelet, and a thin gold chain with a small cross completed the trove. He peered into the depths of the computer's innards. "Nothing more."

Freitan turned and hollered for her partner. "Wong! Soldier Boy found some possible evidence."

Wong appeared. The two conferred over the small pile of loot. "Do you think it's enough to hold Chernobiac?" Wong asked.

"No. Unless we can tie these items to a specific victim, we still have nothing. Let's get the two uniforms in here and really tear the place apart," Freitan said.

So that's what the five of them did, for the next hour. Jake lifted every cushion, emptied every cupboard, dumped out every drawer of bathroom supplies. The house was a mess when it was over, and they had not uncovered anything new.

Freitan surveyed the destruction with her hands on her hips. "I hope that girlfriend of yours has come up with a little more information on the missing persons, such as an inventory of their personal items. If not, it's going to be a bitch to comb through all of those files looking for descriptions to match these odds and ends."

"I'm sure Sophie could filter and collect that. Are you going to release Chernobiac?" Jake asked.

Freitan gave a brief nod, her full mouth folded into a grouchy line. "Already did. Called and had him cut loose at the twenty-four-hour point. But we will be bringing him in again, and following up on that black SUV you spotted."

They drove back to the station in glum silence. Jake spent the time typing with his laptop on his knees, tuning up his case notes and composing a detailed email to Kendall Bix, updating his superior on the situation.

Once they reached the station, Jake headed straight back to the computer lab looking for Sophie. She was nowhere to be found. Tito, the watch officer, told him she'd taken the dogs to the park. "She said she'd just be an hour or two."

Stranded without the Jeep, Jake called Sophie's cell, but she didn't pick up. Stymied, he called Bix on Oahu and simultaneously uploaded his email to his boss.

Bix was all business, as usual. "The parents have some kind of lead. They seem to think it's legit. Someone contacted them, saying they spotted Julie with another couple outside of Volcanoes Park."

"Yeah. That's probably the unsavory couple who robbed her and dumped her in the jungle. The police are holding them, but they are sticking to their story that they just rolled Julie for her cash and dropped her off in a remote area. We then found her hiking gear and clothing further off the road. It doesn't look good." Jake told him about the results of the search in the Travelers' Rest squatter camp. "Both of them are under arrest for robbery and in jail until they make bail, but we don't know what else if anything they had to do with her disappearance."

"Seems like there are a lot of fish jumping but nothing biting," Bix said.

"And I wonder if we're even fishing the right stream." Jake

continued the metaphor. "Sophie is pulling together some data about missing persons trends on the island. Seems to be quite a problem over here. Not just our girl, but a number of others have gone missing. As I documented in my report, we came across a young man who seems like he might have been part of a secondary layer of criminal activity related to the disappearances. But he's working with some others we don't have a clue about. Things are not going well at the moment."

"Let me give you this information about the possible lead. You and Sophie can decide what to do," Bix said.

Jake took out a pen and jotted down the name and address of the possible witness the Weathersbys had found. At least it was something more to follow up on. He ended the call and tried Sophie's cell again.

This time she answered, but her voice was remote and chilly. "I'll be there in an hour."

"What am I supposed to do until then?" Jake snapped. "You have my wheels!"

"That won't be a problem soon, as I've secured my own rental vehicle and a place to stay in Hilo."

"What? That's not necessary! We are still on the job together." Jake tried to keep his voice even. *Sophie was ditching him!*

"As you are experiencing right now, it is necessary for us to both be mobile. I anticipate that this investigation will continue to take us in different directions."

"Come back here so we can talk about this, please," Jake said with deliberate calm, though his heart rate had spiked.

"I'll be back when I'm finished with my business. I'm sure Freitan won't mind your company." Sophie ended the call.

Jake cursed.

Sophie was shutting him out and locking the door. He didn't know why, or what to do about it.

CHAPTER TWENTY-NINE

SOPHIE SLID the phone back into her pocket, and looked up into Dr. Wilson's kind, intelligent blue eyes. The psychologist wore a pretty but professional wrap dress and sat in a comfortable wingback armchair in her counseling office in Hilo. Her sandal-shod foot swung back-and-forth in a gentle arc. "That last bit seemed a little unkind to Jake," she said gently.

Sophie's neck heated and she lowered her eyes. "I don't know why I said that. Freitan has been sexually harassing him. It's really unprofessional." She had barely begun to describe the events that had brought her to Hilo when her phone rang with Jake's call. "Kamani Freitan is a detective we are working with on the case. Anyway, I had to take his call or he would probably have sent the police looking for me."

"Seems like you've got a very dedicated partner, but you are going to some effort to push him away."

"A little more than just a partner, as of last night. Jake and I slept together." Sophie rubbed the numb-but-tingly skin graft on her cheekbone. "I've never understood that American phrase. There was very little sleeping involved."

Dr. Wilson laughed. "Well, you've gotten yourself into quite a pickle now, haven't you?"

"Hopefully not a pickle. Pickles are rather sour."

"Just a phrase." Dr. Wilson shook her head, smiling. "Why don't you begin at the beginning and tell me why you needed this emergency session so much. I was surprised to hear from you, but I'm glad I could rearrange a few things and get you in."

Sophie sighed. "I was planning to talk to you in any case. That was part of the reason I came here to the Big Island. I've had a series of very intense experiences and changes in my life in the last year, and after the latest one, I came here to Hawaii hoping for a little vacation; some time to sort things out, figure out what I was doing next, make sure I was . . . mentally and emotionally healthy after the things that had happened. I had planned to call you and begin counseling as part of that. Instead, I seem to have uncovered another terrible crime." She described the discovery of the body dump, and Jake contacting her about the Julie Weathersby case. "And for the rest of it, I really need your assurance that I have complete confidentiality."

"You do. In fact, since we haven't worked together formally before, I'd like you to sign some things to that effect." Dr. Wilson got up and fetched an intake packet from a nearby file cabinet. She put it on a clipboard and handed it to Sophie with a pen. "You fill those out and I'll take the dogs some biscuits."

Sophie had left the dogs in the waiting area. She filled out the paperwork as Dr. Wilson took Ginger and Tank dog treats from a jar on top of her bookshelf. Sophie's mind buzzed as she filled out the papers on autopilot, then paused to really read the confidentiality disclosures.

She was planning to tell Dr. Wilson about the Ghost.

Everything!

She had to have some objective place to unburden herself. Dr. Kinoshita, the psychologist she worked with at Security Solutions, while an excellent therapist, shouldn't be put in an ethical dilemma by finding out that the company's CEO was a multi-identity cyber vigilante.

Dr. Wilson returned and Sophie handed back the papers.

"Thank you. Now you are officially my client, I am bound by confidentiality except as it pertains to any plans you have to hurt yourself or another."

Sophie shook her head. "No current plans. Though if you'd talked to me a month ago, the situation might have been different."

"Perhaps we should begin there, then."

It took a half hour for Sophie to bring Dr. Wilson up to current events. "As if all of that weren't enough, yesterday I was contacted via text message to meet someone at the park who had information about my mother. I sent Jake to work with the detectives, and I went to the park." She blew out a breath. "The person who found me there was my mother, herself."

Dr. Wilson blinked. "Forgive me. I thought, from your history and things Lei has said, your mother was disabled with depression. Hospitalized, in fact."

"Yes. That has been the fiction that she had created. I have no idea what her real life is like, or where she even lives." Sophie's gaze darted around the spare, comfortable room with its leather couch and armchair, desk, bookshelf, sand garden on the coffee table, and a few paintings. "My mother, by her admission today, does suffer from depression. But not nearly to the degree I've been led to believe. She is actually in espionage, and a member of an elite group of . . . royal guardians, I guess you could call it. The Yām Khûmkạn."

Dr. Wilson sat back in surprise and made a note on her tablet. "No wonder you asked for an emergency session. When was the last time you saw her?"

"Nine years ago." Sophie swallowed—her throat was so dry. "Do you have anything to drink?"

Dr. Wilson got up and went behind her desk to a small fridge. She fetched a bottle of water and gave it to Sophie. "What did she want? There must have been a reason she reached out to you."

"Yes. She wants me to join the organization she works for." Sophie unscrewed the bottle's lid and drank thirstily. When she put the water down, Dr. Wilson was still gazing at her steadily. "I told her I needed time to think about it."

"I would say. Tell me about the encounter."

"She was . . . smaller than I remembered. But she had not aged since I saw her last. She was disguised as an old woman, and had the proper body language and clothing for that, but her face…" Pim Wat was exceptionally beautiful, with wide-set, large brown eyes, high cheekbones, and a full mouth—many of the same features Sophie looked at every morning in her mirror. "She was very cold in her demeanor. Unrepentant about her deception. The only time she showed any regret at all for her treatment of me was when she told me she had traded me in marriage to Assan. For things he could do for the Thai government and our family." Sophie covered her trembling mouth with her hand and firmed her voice. "Pim Wat said she had not known what he was. She couldn't help me once he took me to Hong Kong. He had too much of the power the Yām Khûmkạn needed."

"I wonder that she had the nerve to even approach you." Dr. Wilson's voice vibrated with outrage. "Let alone ask you for any favors."

"She acknowledged that. And appealed to my patriotism. Said that our family and our country was under attack from cyber terrorists, and that my skills were needed. Implied I would be petty to allow our 'personal differences' to keep me from doing the right thing." Sophie tried to still the trembling of her body, but tension shimmered through her like electricity. "I told her I would not give her an answer right away, but that I would look into it. And she got up and left."

"That's all? No attempt to reconcile? To apologize for her neglect and . . . for using you as a bargaining chip to a monster?" Dr. Wilson's eyes were wide with shock and rage on Sophie's behalf.

"She implied regret, and said that everything she did was for a higher purpose. Her attitude reminded me of Connor, but Connor has been more emotional about it. And still he used me, lied to me, and chose his mission over me." Sophie felt the betrayals of those closest to her sucking at her emotionally, dragging her toward that familiar dark pit.

"Connor? Who is that? Tell me about him."

Sophie glanced at the wall clock. "I don't know if I can, today. I have to go pick up Jake and get my rental car before the business closes. Can we meet tomorrow? I must make a decision. This is . . ." she pressed her hands against her belly. "This is eating at me, as Americans say. My depression has been better with medication and all the activity I've been doing, but this is a . . . setback. I just want to get to my hotel room and lie down." She longed for quiet and darkness in which to nurse her pain.

"Of course, it's a setback, a blow. You must always have hoped for something more with your mother. I'm sorry. Some people are simply not capable of it." Dr. Wilson stood up. "I am livid on your behalf. Come here. You need a therapeutic hug."

"If I must." Sophie stood and walked around the coffee table to embrace the petite psychologist. She felt stiff and wooden. She was a robot body with a heart somewhere deep inside, still beating for some unknown reason. But as Dr. Wilson held her, the warmth of the psychologist's firm, gentle touch seemed to penetrate, melting the disconnect surrounding her.

Sophie sagged, and an inadvertent sob erupted from somewhere deep inside.

"It's okay. You must grieve for these things," Dr. Wilson whispered. "Let out the pain so it doesn't cripple you."

"If I start to cry, I'll never stop." Sophie wrenched herself upright and stepped back. "Let's meet tomorrow, please. I will work around your schedule."

CHAPTER THIRTY

JAKE WAS WAITING outside the Hilo Police Department for Sophie when she finally drove up in the Jeep. He'd thought long and hard about what to say, and decided to play it cool. Pretend he wasn't pissed off and freaked out and worried as hell she was going to take off and disappear, like she'd done so many times before. Being clingy, needy, or jealous was lame and never worked with women. Jake had *options*. He had to remember that and act like it. Play a little hard to get.

All of Jake's mental scheming evaporated the minute he got done greeting the dogs, turned around in his seat, and got a good look at Sophie's face.

Her vibrant golden skin tone was ashen; her big brown eyes shadowed and dark, her mouth pinched. That mask she hid behind was in place, but it couldn't hide the pain radiating off her in waves.

"What happened?" He reached for Sophie's hand and peeled it off the steering wheel. Her fingers were icy, and he pressed her hand against his chest to warm it, sandwiching it beneath his. "Something happened. Tell me."

Sophie shook her head. "We need to get to the rental place before five." She yanked her hand away and gripped the steering wheel, eyes forward. "I am getting my own car and I have a reservation for a room downtown. I will take Tank to my place if you don't want to deal with him."

Jake recoiled, absorbing the rejection. *She was hurting.* He had to make it stop. "I won't leave you like this."

"I don't need or want your help."

Ow. That hurt. He forced his mouth to close on arguments, his arms to stay down, not grabbing her and dragging her against him and causing an accident. *He was a cave man, but at least he knew it.*

Jake sucked a few breaths and then turned to the dogs in the back seat. "Hear that, guys? She's taking off and trying to take you with her. Well, I'm not going to let her do it, ya hear? We're sticking together. We've got work to do."

Ginger woofed and Tank pricked his ears.

Calmer, Jake turned to face forward. "Something happened. I respect that you want some space, but I have no intention of letting you blow me off. So, I'll just follow you to wherever you're staying and get a room there too."

A long beat passed by. Sophie gave a tiny nod. "Tank would like to stay with Ginger and we are still working together, so that would be acceptable."

He felt like he'd won a major battle, but schooled himself not to show it.

At the car rental place, she went into the office and got keys. She came back to the Jeep with them in her hand. "I'll take Ginger and my backpack and go now." She was still trying to leave him.

"Not necessary. Just tell me where your room is and I'll bring the dogs and your things." Keep the high ground and make no concessions—he'd learned that in Special Forces.

They locked eyes. His chest hurt at how dead her gaze was. *Sophie was deep in her depression, barely functioning, trying to get to somewhere to hole up.* "It's the Banyan Tree Motel downtown," she finally said.

"I'll be right behind you."

Sophie walked off and located a small blue Ford Focus. She unlocked it and got in. He followed her in the Jeep through the busy streets of Hilo to a side road near the harbor. The motel was three stories of cinderblock painted the green of a hospital hallway, deep in the shade of a massive banyan. They parked and went into the small office without speaking.

"Checking in," Sophie said, and presented a credit card.

Jake pushed her hand aside and handed the clerk the Security Solutions business credit card.

"Both rooms on this card, please. Adjacent if you have it," Jake said. "Is this place dog-friendly?" He held up a hundred-dollar bill.

"It is now." The clerk grinned. He assigned Jake the room next to Sophie's, ran the card and pocketed the cash.

By the time Jake got his stuff moved in and the dogs installed in his room, Sophie had drawn the drapes on her side. He didn't see any light around the door, and it was locked.

She didn't answer when he knocked.

She hadn't even taken her backpack inside the room.

This was bad.

JAKE CALLED for a pizza delivery and took the dogs out for a run before bed. Back at the motel, he couldn't shake his worry when she didn't answer the door for the pizza, either.

Only one person he knew had successfully dealt with Sophie when she was like this: *Marcella.*

"Hey Jake. What's up?" The beautiful Italian FBI agent always sounded so cheerful. *Why couldn't he have fallen for a woman like her?* Marcella was awesome, and what you saw was what you got. But Sophie? There was no end to the depths and layers of Sophie.

"I need your help. Sophie and I are on the Big Island on a job, and something happened to her today. She won't talk to me. Tried to ditch me. She's holed up in a motel room with the drapes pulled, and won't answer the door. She's not eating. I'm looking for advice." He rubbed his face in frustration.

"Oh, damn. Sounds like she is in one of her depression cycles. Usually there's a trigger of some kind. Did anything unusual happen?"

"Yeah. We slept together last night, for one thing." Jake stumbled to a halt, flushing hot and cold with embarrassment.

"Oh-ho. I kinda saw that coming."

"It was really good. I mean, it was mutual, you know? Sophie was into it. But this morning, she began pulling away. I was expecting that, it's her style, so I wasn't happy but I wasn't really surprised either."

"Did you guys have a fight or something, afterward?"

"No. She was withdrawn but I didn't push; I expected she needed space and the case we're on took us in different directions during the day. I went on a house search and Sophie worked at the police station and then went to the park with the dogs. When she came to pick me up . . . I could tell something serious had happened. Maybe someone called her, did something to her. I don't know, but she's in a bad place."

"Let me try to phone her. I doubt she'll pick up; she usually turns everything off, closes the curtains, and goes to bed during one of these episodes. Last time she had a really bad one was when her boyfriend was killed."

"I remember that, of course. Call me back, ok?"

"Will do." Marcella ended the call.

Jake hated being so helpless, so useless.

He dropped to the ground and did one-armed pushups. Right side, left side, then a couple of hundred crunches. Not tired yet, he did lunges and burpees. Someone banged on the ceiling from below, so he lay down and did bicycle sit-ups until the phone rang.

His phone buzzed. "Tell me something, Marcella."

"The person she met in the park was her mother."

"Oh shit." Jake sat up on the bed and tried to calm his ragged breathing. "They are estranged, right?"

"Yeah. Sophie hasn't seen her mother in nine years. Supposedly, Pim Wat Smithson was catatonic in an institution. Turns out she's not as depressed as she pretended to be. Everything Sophie thought she knew about her mom is a lie."

"What did her mother want?"

"Some sort of reconciliation, I guess. Sophie wouldn't say. But it has thrown her for a loop."

Jake ran a hand through his hair, grabbing it in his fingers and giving a rough tug. "I can deal with it as long as it's not my fault."

"Well, Jake, depression is a chronic illness. It's no one's fault." Marcella sounded completely matter-of-fact, and he was relieved at the implicit acceptance there. "When she's been in her hole too long, and I think anything more than a day is too long, I break in, open the drapes and turn on the lights, make her get in the shower, feed her, and give her something to do. Once she's moving, she seems to get better. But she won't like it. Don't expect hugs and kisses or gratitude."

"Duly noted. Thanks, Marcella. I'm glad she told you what the problem was. I hope she trusts me enough someday to tell me what's really going on with her."

"Sophie is a complicated woman. She's got more baggage than a freight train. If it's not too late, you should run." Marcella softened her words with a laugh.

"Not gonna run. And it's already too late." Jake laughed too. "So now you know how I feel about her. Thanks again."

He ended the call and stared at the closed door between the rooms.

He'd give Sophie until tomorrow morning to come out; and then he was going in.

$$\text{⁂}$$

Jake woke at six a.m. and took the dogs for a run around the spectacular horseshoe of Hilo Bay. The palm trees stood still in the morning calm. Mynahs hopped and chattered on the smooth, mowed expanse of the park. Gentle waves lapped at the jetty. Jake tried to find peace in the beauty, but he was too disturbed. What was Sophie's mother doing in the United States?

Jake had a lead for them to pursue, a good reason to roust Sophie out of bed. He planned his strategy as he took a shower and shaved in the little bathroom in the seedy motel.

He knocked on the connecting door when he was dressed and ready, but there was no reply. He took out his toolkit, extracted his lock picks, and two minutes later, stepped into her room.

The darkness was complete—only a line of light showed beneath the pulled blackout drapes. He spotted the mound of her, pressed up against the wall, as he shut the door.

The plan he'd had, to rip open the curtains, tear off the covers, and roll her out of bed—suddenly seemed way too cruel.

He walked over, stumbling a little in the dark, and leaned over to whisper in her ear. "Sophie."

Sophie didn't move. Her sweet, unique scent enfolded him.

He touched her bare shoulder. The rest of her naked body was buried in the cheap hotel comforter. Her skin was as cold as it had been yesterday.

Operating on instinct, Jake lifted the covers and slid in behind her, wrapping his arms around her, pulling her close, tucking her head under his chin. She was as passive and unresponsive as a doll.

Jake shut his eyes, willing the energy and vigor that filled him to flow into her. Maybe it would just seep out of him somehow. In any case, he was warm and she was cold; whatever he could give her, he would.

CHAPTER THIRTY-ONE

Sophie felt Jake get in beside her, surrounding her, his warmth beckoning her back from that dark place deep inside herself, that familiar gray desert where nothing mattered.

Jake had always been intrusive. He was so irritating that way, big and loud and *pushy*. He would not leave her alone. He was trying to break into the protected fortress of her heart. *He was dangerous.*

But he was so warm. One of his big hands stroked her head. "Your hair feels so soft. Better than petting the dogs," he whispered in her ear. *Such a way with words.* Sophie would have smiled if she could have come back enough to do that.

Jake settled her closer, shifting her into his chest, her head pillowed on one of his biceps. He gave a deep sigh as if giving up all his tension. She felt him relax, the thick hard muscles that created so much heat around her going soft and vulnerable. A few moments later, she felt his slow, even breathing as he slept, the metronome of his heart beating against her back. And soon she slept too.

SOPHIE WAS OVERHEATED, and there was a weighted blanket holding her down. She struggled to lift it, and woke suddenly.

The hot weighted blanket was Jake. His arm was draped over her, so heavy that it smothered. She could feel him behind her and around her. Deep rumbling snores lifted the hairs beside her ear, making her smile.

He had vanquished the darkness.

Yes, she could still feel the depression around her, flapping its ugly wings, trying to drag her back down—but the sickness was pushed back, manageable. She could breathe, she could move, she could think.

A change in Jake's breathing signaled he was awake too. One arm was underneath her so her head was resting on it, and the other, draped over her waist. His hand began to move, sliding lightly up and down her side.

Sophie shut her eyes and let herself enjoy the tingling sensation, the awakening of her nerves. After being in her robot body, it felt like circulation returning to a limb that had fallen asleep. His hand slid from her waist to her hip, down her leg, back up again to her shoulder, cupping the round of her deltoid. Nothing inappropriate, unless breaking into her room and climbing in bed with her naked and him fully dressed, holding her and taking a nap with her was inappropriate. And somehow, he'd pulled her back into her body by doing so.

First aid by hugging. That's what he'd done.

She wanted to feel alive, healthy, cherished; and Jake made her feel all those things.

Sophie turned in his arms and breathed in the lemony fresh scent at the apex of his collarbones. She kissed the smooth, tender spot under his freshly shaved chin, the granite knob of his jawbone. She reached up with a hand and tilted his face down so that their mouths could meet.

They spoke, for a long slow time, without words, though getting his clothing off was a bit of a bother.

Afterward, Sophie waited for Jake to make a joke. To tease her, even to nag her to get out of bed, take a shower, eat something—after all, it must be at least ten a.m. on a workday. But he said nothing, just lying beside her, stroking whatever skin he could reach, which was most of it.

His silver-blue eyes in the dim light were the exact color of the mourning doves that were so common in Hawaii. She couldn't look at them for long, and finally got up to shower. Jake went to his room to do the same.

She dressed and opened the curtains. Both dogs were on the other side of the connecting door, scratching to join her, and Jake opened the door. Ginger launched herself onto the bed and licked Sophie's face. "Bad dog! Get down!" Sophie scolded. Ginger hopped down and began wrestling with Tank. The two crashed into the TV stand, making the appliance rock perilously.

"You'd think they hadn't been out, but I've taken them for a run already," Jake said. "I have a new lead for us to follow up on today. I wonder if you're up for a drive. This contact is somewhere in Hilo, a witness that emailed the parents that she saw Julie after she disappeared from Volcanoes Park."

Sophie needed to get to the secure online police station internet to use DAVID to search for her mother and information about the secret Yām Khûmkạn organization; but it would be a good idea to get out and shake off the cobwebs of her depressive episode before she went back into that triggering swamp.

"I need some food first." Sophie's stomach growled loudly.

Jake smiled. "I tried to get you to eat pizza yesterday but you wouldn't answer the door. The dogs got the rest of it when I was out of the room. I'll take you to breakfast."

CHAPTER THIRTY-TWO

JAKE PULLED the Jeep out of the breakfast restaurant's parking lot and out onto the busy thoroughfare leading through Hilo. Sophie had eaten a good breakfast. Her color and energy were better.

Jake felt victorious. His chest gave an almost painful twinge every time he thought of why they were late getting on the road. Happiness this extreme was hard to take.

He had made her feel better. He had brought her out of that coldness. She had turned to him, initiated making love. He couldn't think about it much or his skin would burst with exhilaration.

Was this what being in love was like? He'd thought he'd experienced love before, but he'd never felt anything like this.

Jake stole a glance at Sophie, and she met his eyes. A little smile played around her mouth. "What?"

Anything he said would only reveal what a sap he was, and it might even scare her off. "Nothing."

"What is going on between you and Antigua?"

Jake frowned. "I told you. We broke it off."

"Why?"

"She wanted more. I didn't. The usual."

"The usual. Aha." Sophie rubbed her cheekbone where the scar was. "Then you're okay with our arrangement being more of that 'usual'?"

Just like that, she crushed him.

Jake opened and closed his hands on the steering wheel and lightened his voice with an effort. "Sure. Partners with benefits. Thought we were clear on that already."

"Good. Just making sure there are no misunderstandings." Sophie's hand dropped to his thigh. She massaged the thick muscle there. "Because I have every intention of making use of those benefits. Often, in fact."

His body was not averse to this idea even if his emotions were out of control. Jake forced a laugh, removed her hand. "You're distracting me. I don't even know where we're going. I have to pull over and program the GPS."

Jake navigated to the side of the road and fumbled with his phone.

There was a buzzing in his ears. The exhilaration of a moment ago felt like a heart attack as pain shortened his breath and stabbed his chest. Was this how Antigua had felt when she broke up with him? If so, *holy shit, ow!*

Tank thrust his head forward from the back seat and nudged Jake's elbow, as if sensing his distress.

Regroup, retrench, re-strategize. Never give up. You can win her, Jake, but not head on. You have to accept where she put you; she doesn't feel safe having feelings for anyone right now. You understand that. It has to be okay. You're strong enough to do this. Don't lose sight of the goal.

Sophie was his mission. He knew how to do missions.

"Tell me about this witness." Her voice was cool and businesslike, and that helped.

Jake cleared his throat. "Don't know much. Bix gave me the name, address, and phone of a female contact, Shirley Mandig, who claims to have seen our victim after she disappeared from the park."

"So you told Bix that this was likely before they abandoned Julie in the forest area?"

"I did. Bix seems to think it was after, by the timing the witness described—it was dark, the night of the day they took her. The witness was unclear on when that was, exactly."

"I wonder how she recognized Julie Weathersby."

"Bix confirmed that the Weathersbys have hired a firm that specializes in PR campaigns for missing people. They've plastered the area with posters of Julie. They've got a lot of social media going." Jake shook his head. "What a thing to find a market niche for."

Sophie shrugged. "As long as it helps. All of these kinds of things take time, resources, and manpower. I'm glad they don't expect us to do all that, too."

They wended through downtown Hilo towards the suburbs at the back. The houses became small ranch style dwellings, many of them with fenced yards and opulent displays of orchids, ferns, and other tropical growth. The warm humidity of Hilo lent itself to supersized plants and shades of green everywhere.

Shirley Mandig's home was typical of the area. Set off of a small, residential side road, the dwelling was a plantation style cube with a lanai in the front, thick with potted orchids. They parked in the drive-way, settled the dogs with cracked windows and water, and walked up three wooden stairs to the front porch. A small yappy dog announced their arrival from inside the house.

Jake knocked, and both he and Sophie held up their Security Solutions IDs for the woman to see when she arrived to look at them through a screen door. "We're here to talk to you about your sighting of Julie Weathersby."

The middle-aged Filipina woman wore a purple velour sweat suit, a ton of gold jewelry, and house slippers. Her quizzical look cleared up, and she opened the door. "Please, come in."

The dog, a fuzzy, indeterminate breed, sniffed around their legs as Jake followed the woman's square-hipped figure into the house.

She gestured to a dining room table, and they took vinyl-covered chairs and sat. A sharp tang of vinegar flavored the air. Sophie pointed to a cutting board, covered with green mangoes in various stages of disembowelment. "Are you making pickled mango?"

Mandig nodded. "I am. Every year the tree in back drops more mango than I can give away, so I harvest early. I always leave some of them to mature, but pickled mango makes a good Christmas gift. Let me get you some tea."

The two women chatted about the making of strange foods as Jake assessed the modest kitchen, not upgraded since it was built in the 1970s, if the avocado-colored appliances and fake brick linoleum were anything to go by. Mandig brought Jake a cup of hot tea. He smiled and sipped it, to be polite.

Surprisingly fragrant and sweet, the tea was delicious. Jake slurped and finished it, and finally, during a lull in the conversation, he addressed Mandig where she stood at the cutting board, peeling green mangoes.

"Tell us about seeing Julie Weathersby."

"Oh, so unexpected. I never know what to think." The woman's voice had a lilt of pidgin. "I work at Volcanoes Park gift shop. I was heading home from work, and I saw this woman staggering down the road. She waving her arms. She was wearing only bra and panty. I thought she was drunk. I admit, I was small-kine judgmental." The knife she was using to cut the mangoes whacked into the cutting board. "I wish I had stopped, tried to help her. Seeing her like that, I just thought she . . . I don't know what I thought."

"Was there anyone chasing her, or with her?" Sophie asked sharply.

"No. She was alone. She maybe was trying to get help. I don't know." Mandig's voice had gone low.

"We know Julie was robbed and abandoned on the side of a road. We found her possessions and clothes and they are at the Hilo Police Station. This is the first confirmation we've had that she's alive," Jake said, keeping his tone warm and complimentary. "Very important news. Thank you for coming forward. Can you identify the area where you saw her?"

"I did notice it because it was so funny-kine to see someone out in that area, no clothes, li'dat. She was walking toward Hilo on the side of the road. I remember thinking that if I had to call anyone for her I should know where she was. So I noticed the mile marker, but I never had no bars, so I never called the cops." She named the same road the Weathersby girl had been abandoned on.

Jake and Sophie exchanged a quick look and Jake took down the mile marker number and the street name. He thanked Mandig, and they stood up and headed for the door. Mandig held up a jar of mango. "You like?"

"Thanks." Jake took the jar. "You've been very helpful."

Sophie was right behind him. She touched Mandig's arm. "I hope you will stop and do the right thing in the future if you see an almost naked woman waving for help. She was probably trying to escape her attackers and running for her life."

Mandig ducked her head and crossed herself in a very Catholic gesture. "I pray that girl is safe and that God forgives me for driving past her."

"Well, at least you called to report it. That's something." Sophie pushed out ahead of Jake, and let the screen door bang behind her. The woman's soft face crumpled and her chin wobbled.

That was his girl Sophie. Never one to varnish the truth or coddle anyone's feelings. Jake smiled at Mandig. "Thanks for the mango. I'm sure it's delicious." He restrained himself from saying anything further. Nothing would help. "And thank you for contacting us." He turned and followed Sophie out to the Jeep.

CHAPTER THIRTY-THREE

SOPHIE'S PHONE alerted her to an incoming text as she reached the vehicle parked in Mandig's driveway. She took the phone out of her pocket and checked it as she waited for Jake to unlock the Jeep.

The text was blunt and to the point. *"This is Connor. I am hard at work on the Witness Protection leak. I expect to know more by next week. If you want to call me for information to share with the detectives, you can reach me at this number."*

Sophie's stomach dropped.

The last thing she wanted to do was speak with Connor—but she *did* want to know who had killed that family. And it would be great to have something to share with Freitan that would lend her and Jake credibility.

But was it worth it to have to talk to him?

"No way." Marcella's voice said in her mind. "Don't talk to him. Don't give him a way in."

Sophie quickly texted back. *"I want the information. Send a file to me through DAVID so I can inform the detectives of anything that will be useful. I know everyone on the investigation will appreciate it."*

She wasn't going to say she would appreciate it. She wasn't going to say anything personal.

But a little part of her was glad that something would be done about that breach in security that was leading to so much loss of life and legal implications.

Jake arrived and unlocked the Jeep. "You didn't have to be so hard on that woman. She was probably afraid to pick up someone acting crazy on the side of the road when she was all by herself in her car. Lotta meth heads around here."

"I have a bad feeling about what happened to Julie Weathersby after Mandig saw her. Why is Julie still gone? Why hasn't there been a ransom demand if someone has her? I think she's dead." Sophie got into the Jeep. Doggy smells surrounded her. Wagging tails thrashed the inside of the car.

"I've had a bad feeling ever since we found her backpack and boots. I thought we'd find her body after that."

"We still might. And now we know where to look." Sophie folded her hands on her lap. The last of the good feelings left over from being with Jake that morning had evaporated.

They drove in tense silence to the turn off they had last made in a pouring rainstorm. The area looked much prettier in sunshine; spears of light penetrated the jungle canopy overhead and trailing vines made decorative curtains from the trees. Sophie noticed ripe passion-fruit growing wild, the yellow spheres as random and eye-catching as Christmas tree balls against the shades of green.

"There's the mile marker." He pulled the Jeep over onto the shoulder near the mile marker Mandig had named, being careful not to get too close to the drainage ditch beside the road. "She said it was on the right."

"Let's let the dogs out," Sophie said. They were at least a mile from where they had found Julie's backpack. *This would have been rough terrain for Julie to traverse, barefoot and at night.*

The stream gurgled beside the road, and the streetlights along the way were far apart. Sophie could imagine the young woman's terrified flight after fighting off attackers, getting to the road, and trying to attract the attention of a passing car. "If I were her, I would want to stay off the main road in case my pursuers came after me. I would work my way along the edge of the road, hidden, and come out to try to flag down cars but stay hidden unless I was sure they were not the perps." Ginger, on her leash, nosed in the long, tangled grass beside the road. She tugged toward the ditch hidden by the grass.

"Sounds reasonable." Jake let Tank out, but kept him on his leash. The two of them walked slowly along the road, stopping to look around the area periodically.

Ginger gave a sudden, sharp bark, and yanked hard on Sophie's arm, displaying the same intensity she had when she had discovered the body dump. Sophie's stomach knotted around her breakfast as the dog dragged her down the road, several hundred yards from the mile marker. Ginger jumped off the pavement toward the overgrown ditch and thrust her face down into the trench, digging at the shielding growth with her paws.

The smell of decomp hit Sophie's nose, and she recoiled, covering her mouth and nose with a hand.

She didn't want to look.

She didn't want this to be the outcome of their search for a vibrant young woman.

Jake arrived. He pushed her back. "Let me see."

Sophie let him, giving in to cowardice. She hauled Ginger back and sat on the nearby pavement.

Jake parted the heavy plant growth, looked down into the ditch, and turned back. His eyes were the dark gray of storm clouds, and his mouth was tight. "It's her."

Ginger leaned against Sophie, panting, her jaws open in a happy grin, her tongue lolling. *The dog had found what Sophie was looking for, and expected praise.* Sophie stroked Ginger's chest, her shoulder, her silky ears. "Good girl." She couldn't say that phrase without hearing it in her mother's voice. *"Good girl."*

Jake took his phone out, checking for signal, and called the detectives. Sophie could hear his voice but the words were jumbled, a distant thunder, meaningless.

She took a few more deep breaths of fresh air, braced herself mentally, and moved forward to look.

The body lay face down, an inch or two of water running over it. Good-sized rocks had been used to hold the corpse down beneath the flow. The nude, bloated body was dressed in a black bra and panties. Long brown hair streamed like water weeds. The water somewhat quenched the smell, but not entirely.

Guessing by the bloated level of decomposition, Julie had been dead a week or so. That fit with the timeline they'd established. *"May her killer be broken on the wheel of karma, frying in hell for eternity,"* she cursed softly.

Ginger, nosing around beside Sophie, lifted her head to sniff the air. She gave a loud bark and charged off again, yanking her leash so hard it tore the skin of Sophie's palm. The dog galloped down the road, the leash bouncing off the pavement. Tank, excited by this new game, broke loose from Jake and ran after her.

Sophie stood up. "Ginger!"

Jake shook his head. "That dog is ridiculous."

"Not if she is finding another body," Sophie said. "She seems to have a nose for cadavers."

Jake shot her a quick glance, and then squeezed her shoulder. "This happened long before we got here. We're helping by finding them."

"Too little, too late. A good American saying," Sophie muttered.

"Go. Fetch those dogs. I will stay with the body until the detectives get here," Jake said. "Call me if you find anything."

Sophie nodded, and jogged down the road.

When she caught up with her dog, half a mile or so away, Ginger was down in the ditch, splashing, barking and digging at the grate of a culvert passing beneath the road as Tank looked on.

Sophie caught her collar, and Tank's, and pulled both dogs back and away from the ditch. She tied the animals to a nearby tree.

She needed to see what was down there. There was a good chance something had washed down the ditch and come to rest against that grate, and the flowing water and overgrown bushes hid what it might be. She took off her shoes and socks, rolled up her yoga pants, and pushed down through the bushes toward the grate shielding the culvert.

The pile of submerged human bones pressed against the metal by a flow of water was anticlimactic after the intense emotion of finding Julie's body.

Sophie got out her phone to try to call Jake or the detectives, but couldn't get a signal.

She climbed back out of the ditch, smoothing her muddy clothing and rinsing her scratched hands, and sat down with the dogs.

Was the stream a dump site? It certainly seemed possible. Maybe they were about to solve some of the disappearances. But who was behind them? One serial killer, or some kind of crime ring?

Julie had been dumped off by the couple who robbed her. Then she'd been attacked and stripped of her clothing. She had escaped, and been captured again. Was it the same couple doing all of it, or multiple perpetrators?

No one had benefited from Julie's death that Sophie could tell, at first glance at least. Her parents hadn't paid a ransom; they'd never been contacted. Chernobiac had been fishing to extort but hadn't implemented his scheme yet; and who were the people driving the black SUV that took Chernobiac's cash?

The unmarked SUV that Freitan and Wong drove sped by, a light flashing on the dash. Sophie continued to wait as the medical examiner's van and a squad car soon followed.

Finally, Jake jogged down the road toward her. Sophie rose and walked toward him, and he saw the answer on her face. He lifted a walkie-talkie they must've given him and said, "Sophie found something more."

CHAPTER THIRTY-FOUR

JAKE TOOK his sweatshirt out of the Jeep and wrapped it around Sophie's shoulders. She was hunched in on herself, clearly taking the girl's death hard.

Jake felt it too, a numbness in the extremities, a lead ball in his belly. They watched from a distance as Freitan and Wong directed the uniforms to secure the area and the ME, clad in rubber boots and a coverall, got down into the stream with the body.

More vehicles arrived. Several police officers, dressed in waders, started down the narrow stream with poles in hand to probe for more remains.

"This could be major," Jake said.

"Yes. There might be more bodies here." Sophie's phone dinged and she glanced at it. "Can you give me a ride back to town? I'm supposed to meet Dr. Wilson for a counseling appointment I set up yesterday." She sighed. "I should have taken my own car."

"It's no problem." Jake really didn't want her going off on her own without him. "Well, you'll have even more to talk to her about today."

"Yes, unfortunately. I had planned to . . . do more research before I met with her. But I haven't had time."

"It's been nonstop, yeah. Hop in the Jeep. I'll tell Freitan where she can reach us if she needs anything more."

Sophie nodded and headed toward the Jeep with the dogs.

Freitan was conferring with the ME on the muddy creek bank as Jake walked over to the detective. "Hey. We have to go back to town for an appointment. Anything else we can do to assist?"

"Nah. You two have done quite enough. Or I should say, that Lab has," Freitan said. "She could be a cadaver dog! Was she trained or something?"

"Not that anyone can tell," Jake said. "She's a rescue dog, and generally badly behaved." He pointed to the waterlogged corpse as it was being lifted into a body bag. "That was our client. How would you like us to inform the parents?"

"It's a murder investigation, now. We will do the informing. Preferably in person. What you can do is get the parents over to the Big Island. Tell them there have been some developments and the police need to talk to them personally, ASAP. We'll take it from there." Freitan was abrupt but no longer condescending as she met Jake's gaze squarely. For once, she wasn't eying him like a steak at a barbeque.

"Really appreciate your breaking this open." Wong said. "Can we get the contact info for the witness that tipped you to this location?"

Jake scrolled through his phone to Mandig's contact information and sent it via text over to Wong. "We'd like to keep helping however we can. And please let us know of any new developments —like if you find any more remains in this stream. Sophie's really into solving some more of the missing persons cases."

"We'll let you know," Freitan said. "Stay close."

Jake headed back to the Jeep.

Sophie was already seated inside, texting, but she put her phone away with a furtive gesture as soon as he arrived.

Not good. He'd lay money that she was in touch with Alika right now. His mood darkened.

"Just partners with benefits," he muttered as he got in and slammed the door. "Not a bit fucking jealous."

"What did you say?" Sophie's eyes had dark circles under them and her honey-brown skin had that gray cast it got when she was stressed. He checked the digital clock on the dash—it was two p.m. *Time had flown when they weren't having fun.*

"You need something to eat before I take you to Dr. Wilson," Jake said. He turned on the Jeep and the engine roared in a satisfying way. "You look peaked."

"You are not my parent to worry about my eating habits. And what is peaked?"

"No, definitely not your parent. Peaked is . . ." His mother had used that term when he was little. "A Midwestern thing. Means you seem weak. Sickly, I guess." Jake pulled the vehicle off the shoulder, frustrated. "My mama thought food was the answer to every illness, and I like to see you eat. So, sue me."

"I see no purpose in suing you for such a silly thing." Sophie petted his leg like he was one of the dogs. "Your mama was likely a wise woman to raise such a competent son."

"Is that a compliment?" Stupid as it was, her petting and praise perked him up. "I live for the crumbs of your positive regard."

"Such big words!" Sophie batted her eyes. "You astound me, Jake."

"I may be a Neanderthal, but I did go to college. Majored in political science. I even read several Cliff's notes of the classics."

"I like big words, Jake." Sophie petted his leg a little too close to the groin this time, and he almost swerved off the road.

"Watch those hands or you'll have to pay the price," he warned. She laughed, and it was good to see a little color come back into her face.

"I *am* hungry. Perhaps we could buy one of those nutritionally unsound *musubi* things on the way to Dr. Wilson's office," she murmured. "I do wish we could have a more active role in the investigation. I am annoyed by this private role. But I could not stay in the

FBI when they were trying to take ownership of DAVID. And I got frustrated there too, with the kinds of cases I had to keep working."

"Tell me more about that." *Keep her mind off the bodies, keep her talking.* "What's going on with your patent application?"

"It's moving ahead. The FBI has relinquished its bid for ownership with the advocacy of my very competent lawyer. But it's a slow process. And the issues of consent and confidentiality . . . I don't know if they will ever be resolved."

Jake patted her leg this time. "I have faith in you, my intellectual logophile."

Her smile was his reward. He was definitely going to be throwing around more big words.

CHAPTER THIRTY-FIVE

Sophie was somewhat restored by an energy drink and convenience store *musubi* by the time Jake dropped her off for her appointment at Dr. Wilson's office on a side street near Hilo Bay.

Sophie waited in the tiny anteroom with its rattan loveseat, potted fern, and walls painted a soothing blue. She picked up her phone and continued the text Jake had interrupted. She had started to reply to Alika's inquiry asking how things were going on her hike. *"I have not had the restful trip I hoped for when you dropped me off. Jake and I found the body of our client today. Very sad. I dread telling the parents. And there are many missing people here. We might have found another body dump."*

"What the hell?"

"Yes. This island has too many people who have disappeared for it to be a normal pattern. I suspect a serial killer. We have just begun to scratch the surface with finding the body of our client, and some additional bones. Ginger is quite a cadaver dog, it turns out."

"Do you need help?"

The question mark of Alika's inquiry pulsed at her. *Did* she need help?

Yes, and no.

She didn't know what to do about her personal life, and he would do nothing but confuse her further. She shuddered to think of Alika and Jake in the same room. The lunch her father had hosted on Oahu at the Honua Pub had been barely tolerable; the two seemed to have taken an instant dislike to each other; unusual particularly for Alika, who got along with everyone.

The inner door opened, and Dr. Wilson stuck her head around the corner of the jamb. "Please come in, Sophie." The psychologist looked tidy and composed, her blonde bob feathering around her face. "How are you today?"

Sophie entered the room. She was still muddy and sweaty from wrestling the bushes near the stream, and her scratches itched. She resisted an urge to rub the sore places. "I have had an eventful day."

"As if yesterday were not enough." Dr. Wilson seated herself in the lounger and picked up her clipboard, pen poised. "Have you had a chance to investigate your mother's secret organization? I was Googling around last night, and there was a rumor of something, some kind of palace guard, that was established to take care of the Thai royal family millennia ago. Maybe this is a modern version of that."

"I haven't had a chance to do anything further." Sophie shook her head, smiling slightly. "After I left your office, I picked up Jake at the police station. We got my rental car, which I haven't even had a chance to drive, and went to the motel here in Hilo where I'd rented a room. I admit I collapsed. Had a relapse of my depression."

"Tell me more about that. Since you are a new client, it would help me to know a little bit of your history with the disorder."

Sophie filled the psychologist in briefly, describing her episodes of depression since she was a teenager, and how it manifested.

"Yesterday evening I went to bed in the motel before it was even dark outside. I was deep in it, not really able to do anything else. Jake left me alone, but in the morning, he . . ." To her embarrassment, Sophie felt her cheeks and neck heat up.

"He did what?"

"Jake got in bed with me. Just held me. We fell asleep, then I woke up, and I felt better. I wanted to . . . be with him. Physically."

Dr. Wilson definitely had what Sophie had heard called a twinkle in her eye as she leaned forward, smiling. "I take it that some sexual healing took place."

Sophie rubbed a scratch on the back of one hand. "I'm not familiar with that phrase, but I could imagine it being called that, yes." She struggled to find words to explain. "It was very good. Very healing as you say. Jake has agreed to my terms that we are merely partners with benefits. We are not a couple. We talked about it this morning."

"Oh, he's agreed to that, has he?" Dr. Wilson's eyebrows had raised high in a skeptical way. "Tell me more about Jake. He seems to be quite a character."

"Oh, indeed he is. Jake is large."

Dr. Wilson burst into laughter.

Sophie fanned hot cheeks with a hand, smiling. "I didn't mean that as an innuendo. But Jake is large physically and he has a commanding personality and presence. He has always irritated me by getting too personal. He is intrusive and bossy, and used to try to control and protect me. He made sexual comments and overtures that I declined. But as time has gone on, I find that I like him more than I ever thought I would. And he has learned that being treated like a sex object is unpleasant. Detective Freitan has been harassing him and he has learned a lesson from it." Sophie glanced at the clock over the psychologist's head; they still had plenty of time. "I have always found Jake physically attractive."

"You'd have to be dead not to find Jake physically attractive," Dr. Wilson said. "I met him on Oahu when I was doing some consulting for Security Solutions. I may be twice your age, but I'm not dead."

Sophie nodded. "I believe Jake's attractiveness is biological in nature. Evolution favors powerful males with survival skills. Women are drawn to those who will be able to sire strong progeny and protect them during vulnerable pregnancy and the extended period of child rearing for humans." She blew out a breath and sighed. "But Jake is also funny, and generous. He is loyal, and focused when he has a goal. He is a creative problem-solver, much smarter than he at first appears. All of these are attractive traits."

"You're talking about him as if he were a research project," Dr. Wilson said. "As if you need to justify any involvement with him. And if all these things are true, why don't you want anything more than "partners with benefits?" She made air quotes.

"Because I don't want to be in a relationship right now!" Sophie burst out. "I don't trust myself. I make bad decisions about men."

Dr. Wilson sat back, frowning. "Tell me more about this."

"First Assan, who I agreed to marry even though I didn't love him. I was attracted to him, yes. He was older, and sophisticated. He was good to me in the beginning. After Assan and his tortures, I didn't date anyone at all for five years until I slowly began to have feelings for Alika as I got to know him through coaching me at Fight Club. Then, it seemed like something was happening with us, and Assan destroyed it. Destroyed *him.* We broke up. And then . . . Connor fascinated me." Sophie looked up into Dr. Wilson's bright blue eyes. "You have to keep what I'm going to tell you in the utmost confidence. It's an open investigation, and I know things that I don't want to have subpoenaed."

"You signed the confidentiality paperwork yourself. You are as protected as I can make this. I won't take any notes on this topic. In fact, if you would like to see my notes after the session, you are welcome to."

"I trust you, Dr. Wilson. And that's what I'm going to tell you: my first lover after Assan was a cyber vigilante mastermind who calls himself the Ghost."

"That's quite an opening line, Sophie!" Dr. Wilson smiled. "Where have you been all my life! I should pay you to talk to me, because of how interesting all this is!"

"I'm glad I could provide amusement. I myself have found the situation less entertaining." Sophie told Dr. Wilson the series of events that had led to her involvement with the Ghost.

"That's quite a tale, and I can see why it would put a damper on your belief in your own judgment. But on the other hand, Connor seems to have genuine feelings for you. You two were caught in a moral dilemma that separated you. He seems to have been quite a remarkable man, as are Jake and Alika. If anything, your problem is that you have too many great choices."

"I have to agree. And this is why I don't want to be in a relationship with anyone right now. I just don't think I know what or who is good for me in the long run. But in the short term, I like having sex with Jake. It makes me feel better."

Dr. Wilson muffled a snort of laughter behind her hand. She dabbed her eyes with a tissue and composed herself. "Don't blame you a bit for that. Good sex is definitely an activity that can help battle depression. I just worry that it will lead to . . . hurt feelings. On either end."

"Oh, I already know Jake has other women. On our last job he was sleeping with Antigua, the estate manager." Sophie remembered the breathless feeling she'd had when Antigua told her the two were physically involved. "I didn't like hearing it, but mostly I think because he didn't tell me; Antigua did. And I was with Connor then. Now . . . I have to trust that Jake is okay with our arrangement and will not be too possessive. He says it is okay." She sighed. "And I still have feelings for Alika. He came back into my life on my last job." She described the series of events on Kaua'i. "We kissed. But never agreed upon anything further. I got the feeling, though, that he still cares for me. Always has, even though we broke up."

"One of the things you said was that you didn't think you would have gotten involved with the Ghost if your relationship with Alika had worked out. What if that changed? Why don't you tell me more about Alika and how he was and is different than Jake?"

"Alika is different because first he was my coach and my friend. I was always attracted to him; anyone would be. He is a beautiful man inside and out. But for the longest time, I didn't know he thought anything of me beyond friendship and our coaching relationship. Alika is restful. He makes me feel safe. He is sexy and attractive, but in a different way than Jake or Connor. Each man has his own unique presence that seems to bring out something different in me."

"You seem to think you should decide right away who to be with. Maybe you are still recovering from Assan . . . and are still too damaged by what happened with him to really know."

"I don't think so." The more Sophie thought about it, the more certain she became. "I have been out from under Assan for five years. Yes, he attacked me and the men I was dating, but ultimately, I beat him. This is different. It's about who I am becoming, and who is right for me, not just now but in the future. Only I have no idea what that future will be, and I'm still trying to discover who I am, away from Assan and his shadow."

"So trust that the men in your life are big boys. They will choose their own responses to your honesty about what's going on for you."

"But it is very stressful not knowing. I don't want to break anyone's heart. Mine was broken when Alika was beaten, and again when I thought Connor was *dead*." Sophie spat the word out in remembered pain. "Connor let me think he was dead! How could he do that?"

"Why did he do that?"

"He said it was so that we could get a fresh start without each other, since the Ghost's mission was separating us. He said letting me think he was dead seemed kinder than breaking up because of his ideals. And then he found he missed me too much, and he wanted me to forgive him. I cannot." Sophie's lips felt numb as rage at the betrayal coursed through her body. "I will never trust him again. And yet . . . I reached out to him because of this case."

"Oh really?" Dr. Wilson got up and went to the small fridge in the corner of the room. She removed two water bottles and handed one to Sophie. "Go on."

Sophie told Dr. Wilson about the discovery of the body dump in Kalapana. "The detectives confirmed that the family I found was in Witness Protection. They were cut out of the case, but there is a leak in that organization that's leading to the assassination of witnesses. Connor loves that kind of case, and can do more to fix it than anyone else. He just texted me that he was working on it. Wanted me to call him to get information for the detectives."

"So he is using the situation with you reaching out to him to gain personal contact with you. I want to challenge you that some part of you knew it when you contacted him. Knew that, and wanted that involvement."

"Perhaps." Sophie didn't want to go there. "More occurred today. Ginger found the body of our client."

"No wonder you haven't had time to research your mother! Good Lord, woman." Dr. Wilson took a dramatic swig from her water bottle. "I'm exhausted just hearing all of this. How did that come about?"

Sophie told her. "Ginger found the bones of another victim, too. The investigators are treating the stream as if it might be another dump site."

Dr. Wilson frowned at the clock. "I'm sorry, Sophie, I could talk with you all day and it wouldn't be enough—but I have another client coming. Can we meet again tomorrow? I would like to keep our momentum. I'm sure I can bill some of this to Security Solutions as post-trauma counseling, if that's a concern. I do contract work for them on occasion."

"That would be fine." They set a time for the next day.

"I can hardly wait for the next installment of *As Sophie's World Turns*. Please, try to find out more about your mother and her organization before our next meeting. Don't let all of this other stuff distract you, and believe me, it may feel more compelling to you, more immediate. But the situation with your mother really requires some deeper exploration, and I encourage you not to shy away from that. When did she say she needed an answer?"

"She said she would wait to hear from me. She gave me a phone number." That number seemed to be burned in glowing digits into Sophie's memory. "You are right. I wish to avoid everything to do with my mother."

"But I will help you. Together, we can navigate this. And your love life, too."

Sophie hugged the psychologist spontaneously as they headed for the door. "Thank you. I feel less alone."

CHAPTER THIRTY-SIX

EVENING WAS CASTING long shadows over the dense jungle area of the crime scene as Jake pulled up in the Jeep. Sophie had told him she would take a rideshare back to the Banyan Tree Motel and pick up her rental to re-join him after her appointment with Dr. Wilson, so he decided to go back out to see if any further discoveries had been made, and just insert himself back into the investigation.

Detective Wong detached himself from a cluster of law enforcement personnel and met Jake near the Jeep. "We found two more bodies. Much more decomposed than your client. The chief has ordered a full survey of the ditch and the surrounding areas to find any further remains."

"Aw, man. I hope that stream wasn't feeding into some drinking water reservoir," Jake said. "But it looks like we might be able to cross a few more names off the missing persons list Sophie has put together."

"That's if we can identify them." Wong gestured toward a large plastic tub. "This one is so far gone it came apart when the ME tried to move it."

Jake held his breath against the smell as he looked in. Bones gleamed amid a sludgy mass that seemed to be liquefying before

Jake's eyes. "Nasty. Definitely going to need to use dental records to check who it is."

"That's what we're counting on."

Freitan strode up. "Well, we seem to have hit a body dump motherlode. We're going to search until we run out of light, and then pick it up again tomorrow. If you want to come to a team meeting to strategize, we are meeting back at the station in about an hour."

"I know Sophie will want to be there too. What can I do to help?"

"Put up crime scene tape. We're cordoning off the entire creek, and that goes on for quite a way along the road."

Jake didn't resent the lowly task, but he was glad he had put on his usual worn black ripstop combat pants and waterproof hiking boots as he tromped through the long grass and heavy bushes, unrolling a large spool of tape with another officer.

"I hope someone called the water department," he remarked to the uniform working with him, a sturdy young man whose nametag read RAMIREZ. "This stream is heavily contaminated."

"Even the governor of Hawaii has been alerted by our station chief," Ramirez said. "The situation with missing persons on the Big Island has been declared a state of emergency."

Interesting that Ramirez was the one to tell him such important news, not the detectives working the case with him. Jake wondered if it was just an oversight, or if Freitan and Wong were intentionally cutting him and Sophie out of the loop. That would be a mistake, with Sophie's connections to the FBI and her access to the DAVID program's sophisticated analytical capabilities.

"Has the local news gotten ahold of this yet?" Jake asked.

"Hope not. We don't need this kind of publicity," Ramirez said. "Spooks the tourists."

"Maybe they need to be spooked." A measure of greater caution might have saved Julie Weathersby's life. Jake dreaded phoning the parents; but he needed to get it done before the meeting. "Hey, mind carrying on without me? Got an important phone call to make, and I need to get somewhere with a strong signal."

The corner of the side road that turned off toward the crime scene and the main highway was the closest place Jake could pick up a good enough signal. He called Bix first to update him on the situation, which took a while. "Sophie and I will be going to a team meeting at the Hilo PD Station. The detectives working the case want me to get the parents over here without alerting them so they can be told the news formally and be interviewed. What's your take?"

"Damn shame. Poor girl. That said, let's do a conference call. I want to be sure we cover all our bases. In my experience, parents of murdered children are angry and looking for a scapegoat. I don't want it to be us."

"Don't much see how that could apply when Julie was killed a week ago, and we did the family and Hilo PD a service by finding her body," Jake said. "But all right. I'll reach out and add them to this call."

He punched in the Weathersbys and added them to the call. He was relieved when Julie's father picked up; he'd dreaded speaking to Mrs. Weathersby, with her soft wet blue eyes that reminded him so much of his mom.

"Aloha, Mr. Weathersby. This is Jake Dunn from Security Solutions. There have been some new developments in your daughter's case. I'm on the line with Kendall Bix, and we've been asked by the Hilo detectives to see if you and your wife can come to the Big Island and meet with them."

"Not a problem, Dunn, because we are already in Hilo," Weathersby said. Jake could picture the man's ruddy face to match his hearty tone. "We are working with the FindUsNow PR folks to get the word out about Julie, and they recommended we come to the Big Island to share with the local news and such here."

"Perhaps you might have let us know that, Mr. Weathersby," Bix said testily.

"And regardless, please wait to hear from Detectives Wong and

Freitan," Jake interjected. "Don't speak to any news reporters, please."

"Why not? We are trying to alert the public so that if anyone has seen her they'd let us know . . ."

"Please, Mr. Weathersby. There are elements in play that you may not be aware of. We need your cooperation on this," Bix said forcefully. "You are paying us for our advice as it pertains to your daughter's case. Please take it."

"Mallory from FindUsNow says differently," Mr. Weathersby said. "He says the more of a stink we raise in the media, the more attention our daughter will get."

"Can I get a number for Mallory at FindUsNow?" Bix asked. "I think we should all get on the same page."

Weathersby provided the number and reluctantly agreed to cease his efforts to get the media involved.

Jake shook his head as Weathersby disconnected, leaving him on the line with Bix. "I hope you can get that PR firm to rein it in. This case is about to go nuts when all those bodies hit the news, and if the media gets its hands on it and a leak is traced to us in any way . . ."

"You don't have to tell me," Bix said. "Two steps ahead of you. Now get to that meeting with Hilo PD."

"Roger that, boss." Jake ended the call. He put the Jeep in gear, following Wong and Freitan's taillights as they headed back to the station for the meeting.

CHAPTER THIRTY-SEVEN

SOPHIE ENTERED the conference room at the Hilo Police Department, carrying a tray of sushi from Foodland. She had learned from her time in Hawaii never to arrive at a social situation without bringing food. After she got the call from Jake to meet at the station, she'd speculated that the detectives would be hungry and tired from their labors of the afternoon.

She was right. The law enforcement team descended upon her offering like a flock of sparrows on a rice field. The group consisted of Freitan, Wong, Captain Bruce Ohale, and several other unknown staffers. Coffee was passed around in a metal carafe, and Sophie filled a Styrofoam cup with some of the inky brew, needing to get her energy up a bit after the session with Dr. Wilson.

Jake arrived, vibrating with his usual energy as he greeted the room. "Our supervisor and I spoke with the Weathersbys. Turns out they are already on the island, staying at a hotel in Hilo on the recommendation of a PR firm, FindUsNow.com. Have any of you heard of it?"

"Nasty bunch of vultures, preying on families' hopes," Freitan said. "I am not a fan."

"Bix has a meeting scheduled for tomorrow with Mallory of

189

FindUsNow. Hopefully, we can all get on the same page. It would not be good for the news to find out about all these bodies," Jake said.

"Perhaps you want to control the message the public gets." Sophie made eye contact with the station chief, a burly middle-aged Hawaiian man with a bristly buzz cut and very tiny wire-rimmed readers balanced on his wide brown nose. "Hold a press conference and make an announcement."

"Not until we have some leads," Captain Ohale growled. "Everybody keep your lips zipped."

Sophie cleared her throat. "Have you considered calling in the FBI's Behavioral Analysis Unit? They might be a good resource if we are dealing with a serial."

"Hell no." Freitan snorted. "We've got it right now, thanks very much."

"About a bigger item." Ohale leaned forward, resting the tips of meaty fingers together. "Someone tipped off the governor about our missing persons list, and the situation has been dubbed a statewide emergency. You wouldn't know anything about that, would you, Ms. Ang?"

Sophie's eyes widened in surprise. "Of course not, sir. The only people who know I was working some bigger numbers on the missing persons situation are Freitan, Wong, and my partner, Jake Dunn."

All eyes turned to Jake, who lifted his hands in a surrender gesture. "Don't look at me! Sophie and I have been running our asses off. Hardly had time to breathe, let alone stir the shit to tip off anybody. Our supervisor Bix is on us because we haven't kept him updated, and now our client's body has been found. So we aren't even on the job for much longer." He looked around the table. "I hope you found our contributions helpful. Such as finding a serial robbing tweaker couple that might be murderers, uncovering an extortionist, and discovering multiple bodies."

A beat passed by, and Ohale gave an abrupt head nod. "Your help is noted. Let's start over again with full introductions, then I would like Detective Freitan to facilitate a review of the situation that has led to our current discovery."

Sophie took out her laptop, and looked to the station chief. "All right if I take some notes, sir?"

"No Internet. And shoot us a copy before you do anything with the notes," Ohale said.

Sophie nodded. *The level of concern about the apparent leak was merited.* She was relieved to have keys under her fingers again and something to do with her hands as Freitan got up and went to one of the whiteboards on the wall.

Sophie noted the names of those present as they were introduced: Freitan, Wong, Jake, Ohale, a round, genial Filipino man introduced as Hilo's District Attorney Sam Queiros, and Detectives Latimer and Lono from nearby Puna District.

The meeting got underway with a brief mention of the body dump Sophie had initially found. "I'll just summarize the progress with that so far. We don't think that the murdered family is part of this current investigation," Freitan said. "The 'Jones' family was in Witness Protection. The Marshals Service has taken over that investigation, and is working on a leak that's been leading to exposure of some of their witnesses here on the Big Island. We are no longer involved, except as pertains to processing crime scene evidence and whatever they ask us to do. And now, to our current case."

Freitan turned to a large portable corkboard, which she propped against the whiteboard. Photos of people involved with the case were tacked to it. "Ms. Ang and her handy cadaver dog Ginger, along with Dunn here, are working the disappearance of Julie Weathersby because the parents went ahead and hired Security Solutions. Since these two paired up, the action on the case has been nonstop. They tracked a couple who had targeted and robbed Weathersby out at that encampment at Oceanview, Travelers' Rest." Freitan tapped mugshots of Holly Rayme and Jim Webb. "We still have Webb and Rayme in custody, and these two tweakers appear to have been robbing and rolling on a regular basis. They could be killers too, though our search at their squat didn't yield anything tying to a particular case." Freitan paused to slurp from her mug of coffee and went on. "Dunn and Ang also found a young man named Paul Chernobiac who has, at least, been a part of shaking down families of the missing. Chernobiac seems to have ties to unknown partners; Jake and Sophie reported being pursued by a black SUV when they went to check his address." Freitan pointed to Chernobiac's innocuous-looking photo.

"Hilo PD neither authorized nor sanctioned any illegal search of Chernobiac's property," Wong chimed in. "But when our team went to search the premises with a warrant, the bag of cash Ang and Dunn had reported seeing was missing. We didn't have a confirmed connection between Chernobiac and any of these crimes, so he was released after twenty-four hours."

"So you searched Chernobiac's premises illegally?" Chief Ohale asked Jake.

Jake gazed back at him levelly. "We neither confirm nor deny such an action might have happened."

The detectives snorted with laughter and Freitan picked up the thread. "Today's discovery of four bodies, one of them tentatively identified as Julie Weathersby, has led to an expansion of the investigating team. Wong and I have no problem asking for help from the FBI at this point. It seems like we have a serial here, maybe even a serial with an organized underbelly of secondary crime feeding off of the victim's families."

"I have a question." Detective Lono was a rugged-looking mixed Caucasian Hawaiian in a long-sleeved hoodie with a tattoo showing on his neck. "I usually work vice, and I'm wondering why we've been drafted to be a part of this. We have our own cases that will be neglected for this business here in Hilo."

"Short answer? Because I asked your Lieutenant for more manpower. We need to take these missing persons cases more seriously, and we wanted some investigators with connections to the drug and vice trade in the area," Ohale said. "We need to respond as aggressively as we can with the governor's eye on the situation. I think we might find that there are a combination of different scenarios leading to what apparently seems like one trend."

That seemed to sober the two from Puna District. Wong stood up and handed out packets of photocopied paper. Sophie took hers, scanning it and finding details from the bodies as Freitan said, "We are trying to identify the three sets of remains that we found in the stream. Dunn and Ang took a look at the female body and superficially, it matches the description of Julie Weathersby."

"Too bloated to be totally sure," Jake said, "but the coloring and height are right. Our witness Shirley Mandig identified Julie Weathersby, recognized after the fact through social media, as the girl in a black bra and underwear that she saw on the side of the road. Ultimately that led to our discovery. Julie Weathersby's parents are already on the island and will be asked to confirm the identity."

Sophie gave a little inward shudder at the thought of being asked to identify a child's body after it was submerged for a week. Hopefully, the Weathersbys had strong stomachs.

"We still may need to use dental records and DNA to confirm if the parents can't identify the body, since the fingerprints are too degraded. The others are older and are going to be more difficult. One of the first tasks we need to do is obtain dental records of all of the possible missing within the time frame that the medical examiner gives us for these bodies," Freitan said.

The meeting devolved into the minutiae of who was doing what, none of which involved Jake or Sophie. Sophie continued to take notes, but sneaked a look at her partner.

Jake sat across from her, leaning back in his chair, his big body relaxed, his eyes half-closed, his fingers laced on his flat belly. He'd looked sexy and sleepy like that in her bed.

His eyes shifted over and met hers. *He was remembering, too.* Heat flushed the back of Sophie's neck and she looked down at her laptop.

Jake coiled forward deliberately and set his elbows on the table. "If I may interrupt for a moment. Ms. Ang and I would like to continue to support the investigation, but with our client most likely deceased, it seems we might be out of a job."

Ohale inclined his head. "You two can go. We will let you know when we have an interview set up with the parents."

"I anticipate that tomorrow," Freitan said. That patronizing edge she got to her tone was back, and Sophie frowned as she went on. "I'll text you when. You can attend and watch, and afterward, provide emotional support to your clients when we are done with them."

"So nice of you to include us." Jake's tone was heavy with sarcasm. He stood up, and Sophie closed her laptop and did the same.

Ohale looked up at them over his wire-rimmed glasses. His gaze and tone were sincere. "You've been a big help. Our whole team appreciates it, right, Freitan?"

"Yes, sir. These two earned their cheddar," Freitan said reluctantly.

Cheddar? Some colloquialism for money, no doubt. There were so many.

Wong inclined his head. "Thanks, guys. A pleasure working with you."

"We intend to see this through as far as the family will let us," Jake said. "Talk to you all tomorrow."

Sophie lifted a hand and walked through the door Jake held open for her. He touched her back as they exited the conference room and leaned close to whisper in her ear. "How about a bite to eat, and bed? We've had a long day."

Goosebumps rippled across Sophie's skin where he touched her. "How about showers and takeout, instead?" she countered. "I'm too tired for anything but food and bed."

"Perfect." Jake's smile was wolfish.

CHAPTER THIRTY-EIGHT

JAKE TOOK a shower on his side of the motel room, while Sophie did the same on hers. He paid for a Chinese food delivery, and carried the bag to the connecting door between their rooms, wearing only a towel as he knocked. *She seemed to have liked that before.* Who was he to mess with something that worked?

Sophie opened the door. Jake struck a pose, tightening his abs. "Your beefcake delivery." He held up the bag.

"Beefcake? Not sure what that is, but I wouldn't mind a bite of what's in front of me."

Jake laughed. "Is my Sophie flirting?"

"I am able to learn new skills. Many new skills. But first I need food." She plucked the bag from his fingers. Jake followed her over to the coffee table, tightening the towel to prevent a mishap.

"Did you feed the dogs?" he asked. As if hearing themselves mentioned, the two rascals stuck their heads around the bed inquisitively.

"These two aren't about to let me forget anything to do with them," Sophie said. The dogs advanced, looking hopefully at the Chinese food containers Sophie extracted from the bag and set on the coffee table. "We shouldn't give them anything. Particularly Tank. He needs his digestive system built back up."

They ate on the narrow couch side-by-side, occasionally feeding each other choice bits with the chopsticks. Jake savored the companionship as much as the food. Just knowing how well they had worked together today satisfied him on some deep level.

Sophie's phone buzzed, dancing a little circle on the coffee table. She picked it up. Her brows drew together in a frown. "It's . . . someone important. I have to take this."

Sophie pressed the phone to her ear. She got up and walked into his room, and shut the connecting door firmly between them.

The good feelings Jake had been reveling in evaporated. "Son of a bitch." He threw down his chopsticks and picked up the Kirin beer he'd ordered with the meal, taking a long swig to cool his temper.

Who was she talking to that she wouldn't tell him about? Alika? That helicopter-flying businessman was going to snake his woman right out from under him if Jake wasn't careful.

He didn't know what to do.

Sophie had told him they were partners with benefits, nothing more.

She had told him being jealous was a turn-off . . . but the thought of her and Alika together made Jake want to rip something apart. He'd managed to keep his attitude in check when she was dating that Todd guy, but barely.

Maybe he wasn't okay with this situation, after all. Maybe he couldn't do "partners with benefits" casual sex, at least with Sophie. He'd certainly had no problem with that in the past.

But the secrets she was keeping, just like the many times she'd abandoned him, didn't feel good. Jake wasn't keeping anything from her.

Getting Sophie into bed had been a place to start. If he could make her feel good, he could build a connection, and maybe she'd come to feel the same way about him . . . but it didn't seem to be working.

She was the one who made *him* feel good, even when he was just trying to get her out of her depression, make her lose herself in pleasure. And every time she shut him out, put distance between them, told him he didn't matter, it hurt worse.

But what was the alternative? Breaking things off?

They'd barely gotten started. He couldn't wait to touch her again, couldn't stop thinking about how she felt, tasted, sounded, sighed. All day, little memory bits from their night together had come back to distract him. She had come to mean way too much for him to just turn off feelings that had been building, on his side at least, since the day they met.

If only he had someone to talk to.

His sister Patty came to mind. Jake was the oldest, and he and his younger sister, Monica, had fought all their lives like wet cats, but his youngest sister, Patty, had always been a friend. She looked up to him, and had been a real cling-on after their father left the family when Jake was a teen. It had taken Mom years of taking Dad to court to squeeze the bottom line out of that selfish prick.

Such a screwed-up cliché. He despised his father. Jake never made promises he couldn't keep, and when he finally settled down, it would be for life—which was why he was extra careful not to get emotionally involved—except that it had sneaked up on him.

"Shit," Jake muttered, and finished his beer.

Patty had married a good guy a couple years ago and had a baby on the way. She might know how to advise him.

Wearing the towel seemed silly, now, freakin' embarrassing, and he couldn't go outside when he desperately needed to move and discharge his angst. *A run would be perfect.* He would just have to go get his clothing from his room . . .

Jake speed-dialed Patty as he finished the last of a container of mu-shu pork.

"My favorite big brother! You never call. Who died?" Patty actually sounded worried.

"Ha! Sorry about that." Jake stood up, bagging the trash so the

197

dogs wouldn't get at it. "I need a little advice, sis." He stowed the bag in a plastic can and put it on top of the TV out of the animals' reach. "I've . . . got feels for a co-worker."

"Geez, Jake, really? Not good. Why do you need me to tell you that's a bad idea?" Patty laughed.

"The thing is . . . I didn't want to like her this much." He blew out a breath, ran a hand through his hair, staring at the closed door between their rooms. "But I've been super into her ever since we met, and I thought it was just the usual . . . I mean she's hot, and we'd bang, and I'd get over the attraction like I usually do, and move on."

"Ew, Jake. Why are you telling me this? I really don't want to know you're one of 'those' guys. I like to think you play that part but aren't really . . . you know. A user." Patty sounded sad.

"Crap!" Jake paced. Tank whined in worry watching him, and Jake ran a hand over the dog's sleek head. "I am not a user. I always make sure the lady gets hers, you know what I mean? I haven't had complaints except that I just can't get serious about anybody. But you know why I can't, right, sis?"

"Because of freakin' Dad. But you're not him, Jake. You'll never be him."

"But I look like him. I act like him. Hell, in some ways I'm a lot like him! And I don't want to be that guy. So I'm up front with the women I sleep with, and it's good times and then goodbye. My last relationship went on a little longer than usual, but we parted ways on good terms, just how I like it. But Sophie . . . Sophie's different. Complicated. We never even kissed until this week but she keeps leaving me and it . . . gets to me."

"You finally really like someone and she keeps abandoning you. Like Dad did."

"You a psychologist or something?" Jake forced a laugh.

"Yeah, kinda. If you kept up with my life a little bit too, Jake, you'd know I'm back in school for nursing. We've got plenty of psych classes."

"I'm sorry, Patty. I'm a jerk." The towel was slipping. He needed his clothes! Screw Sophie using his room; he'd just go in and change. *It wasn't like she hadn't seen it all before.* He turned the knob of the connecting door and pushed it open. "I really do care about you, hon."

Sophie was sitting on the bed, her back to him, curled around the phone pressed to her ear. She was speaking some other language. She looked around and glared at him. He dropped the towel defiantly and flipped her off, stomping over to his duffel and pulling out his clothes. "Tell me more, Patty."

"Well, we all have wounds from our past, and you've got a chip on your shoulder about Dad. Why do you think you went into the Army when he was an officer, too? And then, you had to do Special Forces, and outdo him even though he retired a Colonel."

"Not a bad analysis, Patty. Tell me more from a woman's perspective." Hyper-aware of Sophie, Jake dressed, dragging on briefs and a pair of sweatpants.

Patty continued. "I'm guessing, since women pretty much fall all over you, that you picked someone to fixate on that won't do that. Someone with baggage, or another relationship. Someone screwed up."

"You're a little spooky, girl. That's a pretty accurate description." Jake could feel Sophie's gaze on his torso as he pulled a shirt down over his head one-handed. *Good, maybe she'd regret what she was missing.* "So, what do I do?"

"Well, a woman like that is not going to like your heavy-handed approach. I know you, Jake, and you're relentless when you want something—but maybe you don't really want this one. Whoever she is, she's going to break your heart . . . and that's why you chose her. Because Dad broke your heart, and you're trying to heal yourself. That's why we choose who we do—but at least half the time, we just hurt ourselves all over again. So my first advice to you is, give her up. Walk away. Break it off before she breaks you."

"Hey, don't hold back. Give it to me straight," Jake picked up his running shoes and socks. He walked through the connecting door and slammed it with a satisfying thump so Sophie couldn't miss that he was pissed. "Geez, you're brutal."

"You didn't call me to massage your ego, did you?"

"Nope. But what if I can't walk away?"

"Then play it cool. Make her come to you. Be so good she can't forget you, but don't wait around and beg; don't be needy and clingy. Get a life, and live it. Live it so well she wants to join you in it."

Jake felt his eyes prickle as he thrust his feet into his shoes. "Shit, Patty. You should have been a therapist."

"I love you, bro. Don't ever forget it. You're a good guy and you'll be an awesome partner to someone, someday. Don't settle, Jake. You don't have to."

Jake rubbed his stinging eyes with a thumb and forefinger after he said goodbye. Tank thrust his big square head under Jake's arm and took a deep sniff of his armpit, the stump of his cropped tail wagging.

"You guys want a little after-dinner run? Because I sure do." Jake leashed the dogs and left the little motel room, already knowing what he needed to do.

CHAPTER THIRTY-NINE

SOPHIE WINCED as the connecting door between the hotel rooms slammed and Jake left. "I have to go, Mother. My partner is becoming suspicious."

"I can't wait much longer to have an answer from you, Sophie." Pim Wat's familiar voice still paralyzed Sophie, grabbing her by the throat with a conditioned desire to please and appease.

"I don't understand that, when you waited nine years to contact me." Sophie cleared her throat and strengthened her tone. "And so far, you haven't said anything compelling that makes me want to get involved. I have not had time to research your organization's background due to my current case. But I have a life, Mother, and neither you nor your government have been a part of it." So far, the strange conversation that had begun with her mother's phone call had been a rehash of the strange appeal the woman had made to her in the park. "I fail to see how I benefit from such an arrangement."

"You will be well paid, of course. And you will have a future that is reconciled with your past. You can be a part of our family again. You can come to Thailand and reconnect with your aunts, uncles and cousins."

"None of that is of interest to me, Mother." Sophie wondered why she kept repeating the word "mother." It was as if she needed to remind herself that the husky voice on the other end of the phone was even related to her. "I can visit my family in Thailand anytime I want to. I simply have no interest. I am my father's daughter." Sophie hadn't realized the truth of that statement so clearly until she spoke it. "Dad has been there for me. He didn't abandon me."

"Oh, really? Who hired your nannies? Who sent you to boarding school? All of those things were your father's decision. I wanted you kept at home, with me. And the family."

Sophie vividly remembered the large wooden family compound built on raised pilings near the river. She remembered shared meals, and chasing and playing with her cousins as they ran through the different apartments, or the subunits the family occupied. And she remembered how often there was no one home in her family's apartment, and how she'd been absorbed into her aunt's.

A knife of old pain twisted in Sophie's gut. Her father had always been married to his job, and of course, she had needed care, care that her mother hadn't provided. Frank had wanted her to have an American influence and future; that meant that he had taken steps to ensure that she was acculturated to the Western world.

"He was making sure I was ready to come to the United States when I wanted to. And thank God he did those things, because I couldn't have escaped Assan by fleeing to Thailand."

"You didn't really escape Assan, did you? If you had, you would be a normal woman, perhaps married with some children. But instead you are a stunted and scarred person who cannot settle anything. A mercenary for hire with no honor."

Sophie gasped at the cruel words. "And you are the one who gave me to Assan. I have heard quite enough of your version of persuasion, Mother."

Sophie ended the call, hunching over and curling in on herself. She heard a low keening sound, and was surprised to realize she was the one making it.

That phone call had been as poisonous as a black mamba that had sunk its fangs into her throat.

She got herself under control and glanced at the connecting door. It was oddly silent in the other room. *Jake must have gone out.*

"And I hardly blame him," Sophie said aloud, remembering the riveting sight of his naked body as he changed in front of her while talking to some other woman. Hurt and rejection had radiated off of him in waves as he made a fuss of changing and leaving.

She was never in doubt about how Jake was feeling at any given time.

Sophie slid the phone into her pocket. She wished she hadn't taken the call. *She wouldn't take a call from her mother again.* She got up and opened the connecting door.

Jake and the dogs were gone. The trash from dinner was neatly tidied away, but he'd left a couple of containers of food out for her.

Jake could sleep with the dogs tonight, instead of with her. A twinge of regret lanced her. *It would have been so nice to end the day in his arms, as she had planned.* But that was not to be, because explaining any of this to Jake was impossible, and he was already clearly upset because she'd taken a phone call that she didn't want to explain.

She carried many secrets. That would continue. He had to be okay with it, and clearly, he wasn't.

Sophie drew the drapes, turned the bolt on the door, and locked the connecting door. She switched off the light, stripped off her clothing, and got into bed.

Darkness was a familiar friend that folded her close in its arms, and dragged her down into oblivion.

SOPHIE AND JAKE walked side-by-side into the hotel lobby at the downtown Hilo Bay Hilton.

Jake had unlocked the door between their rooms in order to wake

Sophie in the morning, and had roused her with difficulty. He'd been kind, but withdrawn, and she was barely functioning.

Sophie felt fragile, as if anything might push her back into the black depression. Her skin felt thin and sensitive, as if to touch it would burst it, and all that would come out would be a river of tears. She fisted her hands, suppressing the voice of the depression murmuring how hopeless and cursed she was.

"I wonder why the Weathersbys wanted to see us before the meeting at the station." She spoke for something to say as the elevator rose to the top floor of the hotel. "I am not particularly eager to speak to them about finding Julie's body."

"Part of the job. I'd think you'd have a tougher hide about that by now." Jake hadn't looked at her all morning and he'd barely spoken. She missed the sight of his eyes.

"You forget I worked in the computer lab—I was never a field agent. Our cases have been the most activity outside an office that I've ever had," Sophie said.

Jake gave a brusque nod.

Sophie opened her mouth to ask him why he was so upset, but the elevator dinged. Jake touched her back so that Sophie could precede him out of the elevator, and she felt the tiny, polite brush of his fingertips echo through her body. Moments later, they stood in front of the Weathersbys' room, and Sophie rang the bell.

A young woman wrapped in a white robe opened the door.

Sophie recognized her instantly: *five foot six inches, one hundred and thirty pounds, long brunette hair, blue eyes, freckles on her nose.*

Julie Weathersby.

CHAPTER FORTY

JAKE'S MOUTH fell open in surprise at the sight of the Weathersby girl. He closed it with an effort and visually scanned the young woman wearing a hotel bathrobe. She looked healthy and freshly scrubbed, with no visible bruises or other signs of trauma.

"Oh, I am so happy to see you two! My parents have been telling me all about how hard Security Solutions has been working to find me, and I feel so bad about that," Julie gushed, clutching the toweling at her neck modestly. "But it was Mallory at FindUsNow that got the word to me through social media that I was being considered endangered and missing."

Sophie swayed. She looked ready to keel over in a faint. Jake put an arm around her waist and steadied her.

Sophie had gone to the dark place of her depression since he left last night—he had read the signs by her closed shades and locked doors. He and the dogs had gone to bed alone in his room. Going in to comfort her had been out of the question at that point. Whoever had been on that phone call had jacked her up and his help was not welcome. She'd made that abundantly clear.

"We are a little taken aback to see you," Jake said, because someone had to say something. He extended his hand. "Jake Dunn.

Security specialist. I am very glad to see you, young lady." He injected his voice with heartiness as Julie shook his hand with a slender cool one.

Sophie extended her hand next. "We thought that you were dead," she said flatly.

"Oh no! That's terrible. I'm so sorry for the mix-up. Please, come in. We want to tell you all about it before we go to the police station. Dad wants us all to be on the same page."

"Oh, hello there, Jake and Sophie!" Mrs. Weathersby's soft face, filled with joy, still reminded Jake of his mom. After that talk with Patty, he was overdue to give her a call. "Please come in and have some coffee with us!"

Jake and Sophie walked into the suite. Mr. Weathersby rose from a chair out on the deck overlooking a stunning view of Hilo Bay and swaying palm trees. "What's this about thinking my daughter was dead? We want to make sure we all have our stories straight before we go into the police station."

Jake clenched his teeth, bracing for spin doctoring. Rich people always thought they could rewrite history, and half the time they got away with it. "We're eager to hear what happened to your daughter, Mr. Weathersby," Jake said. "And I hope you'll be considerate of all the work that's gone into finding her, both by our staff and by the Hilo Police Department."

"Oh, we'll tip you," Mr. Weathersby said dismissively. "Now sit down and Julie will tell you what happened."

FREITAN AND WONG didn't look like they had gotten much sleep in the hours since Jake had seen them last. The detectives were down-right grouchy as they sat Julie Weathersby, extracted from her parents' arms, on a chair in the interview room. The parents were calling a lawyer, but Julie hadn't asked for one, and as far as Jake knew, Julie wasn't in trouble—they just wanted any information she had about Rayme, Webb, and whoever had attacked her. The young woman began to cry immediately when Freitan told her they'd be recording the interview. Freitan rolled her eyes even as Wong pushed a box of tissues over to the weepy woman.

On the other side of the reflective glass coating, the observation booth was dim and smelled faintly of the ever-present Hilo mold. The voices coming through the ancient sound system were thin and tinny. Jake's plastic chair was hard, and he resisted an urge to reach out to Sophie as she sat beside him, eyes on the drama occurring in the other room. Her hand was just lying there in her lap.

Maybe touching her was a good strategy.

But only if he could do it without it affecting him more than it did her . . .

Jake was determined to take Patty's counsel. No neediness. No begging. No jealousy. Just being so damn good Sophie couldn't forget him. *Good advice, Patty.* He had a plan now.

Jake reached out and took Sophie's hand. As before when she was in her depression, it was cold and limp. He rubbed slow circles on her wrist with his thumb. He felt silky tissue, bones, and fragile veins. Her pulse picked up as the pad of his thumb moved gently over her skin.

Good. She was feeling this.

And he was still nicely detached. He needed to stay that way.

"Rather than having us ask you questions, why don't you just tell us, in your own words, where you've been." Freitan leaned back and crossed her arms on her chest in classic "bad cop" mode. "Your parents are calling a lawyer like you need to be protected from some wrongdoing. So, what you been up to, chica?"

"We appreciate that you are cooperating with us," Wong's body language was opposite: leaning toward the girl, arms open, smiling and friendly.

"It's all a big misunderstanding. I mean, part of it is." Julie gestured to her clothing, a pair of jeans and a tee that still had creases from packaging on it. "I guess you heard from the Security Solutions people that I was robbed and left on the side of the road?"

"Yes. We even have your friends Webb and Rayme in custody."

"That's great! Those two are total assholes! They pretended to be friends with me, and then took all my money and jewelry. They did leave me with my backpack, though."

"Yes. Then the Security Solutions people found your backpack, boots and clothing, and feared the worst. And yet, here you are," Freitan said.

"Well." Julie chewed her bottom lip. The kid was adorable. Even hearing the story for the second time, Jake was impressed with how she oozed sincerity. "I was so upset after Holly and Jim threw me out of their car. I tramped into the jungle to get away, worried they were going to take the rest of my stuff. They had propositioned me for a threesome and when I said no, that's when they decided to rob me, I think. Anyway, I was out there and just starting to turn around and head back to the road, when this guy came out of nowhere." Julie's gaze cut up and to the left as she recalled the events. "He was way scarier than Jimmy and Holly."

"Tell us about him. What did he look like?"

"Close to six feet. He was a local—you know, dark skin, maybe Hawaiian and something Asian. Black hair. He was fast and strong." Her eyes filled. She blinked and sniffled, and Wong handed her a tissue. "He had a knife and threatened me with it. Made me take off all my clothes and told me he was going to . . . enjoy what he was going to do to me before he killed me." Julie's voice shook and she covered her face with her hands, plastering the tissue to her eyes.

"More details please," Freitan rapped out. "We are going to want you to work with a sketch artist. As much detail as you can recall is really important."

"Anything I can do." Julie wrung the tissue with her hands, shredding it. "Dark eyes. He looked like a local guy, like I said. Someone from here. I had an impression he was good looking, but I was too scared to really notice his features."

Freitan leaned forward, her gaze intent. "Young? Old?"

"In his thirties, I'd say. He had rough hands, like he did outdoor work or something. I remember that." Julie dropped her eyes, wiping her hands on her stiff looking jeans. "He had a pidgin accent. Anyway, I didn't want to take my clothes off, and we struggled until he put that knife against my neck." Julie tipped her head to the side, and showed the detectives a healed scratch beneath her jaw. "Once he had the knife there, I cooperated. I took off my clothes and boots."

"And then what happened?" Freitan was relentless.

"He started to take off his pants, but he couldn't get them down one handed, so he put the knife aside. I scrambled up and ran for it. I figured he was going to kill me; I had nothing to lose. His pants caught on his ankles and I was able to jump over the ditch and get to the road. I ran along the road as fast as I could in my underwear and bare feet. A car came. I waved my arms, and the driver pulled over. I told the guy I needed help; I was running away from someone who had attacked me. The driver let me into the car and we took off."

"Who was this?"

"His name was Terence Chang."

Jake felt Sophie stiffen beside him. *The name meant something to her.* She had reacted to it back in the hotel room, too. She had gone out into the hall to make one of her secret phone calls, and had returned with that blank mask in place. She knew something about this Terence Chang, and so far, she wasn't telling what it was.

Freitan and Wong glanced at each other and took note of the name. It meant something to them, too. "And then what happened?" Wong asked.

"I had nothing. No clothes, no money, no phone. Terence said I could rest up at his place. Get cleaned up. He was really nice. Seemed sorry about what happened to me. Said that there was someone in the area preying on travelers, and that everyone needed to be careful."

"So why didn't you get in touch with your parents? Why didn't you call the police about this man who attacked you?" Wong sounded genuinely concerned and confused.

Julie looked down. Jake could tell she was blushing, even though the privacy film bleached the color out of the scene they were watching. "I was ashamed. I felt like a fool. My parents had warned me many times that it wasn't a good idea to go on my hiking adventure; and all their warnings had turned out to be right. I definitely planned to report it and do all the right things, but I just wanted to recover a little bit first before I had to deal with all of that. So, I didn't call anyone, and then Terence and I . . ."

Who was this Terence Chang? Jake Googled him on his phone, but the name didn't come up in the Hilo area. *Bizarre.* Guy must go to a lot of trouble to keep such a low profile.

"So, you got involved with Terence Chang? Rewarded your rescuer the old-fashioned way?" Freitan's voice was frosty. "And meanwhile, you let your parents think the worst had happened?"

"When you put it that way, it sounds so bad. But at the time, I didn't think anyone knew anything about what had happened to me, or even missed me. I'd only skipped one weekly call to my parents. And I was really just . . . disoriented, I guess. I wanted to stay in the little bubble of safety I found with Terence for as long as I could."

"It didn't strike you as odd that this Chang character didn't encourage you to go to the cops? Didn't tell you to do the right thing about your attacker?"

"All I can say is that I wasn't thinking straight. I finally got on one of Terence's computers and went online. I left and found my parents as soon as I saw the social media posts from FindUsNow that said I was a missing person." Julie covered her eyes with a hand. "I feel so bad. I'm sorry for all the hassle."

Jake had heard all of this before, and it seemed just as lame the second time.

"So this Terence Chang. He didn't coerce, imprison, or in any other way delay your reporting what happened?" Wong asked.

"Of course not. Terence was just amazing. I mean he *is* just amazing." Julie's eyes glowed with infatuation as she looked up at the detectives. "I think we fell for each other so hard that we were both distracted. I lost all sense of time. I admit it. But as soon as I wanted to leave, he took me to my parents' hotel. He has been nothing but a perfect gentleman."

"Interesting that you describe him as a 'perfect gentleman,' when Terence Chang is the heir apparent to the Chang crime family. How convenient that he happened along when he did, and took you in and showed you such a good time." Freitan's voice dripped with sarcasm.

Jake felt a twinge of sympathy for the girl as Julie's face drained of color and her eyes grew wide.

"What?"

"To be fair, Terence himself has never been charged with anything. Claims to be going straight. But his family is at the heart of anything unsavory happening on the Big Island. We certainly know whom to bring in for questioning about the bodies in the stream now," Wong said.

"Bodies? In the stream?" Julie paled further.

Jake and Sophie hadn't told the Weathersbys about the remains found in the roadside ditch, particularly the corpse that looked so much like Julie's. Providing her any information might contaminate the police procedure of her case. But an idea was beginning to nibble at Jake's mind.

He squeezed Sophie's hand and whispered to her. "I've heard of the Chang crime family. Were you calling someone about that name when we heard it at the Weathersbys' suite?"

Sophie nodded, her gaze still on the interview. "My friend Lei Texeira has had dealings with the Changs in the past. I called her to ask about him. She didn't know anything except that Terence is the grandson of Healani Chang, the head of the family."

"What if there is some kind of connection between Rayme, Webb, this ditch killer, and the crime family? Could they even be connected with Chernobiac and that black SUV we saw?"

Sophie finally looked away from the interview to meet his gaze squarely.

Jake hated how pale her full, beautiful mouth was, the ashen tone of her skin, the clammy coldness of her hand. But vibrancy flowed into her as their gazes held, and excitement chased the depression shadows from her eyes.

"I think you might be onto something, Jake. We already know what Julie has to say. Let's go talk to Chernobiac. I don't know how, exactly, but my intuition tells me he's the connecting link."

"Finally. Your gut and my gut are on the same page," Jake said as they pushed their chairs back and stood.

Sophie gave a tiny smile as she passed him. "That's an unpleasant visual."

He bit his lip to hold in a laugh, and the tiny pain felt good. *They were going to solve this case.*

CHAPTER FORTY-ONE

SOPHIE WAS glad they'd taken the dogs back to the motel after their interview at the hotel with the Weathersbys. The dogs had been exercised and fed, and would be fine until they got back. She felt like she had reentered her body as they quietly left the interview observation booth, exited the building, and got into the Jeep.

She didn't know exactly what the connection was between the disparate-seeming elements of the investigation, but she felt that Chernobiac was a key as soon as Jake said it.

Jake turned on the Jeep and the energy of the hunt banished the dregs of her latest skirmish with depression. Gratitude filled her that he had reached out to her, had taken her hand. Now, as he gripped the wheel and pulled out onto the road, she reached over and squeezed the muscle of his arm. "I am glad you are no longer angry with me."

"I don't like it when you shut me out, Sophie." Jake's eyes were the color of iron as he gave her a quick glance. "But I'm determined to respect your signals from now on. When you pull away from me, I am going to let you do it."

That should have relieved her. Instead, Sophie felt a wave of anxiety. She turned and stared out the window. "Space" was what she wanted, wasn't it? For Jake to respect her, not crowd her and demand more than she was willing to give?

Jake guided the Jeep onto the main thoroughfare toward Volcanoes Park. As they moved out of Hilo's congested traffic, he gripped and then released the steering wheel, clearing his throat. "I find I'm not really okay with 'partners with benefits' after all. I thought you were taking Alika's call and talking to him last night. The whole thing made me kind of crazy. I needed to get my head straight, so I took the dogs for a run and thought about the situation." He navigated a traffic snarl, gunning through a yellow light. "I don't like secrets, and walls, and other people being between us. And the more we are together and the closer we become, the less I like it. So, I guess we better end the physical part of our relationship before my jealousy gets to be even more of a turn off."

"I wasn't talking to Alika last night." Sophie concentrated on the one thing she could respond to clearly. Irrational anxiety thickened her voice and constricted her throat.

"I realized that when I came in to change and heard you were speaking in another language. Far as I know, that guy is just another American. But I realized that it wasn't just the possibility that it was him. It was all the secrets and lies and other people that are in your life."

"I haven't lied to you. I just haven't told you everything, and I cannot. And I do not foresee a time when I will be able to. There are forces at work, things in play that do not concern you." Sophie's lips felt stiff and she hated her stilted words.

"Everything about *you* concerns *me*, Sophie. The fact that you don't understand that, and that it's not the same for you . . . well, that's what I'm talking about." Jake's voice was flat and harsh.

"Please don't . . ." She couldn't find words. Fear was choking her. "You matter to me, Jake. I very much enjoyed the things we did together. Physically. I don't want that to end." She twisted her fingers together in her lap. "I don't want to lose you."

Jake reached over and picked up her knotted hands. He kissed the back of her knuckles, and the heat of his tongue gave her a zing. "You won't lose me. But we're not having sex anymore until you're willing to say I'm your guy. Stand up in front of others and say it. Choose me over Alika, and any other contenders that might be out there that I don't know about—dudes who speak lots of languages and drive fancy cars. They're out there. I can smell them."

He didn't know about the Ghost, could he? There was no way he knew that her former lover was still very much alive and in the background.

Sophie fumbled for words. "I have tried to be as honest with you as I can. I am not ready to be in a relationship, to declare myself as you have asked. The last time I did that, my lover was murdered." That would be all that Jake knew. The truth was even worse. "I respect that you need more from me. I'm sorry that I can't give it right now. I wish you were okay with 'partners with benefits.'" She turned her hands to grasp his, and lifted his fingers to her lips for a soft kiss, sucking lightly on his knuckles, feeling him shudder. "Let me know if you change your mind. I may close my drapes and lock my door when the darkness falls over me, but I found your method of therapy most effective. I would welcome such an intervention again, whenever you might choose to implement it."

Jake groaned. "Damn you, woman. You aren't going to make this easy for me, are you?"

"I cannot. The situation is what it is. Secrets will continue, and I am ambivalent about involvement. But I have been as honest as I can be, and I will continue to be. I respect you too much for anything else."

"If I could bang my head on something right now, I would," Jake muttered, and swore.

Sophie was too sad to savor any triumph in their little battle of trying to see who could affect the other more—right now, it seemed too much like they were both the losers. So she used the remaining time as they drove to check her Glock's magazine and strap on her shoulder holster.

They reached the turn off for Ocean View Terrace, and turned up the windy, two-lane highway to Chernobiac's abode. This time, they drove straight up to the driveway and parked in front of the house in the waning evening light.

The sensor light bloomed on, illuminating a scene much like the previous one when they had gone to search the house, but this time, Chernobiac's big pickup truck was parked in the driveway, blocking in his fancy street rod.

"I haven't really thought of how we're going to approach this guy," Jake said, checking his weapon.

"We should just play it by ear, as Americans say," Sophie replied.

"Now you're singing my song." Jake was really handsome when he smiled.

CHAPTER FORTY-TWO

"I DON'T THINK Chernobiac is violent." Sophie rammed her clip back into the weapon and stowed it in her harness. "But it is good to be prepared for anything. I'm surprised he hasn't come out to see who is setting off the motion light."

"Yes, that concerns me." Jake peered up at the brightly lit house. There was still no movement from inside. Maybe the guy was glued to his computers. A bomb could go off and gamer dudes like that wouldn't notice.

"Let's do this." Jake got out of the Jeep and slammed the door, wishing they both were wearing Kevlar and had a backup team. "Chernobiac!" Jake called, as they reached the garage. "It's Jake and Sophie! Come out, we just want to talk."

No answer.

Jake reached the back door and banged on it. "Chernobiac!"

Jake grasped the handle and turned. *Not locked.*

He glanced over at Sophie and met her wide eyes. They both drew their weapons. Jake cracked the door and bellowed in his best military voice, "Chernobiac!"

No answer.

Jake pushed the door wide, keeping covered behind the jamb. The back door opened into the brightly lit kitchen.

A pair of feet were visible in the hallway leading off of the kitchen.

Sophie swore from behind him, something long and involved in one of those languages that sounded like water running over stones.

Jake stepped cautiously into the kitchen, weapon ready. "Let's check the house and then call it in."

Jake avoided looking at the body for the moment as they split up outside the kitchen, checking each room. The place was empty and undisturbed, looking much as they'd seen it last except for Chernobiac's plump body, face down, two bullet holes in his back and a blood pool spreading on the linoleum.

"This didn't happen long ago." Jake squatted beside the body.

Sophie called in the discovery directly to Freitan as Jake pressed two fingers to the man's neck, feeling for a pulse. The skin was still warm, and deep inside the extra tissue, Jake felt a sluggish heartbeat.

"He's still alive!" Jake pulled out his phone and called 911 even as Sophie changed her report to Freitan to include the new information. They waited for the first responders, and it wasn't long before an ambulance bumped up the driveway.

Jake met the EMTs at the door. "Gunshot wound. Two in the back. Looks bad."

The paramedics nodded and ran inside.

A few minutes later, Freitan and Wong pulled up. Freitan raked Jake with an irritable glance. "Care to tell us what brought you out here? We thought you were in the observation booth until we went to lock up after the interview and saw you were gone."

"Just had a gut feeling that Chernobiac and the ditch killer are somehow connected," Jake said.

"We thought we'd come out and talk to Chernobiac," Sophie said. "But it looks like someone else got here first. Cypher might have been someone's loose end, as they say."

"He was someone's something, that's for sure." Freitan jerked her head at Wong. "Let's do a quick search. This house is now a crime scene. We might as well use you two since you were out here, poking around. Get some gloves on and let's get to work."

Jake and Sophie exchanged a glance. There was no getting away from being roped into helping search at this point, though neither of them expected to find anything—they had tossed the place not long ago, after all, and whoever had tied off the loose end that was Chernobiac had likely taken any evidence he'd had.

"If there was anything, it would be on Chernobiac's computer." Sophie headed into the bedroom and called out to them. "It's gone." She reemerged. "I don't know what else might be found here."

"We need something tying him to the bodies. To something! Or maybe his murder is unrelated," Wong said, slamming shut a kitchen drawer in frustration.

"Unlikely." Freitan lifted a piece of carpet to examine the floor below. "I think Chernobiac has something to do with the missing persons, and now we've found some of them in the ditch. Who put them there? That's what we've got to find out."

"The next people to interview should be Webb and Rayme," Sophie said, as the four of them ransacked Chernobiac's living room in a replay of a few days ago. "I think those two might know something about this."

"What could they possibly know? They are barely functioning tweakers," Wong said. "We talked to them. They seem like opportunistic bottom feeders, rolling tourists for drug money."

Sophie glanced at Jake, and catching her cue, he groped to explain the idea that had been forming and had brought them out on this call.

"Here's a scenario," Jake said. "I just want us to try it on for size. So, here's how it goes: Webb and Rayme identify marks. People who have resources and can be shaken down. They are in cahoots with someone who does the killing, after Webb and Rayme turn them loose in the ditch area. The killer does his thing—or, Rayme and Webb are the killers, and the story Julie Weathersby is telling is made

up for some reason. This guy has some connection to the Changs."
Jake straightened, dangling a potato chip bag between his fingertips.
"Stay with me for a minute. It just seems way too handy that Terence
Chang happened along to rescue Julie Weathersby. Maybe he's the
killer and decided not to off her? I don't know. But I do know that
anytime you have a crime empire, you've got people who need to be
gotten rid of. Dealers who rip you off. Suppliers who take bribes.
Meth makers who sample the merch." Jake dropped the empty bag
into a nearby trash can and tipped his head back to stare at the swirly
drywall markings on the ceiling and scratched his chin, considering.
"Chernobiac either gets wind of this operation, or is a part of it. He
shakes down the families of the missing for ransom or reward
money. He deflects them with misinformation and keeps them busy
and occupied. Meanwhile, the bodies are hidden in the ditch, buried
in the jungle, wherever. I suspect you're going to find a lot more in
that area in the coming weeks."

Jake looked around at the detectives and Sophie. Everyone had
paused in the search and was staring right back. Even Freitan was
paying attention. "Anyway, things start to come apart when pretty
little Julie Weathersby gets away from our killer or is spared, which-
ever it is. For whatever reason, maybe because she's a pretty face, or
doesn't fit the profile, or maybe will draw too much heat . . . crime
family heir apparent Terence Chang rescues her. He comes up
smelling like a rose, which could be part of his agenda."

Freitan planted her fists on her hips. "That's a pretty shaky
theory. Where's the motive? What would we need to make it all hang
together?"

"Well, we already have a pile of possible trophies from the back
of Chernobiac's computer. Where did he get those? Who are they
from? If we could match them to the bodies or the missing, we'd
have a better idea of what his role was. But he had those items and
the cash we saw. He posted that ad, ran that website, and was solic-
iting families of the missing. He had some part, I'm sure of it. And
someone tried to kill him for it," Jake said.

"I could find out what his role was if I had his computer," Sophie said. "I tried to copy his hard drive when we were here last, but I didn't have time to get the whole thing, and I haven't had time to go through any of the data I've collected. Rather than take more time for this search, I'd like to go back to the station and do what I do best, which is dig for background information. Maybe I can make a connection between the missing and the physical descriptions from the bodies, get a preliminary guess at their identities by cross-checking dates on which people disappeared with the recovered bodies. And if I could identify the bodies, even approximately, I could look for connections between them and the Changs. There might even be something useful I can get off the partial information I have from Chernobiac's hard drive."

"Do it." Freitan flicked a hand at Sophie. "We'll bring Jake back. Get out of here, computer girl, and find us a thread that ties all this altogether."

CHAPTER FORTY-THREE

Sophie sat down in the air-conditioned coolness of the Hilo PD's computer room. She had yet to find anyone else working in the dilapidated old room when she was there, and she preferred it that way. After the emotional roller-coaster she'd been on, settling in front of her laptop was the best moment of the day so far.

Sophie plugged in her headphones, turned on her music, and cracked her knuckles. She plugged the square black write blocker external hard drive into her laptop's port and imported the data she had been able to harvest from Chernobiac's computer to her own for viewing. She searched through the contents, setting DAVID's parameters to sift for any labeling terms that might help her detect useful information.

While Chernobiac's info was being data mined, she ran a comparison between the database of the missing persons and the estimated date of death posted by the medical examiner on the bodies they'd recovered from the ditch. Those could be within days or even weeks of each other, since not all the missing were reported, but she might be able to match some of the missing information to the bodies, given the approximate height, weight and hair color of the remains.

Looking at the profiles, she was able to come up with three possible matches. They were certainly unrelated as far as type, with age, gender and ethnicity all differing. All of the possible dead were local Hilo residents, not pretty, rich young tourists like Julie.

Maybe Julie was the anomaly, not the "type." Maybe the man with the knife was more of a straightforward assassin; but in Julie's case, he had been preparing to "enjoy what he was about to do."

Running with Jake's theory that the bodies were somehow related to the Chang crime family business, Sophie set DAVID to work coming up with deep background on the possible matches.

A few minutes later she could confirm that all of the bodies she'd tentatively matched to identities were petty criminals with records. Though she was unable to find any direct connections yet, it was a strong possibility that the four bodies found in the ditch could have been part of the Chang empire, disposed of for one reason or another, or preyed upon by the killer for that reason.

Sophie glanced up at the clock. Two hours had already passed. She aggregated the information she'd gathered on the bodies, forwarded it to Freitan and Wong's email, and turned her attention to Chernobiac's hard drive.

DAVID had mined the data she had for red flag keywords, and come up with a file named Gamestop.

Chernobiac probably thought he was being clever. Hopefully he would wake up from his injuries and be willing to cut a deal with Wong and Freitan to confirm all of this, but Gamestop consisted of rows of initials, dates and numbers that looked to Sophie like names and payout amounts. She printed that file too, her mind churning.

She picked up her phone and called Freitan. "Detective, I have information from Chernobiac's computer that seems to verify that he was engaged in blackmail. There are initials but I don't know who they belong to. I worry about Rayme and Webb now. If they were a part of this, if they knew any of the blackmail scheme or had a part in it somehow and someone is tying up loose ends, they might be in danger."

"They're locked up tight in county jail," Freitan said. "But I'll call over and have them moved to solitary. We're still out here at Chernobiac's crime scene but we'll go interview them."

"Can I meet you there?"

"For what purpose? No. The interview room at the jail is small; too many of us will spook them. Besides, isn't your client already identified, and alive?"

"Let Jake go to the interview, then."

"We don't even know that Rayme and Webb are involved." Freitan was getting balky.

"Perhaps you'd like me to close my computer and walk away from this case," Sophie said coolly. "After all, our client has been found. We have no further role in this investigation."

A brief pause. "Ah, no. We'd like you to continue, please," Freitan said, mincing her words as if they pained her.

"We are on the Weathersby family's payroll through the end of the week," Sophie said. "I will endeavor to maximize the effectiveness of my work, and Jake can attend the interview with Rayme and Webb. Thanks."

Sophie ended the call, and opened another window in DAVID.

This time, she plugged in the mysterious name of her mother's organization. It was time to find out more about the Yām Khûmkạn.

CHAPTER FORTY-FOUR

WONG AND FREITAN ended the search and summoned Jake to the SUV. "What's the emergency? I wasn't quite done with Chernobiac's bathroom. Not that I was having any luck finding anything incriminating in there."

"Your partner called from the station. She confirmed part of the theory that we've been talking about. We need to go to the county jail ASAP and interview Rayme and Webb."

"Excellent." Jake rubbed his hands together. "What's the connection?"

"She found evidence of blackmail payments on Chernobiac's hard drive," Freitan said. "But there's still no clear connection to Webb and Rayme; she just thought we should isolate and question them in case they are involved."

Jake grunted affirmatively as he settled in the back seat and texted Sophie. *So you got intel on Webb and Rayme?*

"I'm busy, Jake."

At least she was replying. *"Keep me in the loop, partner."* Jake didn't like how even small exclusions felt big to him. So far, he wasn't doing great at detachment.

"Sorry. I'm focusing on trying to find a connection to Rayme and

Webb, and sifting for whoever took the cash and drives a black SUV. No luck so far."

"Ok. I'm psyched to go to the interview. Thought Freitan & Wong would try to ditch me."

"They did. I pressured them that we only have a couple days of pay left and we have to make them count."

"Well, thanks for that. See you when we get back. We can figure out how to wrap things up from there." The thought of leaving the island and saying goodbye to Sophie curdled Jake's innards into a restless ball.

"Yes," was Sophie's terse reply.

"Sophie thinks whoever killed Chernobiac may also want to silence Rayme and Webb," Jake said aloud.

"That's why we've called ahead and asked for those two to be moved to solitary, though we still have no evidence the cases are connected," Freitan replied.

Hawaii County Correctional Center was a lumpish gray cube surrounded by a heavy chain link fence, topped with coils of razor wire. Palm trees at the four corners of the rectangular area attempted a tropical feel that fell short.

Jake and the detectives got out of the SUV in the parking area marked Employees, and the two showed their badges and Jake his ID at the entry point. "Here to see prisoners Holly Rayme and Jim Webb," Freitan said.

The guard at the booth looked up sharply. "Step inside the sally port, please." The three did so, and the door immediately locked with a heavy clang.

Guards entered and frisked them roughly. Freitan scowled. "Hey! What the hell?"

The corrections officers said nothing, and Jake kept his mouth shut too. Whatever was going on was higher than his pay grade. Once they had all been cleared, the COs left them in the sally port. One of them addressed Freitan over his shoulder. "We are running your prints and IDs."

Freitan put her hands on her hips, pacing the tiny area. "Something's gone down involving our perps. This is not SOP, things are usually pretty casual around here."

Watching Freitan do that relieved Jake of his need to do the same. Moments later the inner door opened, and admitted them to a hallway. They were met by the warden himself, a slender man with a transparent tonsure of hair and a deep, leathery tan. "Warden Scott Biles. Were you the ones to call in the warning about Webb and Rayme?" Biles asked.

"Yes, we were. We're here to interview them about our case," Wong said. "A witness they may be connected to was almost killed, so we thought to be proactive and have them isolated."

"Ah. Well, there's been an unfortunate incident. You can speak to Holly Rayme in the infirmary."

"And Jim Webb?" Freitan still had her hands on her hips.

"Webb is dead. Killed in an altercation on the yard this afternoon. We are following increased security protocol and conducting a full internal investigation."

Jake tightened his jaw to keep from showing any expression. Freitan swore, and Wong shook his head. "We are still seeking a solid connection between this couple and the witness who died. I guess there must be one."

Jake followed the two detectives as the warden led them through a series of badly lit corridors smelling of Lysol. They eventually reached the infirmary area.

They observed Holly Rayme from one side of a glass window threaded with a grid of wire. She appeared unconscious, her thin, sallow face swollen and empurpled. Her hands were bandaged, lying quiet on the crisp white sheet.

"She was stabbed with a crude implement and beaten. We had sent a corrections officer to take her to solitary, but he didn't get there in time," Warden Biles said.

"I'll say," Freitan growled. "Is she in any shape to answer our questions?"

"We asked her who attacked her. She said it was a group of people, she didn't know or couldn't identify who—in effect, she refused to answer. She's stable. You should be able to talk to her just fine. Whether or not she will answer is another question."

Jake slid in behind the detectives as they entered the room, trying to stay unobtrusive and in the background. He folded his arms across his chest and leaned against the wall as the detectives pulled up plastic chairs beside the bed. He didn't want to get sent out and cut off from the investigation at such a critical point. He slid his phone out of his pocket and thumbed on the Record feature to capture the interview for Sophie to hear later.

"Holly." Wong was the one to gently shake the woman's shoulder. Rayme's eyes flew open in alarm, and Wong patted her arm gently. "Didn't mean to scare you. Detectives Wong and Freitan. We talked with you when you were first arrested, remember?"

Rayme's gaze flickered around the room and landed on Jake. "I recognize you." Her voice was sandpapery thin.

Jake inclined his head. "Sorry you've been injured. We were concerned that you might be in danger."

Freitan shot Jake a look, telling him to back off. "We are here to help," she said smoothly, turning to Rayme. "Tell us what happened."

Rayme plucked at the white sheet covering her lap. "I'm not sure. It all went down so fast."

"We had called down to the jail, requesting that you and Webb be transferred to solitary for your own protection after we got new information that might involve you. Webb turned up dead, and you were attacked, both within the same hour." Freitan wasn't pulling any punches.

Rayme's eyes filled and overflowed. She covered her mouth with her hand. "Jimmy is dead?"

"Afraid so." Wong patted her arm again. "They got to him before he could be pulled from gen pop."

"And the reason we called over here was that we thought you

might be in trouble, since someone whacked Chernobiac out at his house," Freitan said.

"Oh God!" Rayme rubbed her eyes with fisted hands. Her voice trembled. "I'm the only one left."

Jake was impressed with how matter-of-factly Freitan had delivered that piece of news, as if expecting Rayme knew Chernobiac— when they still had no evidence that she did. The detectives exchanged a quick glance with Jake. *Now they were getting somewhere.*

"We really want to protect you," Wong kept up the arm rub and soft voice. "What can you tell us about who is trying to kill you?"

"I can't. No." Rayme opened those childish fists and covered her mouth with both hands, as if to keep the truth from emerging. Her voice came out muffled. "I can't tell you anything. He'll kill me if I do."

"Kind of seems like he's going to kill you even if you don't," Frietan said dryly.

They waited a bit for this to sink in.

Sure enough, Rayme dropped her hands and clutched the sheet. "You have to offer me a deal."

"Don't have to offer you anything," Freitan said. "We can just leave you here, and let nature take its course. Makes no never mind to us. One more dead tweaker is one less for us to worry about."

"But don't you want to know what has been going on with Chernobiac?" Rayme's voice rose an octave or two.

"Either you want to talk with us or you don't." The detective studied her short, plum-colored nails, and frowned at a chip she saw on one of them.

"Then you have to protect me. Because he will kill me to shut me up. And you need me to put him away." Rayme's eyes were wide with fear.

"Protection can be arranged," Wong assured her. He turned to Freitan, frowning in exaggerated concern. "Detective Freitan, we have to take care of this poor girl."

Jake worried that Wong was laying it on a little thick, but Rayme's head nodded like a marionette. "Yes! I'll tell you everything if you just make sure he can't get to me."

Freitan shifted in the cheap plastic chair and brushed imaginary lint off her black jeans. "All right. We'll see what we can do. I'm going to record this conversation for future reference." She took out her phone and turned on a Record feature, stating the people present, the date, time, and location, and she Mirandized Holly Rayme.

Once the formalities had been observed, Rayme was in a rush to tell her story. "We had a side hustle going on. Me, Jimmy, Akane Chang, and Paul Chernobiac. It was working great until that Weathersby girl messed things up."

"Side hustle? As opposed to . . . some other kind of hustle?" Freitan's eyebrows made inquisitive arches.

"As opposed to the Chang family's main sources of income. I know it isn't news to you that the Changs are heavily involved in prostitution, gambling, and drugs," Rayme said. "The cops are always hassling them. We got to know Akane because we worked in the Changs' meth factory for a while. Akane is their main enforcer. One of the cousins. He is . . ." Rayme gave a theatrical shudder. "He is not right in the head."

Jake kept his face serious with an effort. Rayme obviously considered herself just fine in her mental capacity. *Apparently insanity had degrees.*

"So, it was a side hustle in that . . . no one else knew about it?" Wong asked.

"Yeah. Paul and Akane met gaming and they cooked it up; it was their own private gig. Later, we got involved."

"How did the hustle work?" Freitan asked.

"Paul did some accounting for the Changs and a lot of online stuff. He identified possible marks for Akane, and later us, through a rideshare company that the Changs have connections with. We were just supposed to rob the folks without getting caught, or embarrass the marks in such a way they didn't report what happened. Jimmy and I had a couple of cons worked out." She looked down and plucked at the sheet again. Jake could well imagine the compromising positions they captured their prey with. "We would shake them down and leave them, or sometimes we'd hold onto them, party with them. It was all pretty fun." Her sharp yellowish teeth, bared in a smile, reminded Jake of a coyote at a kill. "Akane is an enforcer for the family, but he likes his job a little too much. He decided to disappear some of the marks after Chernobiac had shaken down their families for ransom."

Rayme paused, clearly reveling in having their full attention as she preened a bit, combing her straggling hair with her fingers. "Can I get some water?"

Wong handed her a cup with a straw, and she took a sip before continuing. "Jimmy and I had a smaller part in things. We took orders from Paul or Akane. We were boots on the ground to take care of the prisoners, who we kept out at Travelers' Rest, and we were always looking to find more marks we could roll." She took another sip of water, and belched. "Julie Weathersby was ours. She wasn't posting on social media or any of the usual ways that Chernobiac would identify a mark. But once we realized she had super rich parents, we knew we better not let Akane have his fun with her—it would draw too much heat for her to turn up dead. The kinds of people we got the best results with were from middle-class backgrounds. Usually they had some kind of drug problem or something that made them vulnerable. We would do like we did with the Weathersby girl; cozy up, roll them for money, and Chernobiac would contact their families and collect bribes or ransom, and then we'd turn them loose on that stretch of road."

"So you turned victims loose in the jungle without clothes or shoes, knowing that a man who enjoyed killing was going to hunt them down," Freitan said flatly.

For the first time, real shame darkened Rayme's eyes. She squirmed and looked away. "It didn't start out that way. And then, by the time it was that way, we didn't know how to get out of . . . what was happening. But I knew things had to end when Akane got a look at Julie while we were camping together—he came to Volcanoes and stopped by to check her out. I knew he was going to do terrible things to her, and I liked Julie."

Jake flashed to the pretty young woman's open, happy smile. "It seems you grew a conscience."

"And that's a good thing, considering that at this point you are part of a conspiracy to commit serial murder," Freitan said.

Rayme crumpled the sheet in her fists. "We had had enough. Julie dead was going to draw too much attention. So Jimmy called Terence Chang. Anonymously. Told him where and when Julie could be found, and that Akane would be after her."

Freitan's alert gaze seemed to crackle with energy. "Why did he choose Terence Chang? Why not just tip off the police anonymously?"

"Because we didn't want the cops involved. We thought that Terence could control Akane, get him to leave Julie alone. Terence is the head of the family now that Healani Chang died."

"He appears to be going straight," Wong said, frowning. "We haven't been able to connect him to any criminal activity."

Holly Rayme snorted. "Terence wouldn't be much of a crime lord if you could bust him, would he? But trust me, he's at the top of the food chain."

Jake glanced from Wong to Freitan. If this was true, Holly Rayme had just become a very valuable witness indeed.

CHAPTER FORTY-FIVE

Sᴏᴘʜɪᴇ ᴅᴜɢ deep in her online research into her mother's secret organization, confident in the multiple VPNs she had set up that protected her identity and location. The police department's firewalls were a final layer of obfuscation; though she'd hardly found those effective against her own penetrations, having the location end up at Hilo PD would keep anyone from finding her individually.

There wasn't much available about the Yām Khûmkạn online, and Sophie had expected that. If this was a secret organization, then having a website that advertised their services would hardly be smart.

She applied search keywords to DAVID's parameters and got up to do a quick series of sun salutations on densely carpeted floor, limbering up muscles left stiff from sitting too long. She did jumping jacks and push-ups and was completing a series of stomach crunches when her computer emitted a tone, signaling that it had found all available matches.

Freshly energized, Sophie sat back down, put on her headphones, and delved in.

The Yām Khûmkạn was referred to in various articles and books as a "secret military police" a "black ops spy organization" and "the strong-arm gangster organization protecting the elite of Thailand."

Recruitment was unknown. Training was unknown. Length of service, rate of pay, even a clear description of how the organization was set up was unknown—but its existence was confirmed.

Sophie dug deeper, going into the untraceable posts of the dark net. This search yielded more. She was even able to find a site that cataloged coups and assassinations credited to the clandestine group.

So her mother wasn't a raving lunatic—but then, Sophie had never believed that she was.

But she had hoped that, in reaching out, Pim Wat had been making an effort to truly connect with her daughter. *She'd been wrong*. No such love existed.

Sophie had to tell her father.

But how? What untold number of security breaches had occurred because the ambassador had been an unwitting pawn in her mother's schemes?

Perhaps what Sophie needed to do was get more information from and about Pim Wat and the Yām Khûmkạn. Pretend to go along with recruitment and penetrate the organization. See how far the security breach with her father went, what the group's agenda was, and break the news to the ambassador when she had something real to share.

Ellie Smith, the intelligent and capable Secret Service agent she had worked with another time when her own security breach had threatened her father, might be a good place to start to come up with a plan.

But even telling an agent Sophie trusted that she'd been approached could have huge ramifications. If Sophie broke silence now on the subject, there was no telling what the Secret Service would do. They might lock her up, believing that she was involved with the organization. Her life would be scrutinized. Picked apart. She would be detained, questioned. She'd lose the momentum she'd fought for so hard in charting her own destiny.

She had to plan her next steps very carefully.

The Ghost might be someone who could help her navigate this minefield.

No. The thought of more involvement with Connor tied her stomach in knots; she couldn't be indebted to him. She was already sick about losing intimacy with Jake, and missing Alika's solid friendship and support as more secrets grew between them like mushrooms after a rain. She couldn't tell any of this to her law enforcement friends, Marcella and Lei.

She had no one to talk to about this situation but Dr. Wilson.

She'd forgotten her appointment! Sophie glanced at the clock. She should have met the psychologist over an hour ago.

Sophie texted an apology to the psychologist with a request for a reschedule. Clearly, she needed a break to clear her thoughts. "I need exercise," she muttered.

Sophie closed up her computer and detached her headphones.

She could walk the dogs at the park, stretch her legs and get a cup of tea. She texted Jake. *"I'm taking the dogs for a run at Hilo Bay. Let me know when and where to pick you up when you are done working with the detectives."*

She waited a moment for a reply, but there was none. Likely he didn't have phone reception inside the correctional facility, but he would get her message after he was out of the building.

She would have felt better getting a response from Jake. Hopefully nothing was wrong.

THE DOGS BOUNCED and pranced on their leashes as Sophie set out from the Banyan Tree Motel. It felt great to get into the rhythm of running, her heartbeat a thunder in her ears echoed by the smack of her shoes on the sidewalk encircling the park. The dogs pulled at their leashes, one in each hand, playful and excited. The waning light of afternoon slanted the shadows of the coconut palms across the velvety green grass.

Sophie did a lap of the entire park, beginning to limber up as the dogs settled down, their restless energy from being cooped up in the motel dissipating. She passed the bench where her mother had surprised her.

What was she going to do about that?

If Sophie did go in deeper, contact her mother, let her think she was intrigued by the idea of being a part of the Yām Khûmkạn, *she had to talk to the Secret Service first and get the idea approved.* They'd never believe she wasn't a part of it if she went to them later.

But what if they turned her over to the CIA, or even, Jupiter forbid it, the FBI? What if Sophie had to deal with an investigation, and her friends came to know about it?

Her reverie was shattered abruptly as a van roared up onto the sidewalk in front of her, stopping with a screech of brakes. The side door flew open to reveal a dark-skinned man dressed in fatigues with a ski mask on, pointing a silenced pistol at her.

CHAPTER FORTY-SIX

"FOUL GOITER ON A LICE-RIDDEN YAK!" Sophie pulled the dogs back and plunged to the side. She'd been too distracted to see the vehicle coming!

"Get in the van!" The masked man yelled.

"Screw you!" Sophie yelled, reversing direction as fast as she could with the excited dogs fighting her.

The gun spat and Tank yelped in pain, pressing against her legs. Ginger barked aggressively, straining toward the armed assailant.

"I'll nail these dogs if you don't get in. Right now," Ski Mask said.

Sophie squatted, pulling Tank against her to check him over. He'd been grazed, a bloody furrow dug along his back just above the tail. *"Son of a poxy whore!"* Sophie screamed. Red rage blurred her vision. "What kind of a monster are you?"

"The kind that knows how to get a job done." The man took aim at the dog's big square head. "Get in, bitch. We're going for a ride."

Sophie whirled to look around the park. No one was nearby enough to see the drama playing out on the quiet side of the park; old men fished off the pier, children played with their families on the jungle gym equipment, mynah birds hopped on the grass. *And like an idiot, she hadn't brought her weapon.*

"Time's up." Ski Mask fired again, and this time, Tank went down at Sophie's feet with a pathetic yelp that froze her heart. The man swung the gun to point at Ginger. "Want me to do this one next?"

Sophie howled in rage and horror. Her mind shut off as she let go of the dogs' leashes and charged forward. She leaped, bowling the man over backward into the van. She got her hands around his thick throat, wrapped her thighs around his body, and choked him, blind to anything but snuffing out his life.

Immediately the vehicle reversed off the sidewalk, throwing Sophie off the gunman to tumble toward the front of the van, rolling over its bare, corrugated metal flooring with the assailant right on top of her. She scrambled to get out from under him, only to have the vehicle lurch forward, peeling out and tossing her and the dog killer into each other as they rolled backward.

All was a blur of punching and kicking as they rolled around in the empty van as it took corners at a wild pace, banging Sophie and her attacker into the bare metal walls. Sophie finally got an arm around the assailant's throat and pulled him backward in a yoke chokehold, using her hip for leverage—but Ski Mask was still armed. Sophie felt the sting of a blade against her lower back. As she squeezed, the blade dug in further.

She was going to die faster than she could choke him if he pushed that knife all the way into her kidney.

Sophie loosened her grip. The burning pressure of the stabbing blade released. She felt the hot warmth of blood sear her lower back.

Her attacker rolled away as she let go, grabbing his gun up off the floor and training it on her. "Crazy bitch," he wheezed. "I want to do you right now, but there are better things in store for you."

Sophie glared at Ski Mask, panting. "I'm going to kill you for what you did to my dog."

"I can still put a bullet in you. Where do you want it? Leg, arm, or shoulder?"

"Chill out, man," the driver yelled from the front seat. "We're almost to the drop zone. You can throw her out of the van so Chang can have his fun. Did you think this was going to be an easy grab? No. You knew she was a fighter."

Sophie stared into slitted eyes revealed by the ski mask, twisted askew by their struggles. *Maybe she could still take him.*

"Don't even think about it," Ski Mask growled. "I'll gut-shoot you and enjoy watching you die."

Sophie had to ready herself for whatever came next. Her phone had fallen out of the pocket of her hoodie; she could feel it, out of sight and just beneath her hip. *Maybe she could get a call out for help.*

CHAPTER FORTY-SEVEN

FREITAN AND WONG got as much information as they could out of Rayme before the nurse finally shooed them away. The detectives arranged for an extra layer of protection with a guard inside the jail. Once they exited the phone dead zone of the jail building, Jake and Wong waited as Freitan worked her phone setting up meetings with the DA for the following day. She also called Witness Protection to consult with the Marshals, assuring that they would protect the woman until she could testify about Chang.

"A bird in the hand," Freitan said with satisfaction as she slid her phone into her pocket and started the SUV. "Always best to get all the info you can out of a witness when they're willing to talk."

Jake nodded agreement, and checked his own phone. He read a text from Sophie about going running in the park, and his heart did a little flip.

She didn't know about Chang, but he might well know about her, and all the connections she was putting together about him! The Changs had eyes and ears everywhere in Hawaii. Sophie shouldn't be running around alone until Akane Chang was locked up.

He phoned Sophie from the back seat of the SUV—the revelations they had uncovered were too involved to describe in a text. Her phone rang, eventually dumping into voicemail. "Please don't go out without me. I have new information on the case. We need to take some precautions," Jake said into the recording, and ended the call.

"You leaving a message for your partner?" Wong asked from the front seat.

"Yeah. She was taking the dogs for a run in the park."

"Sophie's the key to this case in a lot of ways. She's made the connections between the bodies and the Changs, and she has the info from Chernobiac's computer. I want to talk with her ASAP," Freitan said.

Jake leaned forward between the seats as the SUV got underway. "This is our last couple of days on the job, now that Julie Weathersby has been found."

"Sorry to hear that. You two have been a huge help," Wong said.

"And we want all the data Sophie has been able to put together on the missing persons and anything else that woman has found," Freitan said. "She's quite an effective investigator."

Jake felt a swell of pride in Sophie. Praise from Kamani Freitan was hard-earned. "That she is."

Back at the station, the watch officer raised a hand to the detectives and greeted Jake. "Your partner told me to have you call her. She will come pick you up when she's back from the park."

"How long ago was that?" Jake asked.

"About an hour."

Standing in the entry area, Jake tried Sophie's cell phone again.

This time she picked up, but he heard nothing after his greeting but some muffled background sounds, then Sophie's voice came through, unfamiliarly hoarse with anger. "I'm still going to pay you back for killing my dog."

A man's voice, echoing and tinny. "Not if I do you first. Like I said, where do you want it? Leg, arm, or shoulder? I can do all three, but that would cut down on the fun later."

Jake's heart went into overdrive. Another voice, too distant to make out, yelled something else.

Jake hit *Mute* on his phone so Sophie's end of the line didn't pick up any sound. He ran into the station after the detectives. "Wong! Freitan! Something's happened to Sophie!"

The two stopped near their cubicle and clustered around the phone as Jake put it on speaker. More cursing and back-and-forth came through the cell. The audio was rendered hollow and distant, vibrating with the roar of an engine in the background.

Freitan looked up, eyes wide. "Someone's got her."

"And it sounds like something happened to one of our dogs. I'm guessing this went down at the park, and she's in a vehicle of some kind," Jake said.

"Let's get down to the park and see," Freitan said. The detectives headed for the doors at a jog as Wong radioed their plans to Dispatch. Jake ran in their wake, the phone still on speaker.

If Sophie could, she would give him a clue to where she was.

"I'm going to try to track her phone." He thumbed to the *Find My Phone* tracking app he'd loaded. He'd plugged Sophie's number into it some time ago, but had never used it. A map popped up, showing a moving beacon. "They are headed out of Hilo in the direction of Volcanoes Park."

And then, the signal was lost. The phone went black, and the map disappeared.

Jake snarled in anguish as he jumped into the SUV behind the detectives. "We lost her!"

CHAPTER FORTY-EIGHT

SOPHIE KEPT her gaze on the man's face as the van drove, projecting all the hatred she felt for him. She cursed in Thai, a low monotone aimed to intimidate. *"Slimy bloated stench of demons! Chief among the underworld's soulless slaves!"*

She hoped Jake could hear what was happening. Maybe he could find some way to track her; she had to hope. She moved her hand away from the phone. "I will enjoy throttling you slowly, so you know what's happening and fully experience your death, dog killer. I'm going to make you sorry you ever grabbed me from that park."

The cruel mouth revealed by a slash in her attacker's ski mask gave a slow smile. "You talk too much, bitch."

Sophie stared at Ski Mask, focusing on shutting out the throb of the stab wound in her back. She was good at compartmentalizing, at separating herself from her body, at relegating pain to a mere sensation that didn't deserve her attention. She had Assan Ang and his tortures to thank for that ability. She needed to conserve her strength and be ready for whatever came next.

And that came sooner than she'd hoped for as the van swung a hard left onto a rough road, bouncing her and the masked man around inside the van. She couldn't see anything about where they were except a glimpse of green trees through the windshield and the small back window.

Ski Mask grinned as they bumped down the road. "I bet you think we're going to the jungle by the ditch. Nah, done with that. We're going somewhere new. The great thing about missing persons is, there's no murder without a body. But we know how wrong that is on the Big Island, don't we?"

"May you die screaming in agony and your pain never be extinguished."

"Whatever you just said, worse is coming to you, bitch."

Sophie half-closed her eyes and looked away from the despicable maggot. *Conserve strength. Don't waste energy on emotion.*

The van drove a little further and then pulled to a stop with a lurch.

"We're here." The driver scowled through his mask at the man seated on the van's floor. "Dump her out so we can get going."

The silenced weapon came up so quickly Sophie was hardly sure she had seen it. The silencer spoke twice with a sound like a melon seed being spat with force. The driver collapsed against his door, a red spray marking the window behind him. "Thanks for driving us here. Now no one will ever know this location."

Sophie palmed the phone into her pocket and scrambled backwards, reaching for the handle of the back door. She pulled it down, but it refused to budge.

"Locked. A basic precaution." Her assailant peeled his ski mask up. He had a surprisingly handsome face with the buttery-brown skin of Asian and Hawaiian heritage. "Akane Chang. Going to enjoy killing you."

CHAPTER FORTY-NINE

THE DETECTIVES' SUV pulled up on the sidewalk at Hilo Bay Park next to a loudly barking yellow Labrador. Jake recognized Ginger, and saw a knot of concerned-looking people clustered around a fallen dog on the sidewalk. Even prepared by the things he'd heard Sophie say on the phone, Jake's heart was still hammering as he jumped out of the back of the SUV and scattered the onlookers. "That's my dog!"

Tank was still alive, whimpering and trying to rise. The big pit bull was held down at his collar by a sturdy man in a fisherman's hat. "We called an emergency vet," the man told Jake as he squatted to inspect the fallen pit bull. "The guy is on the way."

"Mahalo," Jake murmured, stroking Tank's sleek black-and-white head. He had to force his gaze to focus on the wound in the dog's side, a puncture hole between his ribs that bubbled ominously. "He'd better get here soon. Looks like the shooter hit a lung." Jake looked around at the crowd. "The man who shot my dog took my partner. Did anyone see what kind of vehicle it was?"

"White van," an older man said. "Ford Econoline. We didn't see what happened, but the Lab was barking and the other dog was down, so we noticed the van speeding away."

"I got part of the plate," a kid on a bike said. He held up his phone. "I took a video when I saw the van come up on the sidewalk."

Freitan stepped in, holding up her badge. "Detective Freitan. I need that footage." She took the kid's phone and she and Wong clustered close, watching it.

Jake looked around. "Anyone got a rag, a towel, something I can put over Tank's wound?"

The helpful kid peeled off his tee shirt, and Jake blinked back a tear in his eye as he took it, still warm from the boy's body, and pressed it down over the bullet hole in Tank's side. The dog groaned and coughed, and Jake's breathing got tight too, as the suffering animal wheezed.

"Who would do a thing like that?" a watching woman said. "What kind of monster shoots a dog and kidnaps a woman in a park in broad daylight?"

Jake focused on soothing Tank, trying not to think about what might be happening to Sophie right now.

A moment later, a blue-and-white van with Animal Hospital emblazoned on the side and a flashing red light on the dash pulled up. The vet and his assistant got out. "Thank God you're here," Jake said. "This is a rescue dog my partner and I picked up from some folks who are now in jail. He's in a bad way."

"I can see that. We'll likely need to intubate him," the vet directed his assistant. "Everyone, clear the area so we can stabilize this animal and get him to our facility."

Wong and Freitan pushed the crowd back and Jake held Ginger's leash tight as the vet and his assistant worked on Tank.

Freitan touched Jake's arm, and her sharp brown eyes were compassionate. "We have a BOLO out on the white van, but as you heard, only got a partial plate. We're going out to pick up Terence Chang and interview him—he supposedly knows this guy. Want to come?"

Jake was tempted, but shook his head. "I need to stay with the dogs right now. I'll get in touch with you as soon as the situation is under control. Call me the minute you have a lead on Sophie."

The detectives nodded and the two ran to their SUV.

Jake squatted to pet Ginger. She shivered and whined in distress. It would be best to take her back to the motel room so he could follow the ambulance to the animal hospital and rendezvous with the detectives unimpeded.

His phone rang, vibrating with *Unidentified Number*. Jake never picked up for anonymous callers, but this time his thumb punched the button and he put the phone to his ear. "This is Jake Dunn."

"Jake, you don't know me, but I'm a friend of Sophie's. I've been tracking her phone, and she's in danger." The caller had a silky, urbane voice, and the hairs on Jake's neck rose.

The voice wasn't Alika's. *Who was this man?* "I know all of Sophie's friends. Who are you, and why the hell are you tracking her?"

"That's not important right now. She's in danger. Do you want to know where she is, or shall I call someone else?" The caller's voice was impatient.

Jake breathed through a wave of jealous, terrified rage, his mind flashing on the men with money and connections he'd sensed were in her life. *So many shitty feelings!* He hated them. "Tell me now."

"She's in a wilderness area just outside the National Park. I have a satellite phone photo I can send you—there's a dirt track leading to where the van holding her stopped."

"How the hell do you have a satellite photo? Never mind. Send it." Jake scanned the area for the Jeep—*Sophie had likely driven here from the motel.* He spotted the boxy black vehicle, spattered with mud, in the parking lot nearby.

"Sending it now," Sophie's secret stalker-friend replied.

Jake pressed the phone to his chest to muffle the audio and turned to the vet. "My name's Jake Dunn. I have a lead on my partner's whereabouts and I need to follow up. Call me at this number the minute you know anything about how Tank is doing." He rattled off the number, and the assistant wrote it down.

The vet nodded. "Good luck."

"Good luck to you, too. Save my dog." Jake turned and sprinted toward the Jeep, holding Ginger's leash tightly. His phone vibrated with the incoming photo, and he glanced at it.

An aerial shot, grainy with distance. A thread of a road. A white spot that was the van's roof, almost obscured by foliage. *He'd have to zoom in to see where the turnoff was.*

He put the phone to his ear and spoke to the caller. "Who are you?"

"It's better that you don't know. Just find her. I'll be watching." The caller hung up.

"Fucking James Bond shit." Jake dug in his pocket for the spare key, beeped the Jeep open, and got in with Ginger riding shotgun.

CHAPTER FIFTY

SOPHIE STARED into Akane Chang's brutal brown eyes.

The man had brought her out to this remote location to kill her and dispose of her and the driver's body. He had already shown his willingness and ability to ruthlessly end any life, even that of an innocent animal. She might as well give it all she had, and get it over with.

Sophie drew herself up into a squat, ignoring the wound in her back, and launched herself at Chang as he opened the van's side door.

The man was ready and scrambled out of the van ahead of her, spinning to press the silencer to the tender skin of her forehead.

Sophie stopped. Breathed. She was seconds from death. She shut her eyes and waited for it.

Chang stepped back, and gestured with the weapon. "Get out. Up against the van. Put your hands on the vehicle."

"I fail to see why I should follow your directions," Sophie said. "You're just going to kill me."

"Our fates are never written in stone," Chang said conversationally. "Which is what makes all of this entertaining. Like your little friend Julie Weathersby. She got away, and you're a hell of a lot tougher than she is. So, what's it going to be? Die now, or maybe die later?"

Sophie weighed her options, looking into the black eye of the pistol's silencer.

To live a little longer was always better. If she went for him now, she was a dead woman. "Where there's life, there's hope," Marcella's voice said in her head.

Sophie raised her hands slowly and climbed out of the van. She turned to face the vehicle.

She felt Chang approach, and kicked back viciously with her left leg, glad that she was wearing sturdy running shoes.

Chang yelped as his leg buckled. He hit her with the pistol on the back of the head. Stars exploded in Sophie's vision, and she staggered forward, falling against the side of the van.

Chang grabbed her and flung her to the ground, dropping to put a knee in her back. He cackled like a demented television villain as he wrenched her arms up and zip tied them behind her back.

Her chances of a slow death versus a fast one had just increased exponentially.

CHAPTER FIFTY-ONE

JAKE SAT in the driver's seat of the Jeep and took a moment to zoom in and study the satellite photo. The white dot of the van stood out in an ocean of green at the end of a thread of dirt track, but an inserted photo close-up showed the name of the turnoff from the main highway leading out of Hilo.

"I'm half an hour away, tops," he muttered. He turned the key. The Jeep roared into life. He threw it in gear and pulled out, realizing for the first time that his shirt and hands were covered with Tank's blood. Wiping his hands clumsily on a paper napkin as he drove one-handed, he voice-dialed Freitan. She didn't pick up, but he left a message detailing the new info and took a moment to forward the satellite photo to her and Wong's phone. "I need backup. Meet me at the location ASAP."

Once on the highway, breaking speed limits to get out of town, Jake let himself wonder. "Who was that, Ginger? Who's tracking Sophie's phone? I'm going to find out no matter what happens today."

The dog cocked her head and gave a woof, clearly as confused as he was.

Jake hit his horn, dodging through a red light at an intersection, weaving among other vehicles. Ginger gave an excited yap beside him, her front legs braced, her tongue hanging out like they were going on a Sunday drive. "I should put a seatbelt on you, girl." He reached across and buckled the dog in place. On another day, the sight would have been amusing.

Jake voice-dialed Bix, and was relieved when his boss didn't pick up. He left a brief message on the latest developments. A few minutes later, he spotted the small, bent road sign marked PRIVATE and naming the dirt turnoff outside of Hilo.

The Jeep took the turn too fast, tipping dangerously, as they barreled down a potholed road. They hit a bump, and Ginger yelped, scrambling out of the seatbelt to end up in the foot well. "Should have left you at the park, girl."

His phone toned and he managed to pick up. "Jake Dunn."

"What the hell, Jake? Who sent you this satellite photo?" Freitan's voice was tight with tension. "We just got Terence Chang in the vehicle. He denies knowing where Akane takes his victims."

"Bring him or cut him loose. I need backup. Now. There were at least two in that van, and they have a major head start." Jake hit another bump and the Jeep levitated, out of control. He wrestled the bucking steering wheel and banged his head on the soft top. "Shit! Call an ambulance too. If anyone's alive out here, they're going to need medical attention." He could feel Freitan's indecision over the hissing phone line, and he snarled. "Get your butts out here, Detective Freitan, or you're going to have so many bodies you'll be buried in them!"

"All right, Soldier Boy. On our way. Wong's radioing for backup and ambulance." The detective ended the call, and the calm decisiveness of her reply centered him.

He wasn't alone with the odds stacked against him . . . at least not entirely. He slowed the Jeep, trying to tamp down his fear for Sophie.

Whoever had taken her must know her value to the case, and other cases—*it had to be Chang!* And if he eliminated Sophie, Holly Rayme would be the only witness connecting him to his "side hustle" and his work for the Chang family. Guaranteed there was a contract out on the woman already. They had to get her into Witness Protection, *but what about the leak in that program?*

The white van appeared so unexpectedly that Jake almost slammed into it. The Jeep fishtailed, never the most stable vehicle with its rear wheel drive, and he pulled up against a dirt berm marking the end of the crude road.

Jake turned off the vehicle, palming his weapon and swiveling to check for anyone nearby. Nothing moved. "Stay, Ginger."

The dog whined, but settled back in the foot well, clearly overwhelmed by all the stimulation of the last hour.

Jake opened his door cautiously.

If there was someone in the van, they'd already had plenty of time to draw a bead on him. He stuck his leg out, and, using the door for cover, looked the van over.

The side door was closed. The passenger door was closed. He was a little ahead of the vehicle, enough to peer through the windshield—and what he saw chilled him.

The driver was slumped against the door in the front seat, and a red spray of blood and brains decorated the window.

Not a good sign, but one less perp to deal with.

"Sophie?" Jake called.

A strange stillness lay over the jungle. Not even a bird call disturbed the silence.

Jake crouched, weapon in ready position, wishing he'd taken the extra few minutes to put on his tactical vest. He moved out from the cover of the Jeep's door, closing it carefully to keep Ginger inside, and approached the van.

He moved around the vehicle and checked the interior through the back window.

Empty.

He opened the side door.

The stench of blood hit his nostrils with a coppery tang. His gaze fell on Sophie's phone, lying crushed on the metal floor of the van beside her billed running hat.

"Sonofabitch." Jake spun, searching around the vehicle. *Which way had they gone?* The jungle was thick, pressing in around the vehicles where they'd parked against the berm of bulldozed soil left over from the rough track's construction.

Jake spotted a broken fern, a spot where someone had stepped —*it would take him forever to track Sophie and her assailant through this jungle without a trail!*

But he wasn't the only one who wanted to find Sophie.

Jake reached into the van and grabbed Sophie's hat off the floor. He ran back to wrench open the door of the Jeep. "Ginger! Find your mama, girl!" He held the hat out for the dog to sniff.

Ginger swarmed up off of the floor of the front seat with an excited bark. Jake was barely able to grab the dog's leash as she leapt to the ground, sniffing around the side of the van and then taking off into the area of the broken ferns with a happy snort.

Jake clung to the leash like a lifeline as the dog plowed into the jungle.

CHAPTER FIFTY-TWO

SOPHIE STUMBLED over the large root of a huge *ohia lehua* tree. The tall, white-barked tree with its silvery-gray oval leaves and red blossoms, familiar from going out run-hiking with Lei Texeira a few times. Sophie's friend Lei had learned to identify all the native plants, fruits, flowers, and birds from her Aunty Rosario, a lovely woman recently lost to cancer.

Sophie wished she'd been able to meet Rosario. Another regret in a sea of them. *Maybe this was her bad luck for plucking that lehua flower on a day that seemed like forever ago...*

Odd, the thoughts one had when close to death.

Sophie had noticed before the tendency of the mind to hyper-focus on details that were likely irrelevant, as it tried to escape an extreme situation.

"Keep moving." Chang used the knife to prod her. "And don't pretend I really hurt you with that poke to the kidney earlier. I hardly dented you."

She would not engage. This man was like a cat who liked to play with his food before eating it. Denying him his game might help her live longer.

"There is no trail here." Sophie picked her way around a towering *koa* tree draped in vines. "How did you find this place?"

"Pig hunting. And go left. I've got the location on my GPS." She glanced back. Chang was holding his phone out. "It's a sat phone, so no worries about losing the signal."

The worst moment of this whole ordeal so far had been when Chang smashed her phone after he zip tied her hands. She'd felt the metallic, splintering sound in her very bones, knowing it meant no one could find her by any electronic means.

The Ghost. Maybe Connor could track Chang's active satellite phone . . . *but how would he know about Chang, or anything about where she was right now?* He was out of the country. How could he help her?

She had to help herself. It always came down to that, always would.

Sophie turned her body and trailed her hand along a branch and broke it, bending the leaves downward. Anything she could do to slow her progress and leave a trail that could be followed was worth trying.

"I see what you're doing. And it won't work." Chang grabbed the branch and tossed it away. "The driver is dead and he's the only one who knows where this place is. We are in a private wilderness area no one knows about."

"Can't blame a girl for trying."

"Sure I can. Keep moving."

Sophie had laced her fingers together when he zip tied her, pushing her wrists apart as far as they would go, hoping she could create some space between them. But the old escape trick hadn't quite worked. Even now, she worked her wrists up and down inside the hard, plastic bonds, trying to gain space to pull out one of her hands. Chang had forced her wrists very close together, and the plastic bit deeper into her skin as she tried to move her wrists up or down.

Sophie had to pay attention to her feet, too, as she tripped on roots and trailing vines. The ground was rough, covered with fallen branches, ferns and bushes, and the remains of trees being swallowed into the jungle floor. Even in the extremity of the situation, Sophie noticed the wild red and white hibiscus, the *hapu'u* tree ferns, the exotic saucer shapes of *lilikoi* blossoms, their bright round fruit dangling like unlikely Christmas ornaments. Tiny purple orchids grew in clumps up through the mass of ferns and ginger. Hawaii's native birdsong sweetened the air.

Another day or time, this would have been a beautiful and interesting hike.

Suddenly Sophie felt a draft of heat. She stopped. A tendril of steam wafted up from a crack in the ground beside her.

"Yes. We are getting closer to Pele's heart," Chang said from behind her. "Some say that Pele feasts on blood."

A terrible suspicion curdled Sophie's gut. *They were headed for active lava territory.* Even though this upcountry area of Kilauea Volcano was largely inactive, the area was still riddled with deep steam vents, lava tubes, and even active flows that moved beneath the crust of the earth.

The depression's familiar voice whispered in Sophie's ear. *"Since you've got to go, being a sacrifice to the volcano goddess is at least interesting."*

"No." Sophie muttered aloud, mustering the will to live that always seemed to take so much effort. *"No, I won't die easy. I won't go quietly. I didn't survive Assan Ang to be this monster's plaything."*

"What's that language you are speaking? Tell me." Chang prodded her with the tip of the knife again. Her back felt like one of the little satin pillows filled with sandalwood dust that her aunt had used to store sewing needles.

"I was just telling myself that I didn't survive a sadistic ex-husband who tried to kill me just to become your next statistic." She could feel by his body heat how close Chang was. Sophie coiled inward and threw herself backward, trying for a body slam. *If she could just get him down, she could stomp him . . .*

Chang flung himself to the side with a curse, but she'd connected with him enough to make him stagger. The knife left a line of fire on the outside of Sophie's arm.

"Dammit, bitch! You're making me work for it." Sophie heard the sexual excitement in Chang's voice, in his panting. "You make all the others seem like chopping wood; no fun at all. And this ass." He grasped her buttock, the rough grab shockingly intimate. "So fine."

"Foul swine!" Sophie kicked backward.

Chang dodged, and shoved her in the center of the back so that she stumbled forward. "Just a little further, now, babe."

Sophie noticed the flutter of a green plastic tie, affixed to a branch. *He was navigating through the forest with more than his GPS.* Her mind scrambled for a way to even the odds, to slow him down. The longer he took to get her where he was going, the better chance she had for someone to find her.

Jake's face appeared in her mind, his gray eyes intent with passion as he gazed at her, his hand warm over her cold one. Her chest squeezed. Jake was going to be so frantic to find her. He would blame himself that she had been taken, no matter how illogical it was.

Alika's dear face flashed to mind next. That kiss at the helicopter had truly been goodbye. At least they'd ended their relationship as friends, and saved a young boy together. Tears of self-pity filled her eyes for the first time. *Why couldn't her life be simpler?* Safer? More normal? Alika always made her wish for those things.

Connor's chiseled features appeared last, lit in the blue-gray glow of a computer. The Ghost was somewhere out there, pulling strings like the puppet master he was. *No one knew him or saw the real him but her.* It was a privilege, and a curse. She couldn't help her longing and ambivalence. He was her counterpart.

Each of these men would grieve for her, and she was sorry for that.

A deep, steamy vent appeared beneath her feet, the brink hidden by an overgrowth of grass and ferns. Sophie stumbled, unable to catch herself from falling forward. Chang grabbed her arms and pulled her back from the edge. He stabilized her, his breath tickling the tender hairs at her ear as he chuckled.

"Whoops. Wouldn't want you to fall in too soon." He tugged her by one of her arms, wrenching it in its socket and wringing a cry from Sophie's numb lips. "Right this way." Chang sounded like he was taking her for a picnic, his voice bright with energy and a fillip of lust, too. *He planned to rape her before he threw her into the vent.*

Sophie's resolve hardened.

It didn't matter if she died in the next half hour; all that mattered was that she took Akane Chang with her.

Sophie kept her focus on monitoring Chang as he steered her through the rough underbrush. *She had to be ready when he made his move.*

Even as she thought this, Chang kicked the back of her knee and shoved her forward. Without her arms for balance, Sophie went down face first in a patch of soft, springy grass. Chang landed on her back with his full body weight, blasting the air out of her lungs.

She moaned as his weight crushed her bound arms. Chang settled himself on her. He ground his pelvis into her backside. One hand held the knife at the junction of her jaw and throat, and the other hand slid down her body, pressing his fingers into her intimate places through the tight exercise clothes she wore.

Sophie shut her eyes and detached. She relaxed her breathing, going limp beneath him, letting him have his moment of victory.

Chang's breath rasped in her ear harshly as he tried to work his hand into her tight pants to peel them down. She could feel the revolting hardness of his erection. *"May your penis be invaded by flesh eating worms, and fall blackened off your rotting corpse!"*

"You're so sexy when you talk dirty to me." Chang was not intimidated by her verbal voodoo.

Strategic. She had to think strategic. Face down, with her arms bound, she had no leverage. On the other hand, screwing her in that position was proving to be a bit challenging too, especially with her restrictive clothing. But on her back with her legs free . . .

"Aren't you man enough to look me in the eye while you rape me?" Sophie's voice was muffled by the grass, but he must have heard it clearly because his body stiffened.

"I can do whatever I want with you." Chang shoved himself upright and away up from her body, squeezing the air out of her once again. He flipped her by her shoulder.

Sophie was now on her back, lying on her bound arms, which might have been painful if she had been allowing any pain signals into her awareness. But all she felt was power pumping through her body, and a readiness to kill or die trying.

Chang stood over her, his legs braced wide, exulting in her help-less position—*and that was his mistake.* Sophie whipped up a knee, and kicked him in the balls with everything she had.

The man gave a choked cry and collapsed, falling to one side and gagging in pain, his hands clutched over his mangled manhood. Sophie pulled in her abs and jumped to her feet.

Chang curled up into the fetal position, gasping. Sophie shoved him onto his back with a foot, and he moaned, bringing his knees close protectively, hands still wrapped around his package.

"I've always wanted to really test the effectiveness of a full force kick to a man's groin. But none of my opponents in the ring were ever stupid enough to give me that kind of opening." Sophie pushed Chang's knees aside and knelt on his chest to hold him in place, her fingers scrabbling on the ground for the fallen knife.

Chang gasped for air, his color mottled, his eyes rolling. She got hold of the knife and awkwardly sawed the zip tie while the man writhed and gagged, still completely impaired.

The plastic eventually parted. Sophie shook out her arms, glorying in the tingling of restored circulation. She brought a hand around and put the point of the blade under Chang's chin, poking the skin hard enough to pierce it. Chang shut his eyes, the color draining from his face.

"One good push, and this knife is in your brain. But I think that's a little too good and way too easy a death for a man who enjoyed killing as much as you did. I think you need to answer some questions first." Sophie traced the blade along Chang's throat, scratching the skin and raising droplets of welling blood. "Where else did you hide bodies?"

"Why should I tell you?" He rasped.

"Because, like you said to me—you can die fast, or you can die slow." Sophie felt completely detached from the pain she was inflicting as she sliced off a bit of Chang's ear. He wailed. "Got any last confessions about the locations of other bodies?"

"No!"

Sophie pried Chang's hands off his groin and pressed the point of the knife into the bulge there. Chang gagged reflexively from the pain, but when he got his breath back he spat the words out. "Don't cut me there! I'll tell you."

Sophie lifted the blade slightly, relieving pressure, but the sharp point still pierced the fabric of Chang's pants. He lay perfectly still, and she pressed down again. He yelped. "South Point! I dropped them off the rocks, weighted down. None of them have washed up with the currents that go off the Point—the currents end up in Tahiti."

"How many?"

"Three. They were family business."

"And your recreational killing?"

"There's another vent. That one's in the park. You'll never recover anything from there."

"How many?"

"I didn't like that one since I had to go into the park and that left a record. But Holly and Jim brought their marks to the park and . . . I chased them there." A feral gleam of memory darkened Chang's eyes.

Sophie dug the point of the knife into the man's belly this time. "Was that all?"

"Yes."

Her muscles tensed—*she could end this now.* Gut Chang like a fish. No one would blame her, and it would be no more than he deserved.

Chang opened his mouth to scream as the knife dug into his abdomen.

A flurry of crunching and crackling sounded in the bushes nearby. Sophie whirled to face her attacker, only to be knocked to the ground by a hundred pounds of ecstatic yellow Lab.

CHAPTER FIFTY-THREE

JAKE CONCEALED a burst of relief that felt too much like joy as he took in the scene at a glance: Sophie, bloodstained but basically intact, struggling to get out from under her dog. Chang, moaning, rolling away from Sophie to curl up like a shrimp, his hands over his crotch.

"I might have known you would have things well in hand."

Sophie pushed Ginger away enough to grin up at Jake. "Took you long enough to get here."

"You didn't need me, after all." Jake observed the small wounds decorating Chang. "Too bad we need this guy to tell us where the rest of the bodies are, and give us the dirt on the Chang operation."

"You've spoiled my fun." Sophie stood up. On closer inspection, he could see swelling on the side of her face and that her wrists were lacerated. Blood stained her dark blue tank top from some wound on her back, making dark splotches. A scratch on her arm seeped. "I interviewed Chang on behalf of the police department and got a couple more body dump locations out of him." Sophie's ferocious smile reminded Jake that it hadn't been long since she slashed her ex's throat to the bone. *He never wanted to get on Sophie's bad side.*

Jake rifled in Chang's pocket and pulled out a zip tie. "Rumor has it this guy had a gun, too. Not that it did him any good dealing with you."

Memory clouded Sophie's eyes and she looked away. "He killed Tank, and threatened to kill Ginger, too. That's how he got me into the van, and that's why I promised to kill him."

"Well, double good that I got here in time to tell you that Tank has a chance of survival. I saw our boy into the capable hands of an emergency vet. Now let's get this piece of trash turned over to the cops so we can go see how Tank's doing."

Sophie rubbed her wrists absently as Jake zip tied Chang and hauled him onto his feet. Ginger, nosing in the grass, gave a woof as she located the pistol. Sophie picked it up and pointed it at Chang. "Sure you won't let me get rid of him? He told me what he did with the bodies already. We could drop him in the lava vent and no one would know."

Jake decided to pretend she was joking. "Nope. Not only would *we* know, but we need him to sing for the cops and clear up the mystery of this island's Bermuda Triangle." Jake held out his hand. "I'll carry that for you so you can deal with your dog."

Sophie stared at Chang, clearly considering whether or not to comply. She finally gave a reluctant nod, handing Jake the weapon.

Jake jabbed Chang in the back with it. "Get moving, asshole."

FREITAN AND WONG, along with a police cruiser with backup and an ambulance, met them at the van's parking area. "I thought you needed help," Freitan told Jake. "Looks like you had things under control."

"That's what I told Sophie when I found her. She'd turned the tables on Chang," Jake said. "And she got some information out of him for you."

"Excellent." Freitan gestured to the back of the detectives' SUV. "We brought Terence along since we'd grabbed him and didn't have time to interview him."

Jake glanced into the back of the SUV. Terence Chang stared straight ahead, his expression stony. He had mixed Hawaiian Chinese features similar to his cousin's; the family resemblance was remarkable.

Akane Chang stiffened under Jake's hand at the sight of Terence, and Wong took charge of him, steering the man to the back of the nearby police cruiser. Freitan grinned. "Divide and conquer two Changs. I'm going to enjoy playing these cousins against each other." She gestured for the EMTs. "Can you patch this woman up while I get her statement?"

"You're always so efficient, Detective Freitan." Sophie sat down suddenly on the bumper of the ambulance. "I think I'll rest a minute."

"You can call me Kamani," Freitan said. "Glad you're okay. I need your statement for the record while they're patching you up."

Jake left Sophie dealing with Freitan while getting first aid for her injuries. He led Ginger over to the Jeep and opened the door for her. She hopped into the back, and Jake patted her head. "You're the real heroine, Ginger. Good nose, girl."

He sat in the driver's seat with the door open and called Bix, thankful to get a signal to update their boss. "Everything seems to be wrapping up here, thank God."

"Yeah, the Weathersby contract's up as of this evening, so do what you can with the police and take Sophie out for a steak dinner," Bix directed. "On our expense account. Well done,"

"Thanks, Boss. Sophie's the one who deserves a medal for this one. Thankfully, she's going to be okay, and has her own therapist here, Dr. Wilson, to do a trauma debrief tomorrow." Security Solutions was meticulous about best practice mental health for its agents. "I don't know if Sophie's going to stay on the Big Island longer, or return to Oahu." Jake's phone beeped with an incoming message. He glanced at it, eyes widening—it was *Unidentified Number* again. "Boss, I have to take this call."

Jake clicked over. "Jake Dunn."

"Jake? This is Sophie's friend." The smooth masculine voice was tense. "I see a number of vehicles in the area near the van, including an ambulance. Were you able to intervene?"

Jake kept his voice hard and businesslike. "What's your game, man? How are you watching us via satellite?"

"Just tell me you got Sophie out." The man's urgency and tension broke through Jake's resentment.

"Yeah. Thanks to you and Ginger I got to her before she carved the perp into little chunks and threw him in a volcano vent."

Satellite Stalker laughed, and Jake heard relief in his tone. "She is full of surprises, our Sophie. I might have known she'd turn the tables."

"What's your interest in Sophie, besides spying on her?" Jake tried for a joking tone.

"None of your business. Above your pay grade." Satellite Stalker's tone was coolly dismissive. Jake's hackles rose and his grip tightened on the phone as the man went on, "Tell Sophie she has a friend looking out for her. She knows who I am."

"A friend who tracks her phone and uses satellites to keep an eye on her. With friends like you, who needs enemies?" Jake's neck was hot. "She doesn't need either of us, it turns out."

A short, charged pause.

"Don't get any ideas, Jake. She's spoken for." The line went dead.

"Fuck you!" Jake snarled. *Satellite Stalker could burn in hell.*

Bix had come back on the line. "I beg your pardon?"

"Oh, sorry. Was talking to my other caller." Jake looked up to see Sophie approaching. She walked slowly, wrapped in a silver emergency blanket. Her shoulders were slumped, her head hanging, and she stumbled in the crushed grass. "I gotta go. Our best operative needs some TLC."

He hung up on Bix and stowed his phone in his pocket. Sophie looked in need of a hug. Jake opened his arms. She walked into them, and rested her head on his shoulder.

CHAPTER FIFTY-FOUR

DEBRIEFED, fed, and showered after stopping by to verify that Tank was indeed going to survive, Sophie snuggled in bed with Jake at the motel as the TV played some old movie on mute in the background behind her. She basked in his furnace-like body heat as a chilly, wet Hilo night enfolded them. She couldn't seem to get enough of being hugged and held by him since the ordeal with Chang, and he seemed more than willing. She felt cherished, protected and warm in his arms.

She really would have liked more than that to be happening, though. Sophie slid a hand under Jake's shirt, savoring the feel of his rock-hard abs. Jake gently but firmly removed her hand and put it on her own hip. "I told you my terms. I'm your guy, or no nookie."

"Nookie?" Sophie's brows arched at the term.

"It's . . . erm. My parents called it that."

"I don't know how I feel about you comparing sex with me to the sex your parents had," Sophie said, her mouth quirking up in a smile.

"Ha. Didn't mean to . . . whatever. You know what I'm saying. We talked about this earlier."

Sophie sighed in resignation, folding her hands up under her chin. Jake drew her closer and kissed her forehead, snuggling her against his chest, but with no other body contact.

"Tell me about your parents. I've never asked you about them," Sophie said.

"Oh, they weren't that interesting. Typical Army couple. We moved a lot. Mom lives in Texas now, near my sister who's married with a baby on the way. My other sister lives in Chicago."

Sophie turned away so that he fitted against her from behind. It felt easier to talk without facing him. "You forget. I don't know much about American culture except what I've read." She stroked the back of Jake's arm where it crossed over her waist, enjoying the feel of his springy, blondish hairs. She lifted his hand and looked at the tender blue veins at his wrist, remembering an impulse not long ago to kiss him there. *So vulnerable, a web of fragile life lying over the toughness of sinew and bone.*

Sophie gave in to the impulse and lifted his wrist to kiss the nexus of veins softly as she'd wanted to do then. "Tell me about your father. You never talk about him."

"That's because he . . . left our family. Abandoned Mom, me and my younger sisters. I was fifteen when he came home one day and told Mom he was leaving her for his secretary."

"Oh no." Sophie stroked Jake's wrist, her fingers tracing the many textures. He had a calloused area in the web between his thumb and forefinger, likely from handling weapons or pushing weights. "That's terrible."

"Dad was career Army. Mom was a traditional homemaker who hadn't kept up her job as a teacher because we moved so often with his postings and she had the three of us to care for. I didn't know it until he left, but he was often unfaithful. Mom wasn't even surprised about the secretary. She was just surprised that he had no honor about how he left, or providing for us." Jake sighed. His breath stirred the hairs behind Sophie's ear and she suppressed a shudder of arousal. "I became an investigator the day Mom sat us down and told us he was gone. He hadn't said goodbye to any of the three of us.

Wanted to avoid a scene, she said. I went after him, trying to find out who he'd really been. I didn't like the answers I found."

Sophie felt the rigidity of old pain in Jake's muscles but she held herself still, resisting the urge to soothe and comfort—it wouldn't work. "Dad was eventually forced to pay child support by the court. I . . . had a rough time that year. Became angry, wild. Reckless. Lots of fighting. Deciding to try for Special Forces after high school saved me from getting into drugs or partying, though. I joined up the minute I was eligible."

"You wanted to outshine your father. Beat him at his own career."

"Yes. And I did. But I had trouble trusting people. Women. I couldn't commit. I guess I've been afraid I wasn't capable of it, that I was too much like him."

"Smart to avoid it then," Sophie said.

Jake gave a mirthless chuckle. "I thought you'd agree with avoidance. You have a secret admirer, you know."

"What?" Sophie twisted to meet Jake's gaze. Evening shadows colored them stone gray in the low light of the motel's small bedside lamp. "Who?"

"Didn't you wonder how I found you?"

"I assume you tracked my phone. And then at the van, you were smart enough to know Ginger could find me."

The Lab, lying on the rug at the foot of the bed, lifted her head at the sound of her name. She was mopey without Tank, who was recovering at the animal hospital and would be released in a few days if all went well.

"No. Your phone's signal cut off a few minutes after you answered my call and I couldn't get it again even with the Find My Phone app. I opted to stay with Tank while Wong and Freitan went off to get Terence Chang and try to shake Akane's location out of him. While the vet was stabilizing Tank, I got a call from an *Unidentified Number*."

Sophie stiffened. "Who was it?"

"The dude wouldn't say. Told me that he was tracking your phone and had a satellite picture to share with me that showed where the van that took you was. I tried to ask him more, and he just asked if I wanted to help you, or should he call someone else?" Jake squeezed Sophie closer. She could feel how much he wanted her, a sweet suffering they shared. "I told him to send me the picture, and that's how I found the van. I forwarded the satellite photo to Freitan and Wong and they called for an ambulance and backup. Later, while you were giving your statement, he called again to see if I'd rescued you. He warned me off. Said you were spoken for, and that you'd know who he was."

"Yes, I know who he is." Sophie extracted herself from Jake's arms in agitation. "But he has no claim on me. We are not involved."

"I thought you got rid of all the dangerous stalkers in your life when you killed Assan Ang," Jake said in a dry tone. "That man sounded like money. And power."

Sophie decided to ignore the accusation in his voice. "I told you I had secrets I couldn't share with you. And he is one of them. He is . . . monitoring me. He is not a danger to me."

"Anyone who can use a satellite as his personal nanny cam and lacks the scruples to abide by the law could be dangerous to you, or others." Jake's eyes had gone flinty and his jaw was hard as he propped himself on an elbow.

"I can't talk about this man. I'm sorry, Jake. But trust me when I tell you—I have no romantic interest in him," Sophie said forcefully.

"You've got no romantic interest in me, either, it seems." Jake rolled on his back and stared at the ceiling. "You must like guys with helicopters, then. All I'm saying."

"Are you pouting? Is that what you're doing when your mouth droops like that?"

Jake laughed. She'd come to love that—Jake was never discouraged or downcast long, and his unsinkability was a tonic for her depressive struggles.

"Fine. I was pouting." Jake sat up. He gave her exaggerated

bedroom eyes, fluttering his lashes, and peeled his shirt off over his head, tossing it across the room. He flexed his arms and tightened his abs, striking a pose. "Now I'll just have to rely on my looks and charm to wear you down. Come over here and snuggle with all of this. Platonically. Until you're ready to be my girl and have it all for yourself."

Sophie groaned. "No, thanks. You are beefcake—I understand that word now—and I'm a hungry woman. I'd better go to my own room so I can respect your terms." She walked to the connecting door. Ginger rose and joined her, and Sophie looked back at Jake. "I wish I were ready to be your girl."

"Me too. Now get out of here so I can take a cold shower," Jake grumbled, and threw his pillow at her.

CHAPTER FIFTY-FIVE

S<small>OPHIE</small> <small>RUBBED</small> one of her abraded wrists absentmindedly as she sat in Dr. Wilson's waiting room late the next day. She felt good, considering all that had gone down the day before. She hadn't needed more than a sturdy bandage for the wound on her back, administered by the EMTs at the van. Her other assorted punctures and scrapes from yesterday's ordeal were already healing.

So far, today had been spent wrapping up the case with the Weathersbys and attending a team meeting with the detectives where she turned over all the information she'd gathered on the body dump sites Chang had told her about, and what she'd put together on the missing persons using DAVID. Freitan and Wong had enough to verify the way the "side hustle" had gone down, even with both Changs heavily lawyered up. Hope was high at the station that they'd even be able to unravel the intricacies of the Chang crime operation if they could keep Holly Rayme alive and the Chang cousins would talk. Those were big "ifs," but a good start.

Dr. Wilson opened her inner door and stuck her head out. "Sophie! So good to see you. I was worried yesterday until I got your text." Sophie stood and turned to face the psychologist, and Dr. Wilson widened her eyes. "You look a little worse for wear, my girl."

"I got off lightly, considering the situation that occurred yesterday. Is it all right if this is my official post-incident trauma debrief per Security Solutions protocol?"

"Wow, it must have been a doozy of a day. Whatever you need. Do you want to do some EMDR?"

Eye Movement Desensitization and Reprocessing were the best practices recommendation for post trauma work. Sophie was quite familiar with the technique, a combination of structured question and memory recall accompanied by eye movement guided by a light bar.

"Maybe, but I would just like to sort through everything first. A lot has happened since I saw you day before yesterday."

"Well, let's get to it." Dr. Wilson held the door wide, and Sophie walked in.

Sophie took a seat on the familiar couch, and picked up a fidget toy off of the coffee table. "Do many of your clients play with this while they talk?"

"They do. I find that males, particularly, need something to do with their hands while they talk."

Sophie spun the gadget. "I'm not sure where to begin." All that had happened, including her confusion on a number of subjects, jostled together to stifle her tongue.

Dr. Wilson smiled from her comfortable lounger, a clipboard and pen on her lap. Today she wore a simple scoop-necked dress in a vibrant peacock shade that enhanced her striking blue eyes.

"Why don't you begin where we left off? Tell me what you were able to find out about your mother's secret spy organization."

"I finally had some time to research it online just before I was kidnapped," Sophie said.

Dr. Wilson snorted. "Maybe that's not the right place to start. Why don't you start with the biggest thing that has happened since I saw you last."

"I am trying to remember what had happened before I met with you last. I don't think we had found Julie Weathersby or Chernobiac's body yet."

Dr. Wilson shook her head. "Good Lord. Okay, begin wherever!"

Sophie proceeded to fill Dr. Wilson in on the events of the last few days.

At some point, Dr. Wilson got up and fetched Sophie a bottle of water from her little fridge. She needed it by then, her throat scratchy from talking. "To conclude, the investigation is wrapping up, at least our part of it. Freitan and Wong have what they need for solving many of these missing persons cases. If Holly Rayme will testify and Akane Chang will cut a deal for his confession, they might even have enough to chisel a hole in the Changs' crime operation here on the Big Island."

"That's remarkable. And what about you? Were you able to find anything out about your mother and her organization?" Dr. Wilson had circled back around to the original question.

"Like I said, I finally had time to research the Yām Khûmkạn yesterday at the police station before Chang snatched me at the park. Mother was telling the truth. There is such a clandestine organization, and it does a good enough job concealing its presence that it actually doesn't have much of an online footprint. Even data mining the dark net didn't yield the kind of information I'm used to getting. But while spending time learning about it, I began to be concerned about how to tell my father that Mother is a spy." Sophie laced her fingers tightly together and squeezed. "I have to tell him, and I know it will be devastating. It will also cause a possible national security breach. I will be detained. Questioned. Everything I've done, sensitive information I had access to through my work with the FBI . . . everything could come under scrutiny."

"I'm sorry, Sophie. It's not fair. This was none of your doing."

"That's why I hate this so much. Not only has my mother no love for me and only a desire to use me and my father, she has . . . corrupted my life with this attempt to recruit me. I am in a bind because of it." Sophie gazed into Dr. Wilson's compassionate eyes. "I have worked so hard to be free. To be able to chart my own destiny. That was what this trip to the Big Island was supposed to be.

What my trip to Kaua'i was supposed to be. Instead, I keep finding . . . *pilikia*. Trouble."

"I'm not sure if this is what you want to hear, Sophie, but I have to ask. Is it possible that some part of you wants to find these bodies, solve these crimes, even more than you want to be free? Whether they are missing people, lost boys, cyber vigilantes, you name it—you put yourself into a crime-solving life by joining the FBI, and now, though you are out, you still keep stumbling into hot cases."

"I know. It's so strange." Sophie rubbed the scar over her artificial cheekbone in agitation.

"You say you want to be free. What does that even mean to you? Let's make sure we are on the same page with the concept."

Sophie looked down at her hands. Her short nails were ragged, and the zip ties Chang had put on her wrists had left angry red lines. "I don't know exactly what freedom means. I just know that sometimes I have these feelings. Expansive feelings, like I am flying, like I have found my place in the world, and I do not have to answer to anyone or anything. I am . . . happy. Very happy." She sighed. "These moments pass too quickly. I only get the feelings sometimes, usually when I'm alone with my dog, out in nature. But those feelings are the opposite of the depression. They are the antidote to it."

"But you have told me in the past that you had those same feelings of freedom, of flying, when you were in the cyber world, online. Could it be that what you are doing is already bringing you freedom? Could it be that this feeling of freedom is what some others call fulfillment?"

Sophie glanced up to meet Dr. Wilson's wise gaze. "English has been my second language, though it's quickly becoming my primary one. Maybe the words are more related in my mother tongue, or in Chinese. I do speak five languages, and sometimes concepts get mixed up. But what I know is that I want more of those feelings. I don't want to be depressed anymore."

"Have you been taking your medication?"

"Not regularly enough." The little white pills she'd begun a few months ago were hard to remember to take when so much was going on.

"Please try to make that a priority." Dr. Wilson sat forward, capturing Sophie's gaze. "I would propose that you can have those exultant kinds of feelings within whatever you are doing as a job. What you are describing is *flow*, a phenomenon that occurs with the right mix of endorphins and the attainment of a difficult goal. There's a book about it called *Flow: The Psychology of Optimal Experience*, by Mihaly Csikszentmihalyi, a Hungarian psychologist. You can look it up. People chase after the feeling, but it cannot be bottled—except perhaps as a recreational drug." Dr. Wilson smiled. "And of course, you would be too smart to want that kind of pale substitute."

"This is . . . so good, Dr. Wilson. I want to understand everything that you are saying." Sophie glanced at the clock. "But I don't have much time, and I don't even know what to do next. I don't know what to do about my mother and her proposal. I am considering calling my father's Secret Service protection agent, Ellie Smith, and throwing myself upon her mercy to guide me. Perhaps I will become a double agent, and spy on Mother's organization."

"Dear God. What a can of worms!" Dr. Wilson rubbed her temples.

"It's true. And simple next steps: should I stay here on the Big Island, or go back to Oahu and resume work with Security Solutions? I need to make a living somehow. It's not urgent at this moment. I have savings, and I will be paid for my work on the Weathersby case. But I also need to figure out my love life. Jake told me he wouldn't have sex with me anymore unless I become his girl. In other words, acknowledge that we are an exclusive couple."

"I know what that means," Dr. Wilson said. "And how do you feel about that? About him?"

"Not ready to make such a commitment. I still have feelings for Alika, too, and I don't have room for Jake in my life with all that's going on and how much he would want to be a part of it. There's so much I couldn't tell him, and he hates secrets. To complicate things further, Connor has been tracking me. He called Jake and provided my location via satellite when I was kidnapped, which was how Jake was able to find me before I . . ." Her voice trailed off. "The most troubling thing is not that the Ghost is watching me and monitoring me . . . I am not surprised by that. He told me he was. What I am surprised by is something else."

Such a long moment went by that Dr. Wilson prompted, "And what is that, Sophie?"

Sophie reached out and picked up the fidget toy and spun it. "I'm surprised by how easy it was for me to intimidate Chang into telling me the locations of the bodies he'd disposed of, and how very tempted I was to kill him and dump his body. I'm changing, Dr. Wilson, and I don't know who I am becoming."

"Even though hurting another human being is getting easier for you, it's understandable with the violence you have suffered and the exposure to vigilantism that you are dealing with. In spite of those powerful drives, I am encouraged that you're continuing to grapple with these moral and ethical issues. Sometimes justice isn't simple, not just an eye for an eye. If that were the case, then yes, Akane Chang would have deserved to be dead ten times over. But if leaving Chang alive leads to the downfall of a crime organization that has its tentacles all through the state of Hawaii, then perhaps justice is exactly what you were meting out in handing Chang over to the authorities. They might cut a deal with him, and he might never be punished to the extent we would wish. And still, that might be a greater justice."

Sophie smiled. "I see why Lei always said you were the best therapist. You aren't afraid to be with me as I look my own evil in the eye."

"We are all shades of gray," Dr. Wilson said. "And that's why justice is never simple and seldom easy."

Sophie felt the weight of Dr. Wilson's contemplation, and finally the psychologist spoke. "Well, can you come see me again tomorrow? Our business is not yet finished. I would like to see you resume the trip you came to the Big Island for, hiking and exploring this beautiful place—and coming to talk to me about what you discover, both on the inside, and on the outside."

Sophie nodded. "That feels right to me, too. Thank you. I will decide that much, today."

CHAPTER FIFTY-SIX

JAKE SET his duffel on the sidewalk of Hilo's airport and tugged on Tank's leash. The big pit bull came reluctantly out of the back seat of Sophie's rental car, where he had been ensconced with Ginger. Jake adjusted the plastic cone around his neck keeping the dog from licking the stitched-up wound site left over from the bullet he'd taken. "Come on, boy. We are going home to Oahu. You're going to like my apartment. It's small, but we have a tiny backyard where you can take dumps and bark at birds all day long." After all they'd been through, Jake found talking to Tank totally natural.

Sophie, behind the wheel, raised a hand. "Goodbye, Jake."

Jake's chest felt tight, his throat constricted. It had been almost a week since the events of the Chang kidnapping. He and Sophie had taken time off from Security Solutions to hike Mauna Loa, explore the trails of Volcanoes Park, and even take a tour boat at the crack of dawn to watch the lava dripping into the sea at Kalapana, a mesmerizing sight that Jake would never forget. They'd argued and laughed and enjoyed amazing experiences unique to the Big Island. The friendship side of their relationship was stronger than ever.

But in all that time, Sophie had respected his "terms." She had not given in to his masculine wiles, both subtle and not-so-subtle. He felt her ambivalence as deeply as ever. Leaving her felt awful, a heavy sensation in his body like he was coming down with the flu.

His sister Patty's voice sounded in his mind. *"Don't be needy, Jake. Get a life and live it so well she wants to join you in it."*

He knew Patty was right, but he was leaving Sophie vulnerable to unknown enemies and the attentions of men with helicopters and satellites. He needed to try, one more time, to let her know how he felt. "Can I get a hug?"

"Of course. I love your hugs." Sophie smiled that closed-mouth, guarded curve of her lips that always left Jake wishing he could surprise an actual laugh out of her. If only she would let go more . . . but he knew there were things going on she couldn't or wouldn't tell him, things that hurt her and activated darkness in and around her. It pained him that she shut him out from those things. *Did she think he couldn't handle her problems?*

Sophie got out of the car and came around the hood, opening her arms to him.

Jake crushed her close in the longest hug, burying his face in her neck, relishing the sensation of her strong, springy form in his arms. His feelings seemed to vibrate inside of him, humming along the lines of his body, and he could tell she felt them as she squeezed him back. "I had so much fun with you, Jake. Thank you. For everything."

His smile felt painful as he set her away with an effort, clasping her hands. "Be safe, okay? Call me anytime."

"I'm going to be a lot more than just *safe*. I'm going to be finding out more about who I am as I work with Dr. Wilson. I'm sorry that there are secrets and time apart. But I want you to know I care for you a great deal, Jake, and I trust you. And I don't trust many." Sophie's golden-brown eyes were intent on his.

"It's a start." Jake touched her nose, trying for lightness. "I can work with that. Until I see you again, I won't be lonely."

Sophie raised her brows in question.

Jake indicated Tank, sitting on the sidewalk, panting and looking a little ridiculous in his plastic collar. "I have a new roommate. We're going to be spending a lot of bro time. But if you ever need anything, I'll be waiting."

"I hope you won't be waiting long. I'll be in touch as soon as I know what I'm doing next."

Then Sophie stepped forward and pulled him down for a kiss that he would spend his nights remembering.

Turn the page for a sneak peek of, *Wired Secret*, Paradise Crime Thrillers book 7.

SNEAK PEEK

WIRED SECRET, PARADISE CRIME THRILLERS BOOK 7

Sometimes justice wasn't fair.

Security specialist Sophie Ang stared with dislike at the twitchy blonde woman on the bed in the jail's infirmary. Swelling distorting Holly Rayme's face had gone down in the week since Sophie had seen her last. The woman's face was back to gaunt, blotchy with the green and yellow of fading bruising.

If justice were fair, Holly Rayme would be dead right now. Instead, she was getting out of jail—but at least, not free.

"I am in hell." Rayme picked at a scab on the back of her hand as she addressed Sophie, Detective Kamani Freitan, and Hazel Matsue, a U.S. Marshal brought in to interview her for inclusion in the national Witness Security program. "You have to get me out of here."

"Things can actually get a lot worse for you," Freitan said with her usual bluntness. Freitan, a tall, voluptuous mixed Hawaiian woman, exuded volatility. Ancient Hawaiian chieftesses had accompanied their men into battle, and in another age, Freitan would have been perfectly in character carrying a club ringed with sharks' teeth instead of the police issue Glock she currently wore. "You've been hiding out here in the infirmary, in a soft bed with protection. Your own TV, even. But if that protection is going to continue, we need to know you understand what this is all about."

"Yep. This is all about me testifying against the Changs. Helping you bring down a crime family." Rayme's watery blue eyes blinked. "I had to go through detox this week in this supposed comfy bed with my own TV. You think that wasn't hell?"

"You drug, you lose. And it would have been a lot worse out in general pop," Freitan retorted.

"We know you've been through a hard time, Holly." Sophie stepped forward to defuse the tension between the two as Marshal Matsue looked on, arms folded. "But you had medical support, and you're through the worst of it. You're fortunate. Ms. Matsue here is willing to take you into protective custody, provide you with a new identity, and relocate you until you can testify. You won't have to be in jail at all."

"Yes. I'm here to interview you and explain the program." Matsue was a slender woman with a triangular face. Though she wore black pants, a white shirt and a black vest whose purpose was to conceal her sidearm, Matsue had an innate style that set her apart, conveyed by deep red lipstick and an angular, asymmetrical bobbed haircut. She would have looked as completely at home in Paris or Madrid as she did in this dingy room with its bloom of ceiling mold and smell of Lysol. "Do you understand why you've been referred to the Witness Security program, Ms. Rayme? And that you must comply with our procedures and directives? The U.S. Marshal Service has a one hundred percent success rate at protecting our clients if they follow WITSEC directions and protocols."

"I don't see that I have much choice," Rayme grumbled. "I mean, look at me. Broken ribs, bruised all over my body. I'm lucky to be alive. My boyfriend Jimmy isn't, and I won't be if I don't stick with you guys. I know that much."

Jim Webb and Holly Rayme had been scooped up in an investigation Sophie had just completed that had resulted in the apprehension the Chang family's sadistic enforcer, Akane Chang. Webb had not survived an attack in the general population of the jail once the couple's importance as witnesses became evident.

"I have some paperwork for you to fill out and forms for you to sign." Matsue handed the paperwork on a clipboard to Rayme. "Once we have this done, we can process you out of here."

"Can I turn this prisoner over to your custody?" Freitan asked. "I've got work to do."

"Shortly." Matsue addressed Sophie. "Why are you a part of these proceedings?"

"I work for a private firm, Security Solutions. My services have been retained by a coalition of Chang's victims' families." Sophie's ongoing attachment to the case had been a new development. She and her partner Jake Dunn had wrapped the contract to find a missing girl, and she'd tried to resume the vacation and hiking trip she'd come to the Big Island for. Only days later, she was contacted by her employer to assist in security and support for Holly Rayme. "The families of Akane Chang's victims contracted with Security Solutions to pay for my services to support regular law enforcement."

"The U.S. Marshal Service does not work with private entities," Matsue said frostily.

"You want to work with this chick," Freitan said. "She's former FBI and a computer wizardess. Can't hurt to have her in your back pocket."

"And she's a badass bitch with a mean left hook," Rayme volunteered from the bed. "I happen to know. She and her partner were the ones to find out our part in the hustle with Akane Chang. I'm only saying anything nice because her partner adopted our dog, and I want to stay alive. She can help keep me alive."

Endorsement by these unlikely allies almost made Sophie smile. "I am on retainer, and available to help and support. If you choose not to work with me, I will help from the sidelines. We should at least talk so I can explain how my skill set might be of use to you." Sophie held Matsue's skeptical gaze.

"Well, if that's all, I've got perps to bust and the day's a-wasting," Freitan said. "See you ladies at the trial." She turned and headed for the door, and as her hand touched the knob, an alarm ululated outside. The dome light out in the hallway began spinning, throwing red beams across Freitan. The muffled crack of a gunshot sounded out in the hall.

"Shit!" Freitan drew her weapon and flattened herself against the doorjamb, reaching over to turn the heavy silver bolt, locking the door. "We need to stay in here and guard the prisoner."

"Lower the blind over the window, Detective!" Matsue barked. "Ms. Rayme, get down off the bed and behind some cover!"

Sophie, as a civilian, had surrendered her Glock upon entering the jail and she felt its loss keenly as she helped Rayme, groaning and exclaiming, down off the bed. Freitan pulled the plastic retractable blind down over the bulletproof observation window as Matsue joined her, weapon drawn.

"I've had experience with an attack in a room like this. These beds make good cover." Sophie maneuvered the heavy metal hospital bed sideways into a horizontal position facing the window. "Stay back here with me," she told Rayme.

Steps thundered outside in the hallway. More shots rang out. Yelling added to the cacophony of the alarm. Sophie fumbled her phone out of her pocket. She had upgraded recently to a satellite phone, but when she thumbed it on, *No Service* showed in the window. *"Foul stench of a week-old corpse."*

"What's that you're saying?" Rayme whispered. Her teeth were chattering and her eyes were wide in her multicolored face. "I'm scared too."

"I curse in Thai, my native tongue," Sophie said. "More variety that way." She held up her phone. "Either of you getting a signal?"

"Nope," Freitan said. "But reception's never good in here."

"I can usually get a few bars. This is weird," Matsue said. The women bracketed the covered window, weapons drawn.

Sophie's heart rate was up, but she wasn't unduly alarmed. Three highly trained professionals, two of them armed, were barricaded in with Holly Rayme, and it was likely this disturbance was not even related to their prisoner. She smiled reassuringly at Rayme. "Try to stay calm. We've got you covered."

More gunshots and the thunder of feet in the hallway were not reassuring. Neither was the shout, "she's in the infirmary. Just start trying doors!"

The knob rattled. The door shook under pounding with some metal object as the impacts sent medical supplies piled on the shelves falling to the floor.

Rayme let out a squeal of fear after one particularly loud crash, moving to clutch Sophie. Sophie wrapped her arms around the trembling woman and covering Rayme's mouth with a hand. "Don't let them hear you," she whispered in Rayme's ear.

A flash of memory.

Sophie was the one being held in someone's arms. A hand covered her mouth, and a desperate voice whispered, "don't let them hear you."

Suppressed memory came flooding back, and Sophie's arms tightened around Rayme.

The woman holding her had been her beloved nanny, Armita.

Armita had fought like a tigress when kidnappers broke into seven-year-old Sophie's room, screaming and beating at the men with a broom. Sophie's last sight of Armita had been the nanny, head bleeding, sprawled on the ground as masked men in black carried Sophie away.

She had never seen Armita again.

After the ransom was paid and Sophie was returned, Mother told her Armita had quit because she didn't want to work at a place where she'd be in danger.

Armita had been hurt because of Sophie; and she'd left because of Sophie.

Self-blame had been a heart-splinter of Sophie's ever since. As

Sophie held Holly Rayme's trembling, sweating body in her arms, she let it go. *Not her fault. Just a child.*

Another missing piece from her past to ask her mother about. Her mother, Pim Wat... *Now that was a topic for another day.*

The heavy crash of something metal hitting the covered viewing window made Sophie hunch instinctively over Rayme, protecting the woman with her body as the intruders bashed at the safety glass window, bowing it in and shattering it.

Sophie peeked over their crude barrier. Two lean, dark men in prison orange filled the window's opening, shoving aside the dangling blind with their hands, pushing the sheet of glass, held together by wire, out of the way.

And then Freitan and Matsue were up and firing. Sophie and Rayme curled close, covering their ears as they hid behind the bed.

Ringing ears assaulted by gunfire in a small, enclosed space.

Curses and screams.

The burning tang of weapons discharge.

A long moment passed as silence fell, broken by Rayme's sobbing. Sophie lifted her head to peer out from cover. Matsue and Freitan stood in identical shooting stances, aiming their weapons at the crude opening in the window.

More running, yelling, and gunfire out in the hall, this time passing by. No further incursions.

"Suspects are down." Freitan clicked the deadbolt open. "I'm going to see what's happening." She was out the door before Matsue could object.

The Marshal turned wide, tilted brown eyes upon Sophie. "You two okay?"

"Yes." Sophie tried her phone again. "The jammer is off. I've got a signal."

She dialed 911 and was told that backup was on its way and the riot was almost under control.

Rayme wriggled out of Sophie's arms and adjusted her gaping

hospital gown. "Thanks. Almost seemed like you cared, for a moment there."

"I always do the right thing, no matter how I feel about someone personally," Sophie said. Rayme's mouth turned down. The woman crawled back up onto the bed, and pulled the sheet up over her head.

Matsue came to stand over Sophie. "If what you just said is true, then we will get along just fine." She turned to Holly Rayme, still hidden under the sheet. "Your application to WITSEC is hereby approved."

Continue reading *Wired Secret*: tobyneal.net/WScwb

ACKNOWLEDGMENTS

Aloha dear readers!

Thanks so much for joining me for this latest installment of Sophie's journey into the mysteries of the Big Island's crime scene, and her own mission to understand justice and the path of self-discovery!

It was such a treat to be in Jake's head. Jacob Sean Overstreet Dunn is growing as a person, and it's often a painful process—but in doing so, Jake is becoming a man who really could be a contender for Sophie's heart and might well hold the key to helping heal her.

Freitan and Wong had a bigger role than I first imagined. I met Kamani Freitan for the first time in Unsound (Dr. Wilson's story) some years ago, and remembered thinking then that it would be fun to "work with her" again in the future. The scenes where she made Jake squirm were fun to write, because in my own life I've experienced a good deal of sexual harassment at different jobs and been able to do exactly nothing about it. I've known men like Jake, who think their innuendoes are compliments. Those scenes were my moments of imagining a glorious comeuppance that teaches a guy a lesson he actually learns from—something I've never seen happen in real life, alas. But that's part of why we love fiction, isn't it?

Sophie's mother appearing and introducing a whole new direction for the series was an exciting development that wasn't in the initial outline of this book, and hopefully you aren't too frustrated that we only introduced Pim Wat and her mysterious organization and didn't resolve all the questions it raised. I'm super excited to see where this exploration of a major element of Sophie's life and past takes her next. Many of the questions raised in this book will be answered in the next, so hang in with me for the next chapter of this epic journey!

Thanks go out to my awesome support team, and to you, my readers. You keep me coming to the keyboard with excitement and passion; your reviews, comments, sharing and interaction encourage and uplift me. The life of a writer is a quiet and sometimes lonely one; but all I have to do to know that my writing matters is to open my email or check in with my Facebook Friends group, and I know we're in this together.

If you enjoyed *Wired Justice*, please leave a review on your favorite retailer. They mean so much, so I thank you with a big MAHALO in advance.

Until next time, I'll be writing!

Much aloha,

FREE BOOKS

Join my mystery and romance lists and receive free, full-length, award-winning ebooks of *Torch Ginger* & *Somewhere on St. Thomas* as welcome gifts: tobyneal.net/TNNews

TOBY'S BOOKSHELF

PARADISE CRIME SERIES

Paradise Crime Mysteries
Blood Orchids
Torch Ginger
Black Jasmine
Broken Ferns
Twisted Vine
Shattered Palms
Dark Lava
Fire Beach
Rip Tides
Bone Hook
Red Rain
Bitter Feast
Razor Rocks
Wrong Turn
Shark Cove
Coming 2021

Paradise Crime Mysteries Novella
Clipped Wings

Paradise Crime Mystery
Special Agent Marcella Scott
Stolen in Paradise

Paradise Crime Suspense Mysteries
Unsound

Paradise Crime Thrillers
Wired In
Wired Rogue
Wired Hard
Wired Dark
Wired Dawn
Wired Justice
Wired Secret
Wired Fear
Wired Courage
Wired Truth
Wired Ghost
Wired Strong
Wired Revenge
Coming 2021

ROMANCES
Toby Jane

The Somewhere Series
Somewhere on St. Thomas
Somewhere in the City
Somewhere in California

The Somewhere Series
Secret Billionaire Romance
Somewhere in Wine Country
Somewhere in Montana
Date TBA
Somewhere in San Francisco
Date TBA

A Second Chance Hawaii Romance
Somewhere on Maui

Co-Authored Romance Thrillers
The Scorch Series
Scorch Road
Cinder Road
Smoke Road
Burnt Road
Flame Road
Smolder Road

YOUNG ADULT

Standalone
Island Fire

NONFICTION
TW Neal

Memoir
Freckled
Open Road

ABOUT THE AUTHOR

Kirkus Reviews calls Neal's writing, *"persistently riveting. Masterly."*

Award-winning, USA Today bestselling social worker turned author Toby Neal grew up on the island of Kaua`i in Hawaii. Neal is a mental health therapist, a career that has informed the depth and complexity of the characters in her stories. Neal's mysteries and thrillers explore the crimes and issues of Hawaii from the bottom of the ocean to the top of volcanoes. Fans call her stories, *"Immersive, addicting, and the next best thing to being there."*

Neal also pens romance, romantic thrillers, and writes memoir/non-fiction under TW Neal.

Visit tobyneal.net for more ways to stay in touch!
or
Join my Facebook readers group, *Friends Who Like Toby Neal Books,* for special giveaways and perks.

Made in United States
North Haven, CT
25 October 2022

25905036R00188